Cherry Stem

SOTIA LAZU

This book is a work of fiction.

While reference might be made to actual historical events or existing locations, the names, characters, places and incidents are either the product of the author's imagination or are used fictitiously, and any resemblance to actual persons, living or dead, business establishments, events, or locales is entirely coincidental.

Other Books in This Series
Cherry Pop (Vampire Cherry Book 0)
Cherry Blossom (Vampire Cherry Book 2)
Cherry Pie (Vampire Cherry Book 3)

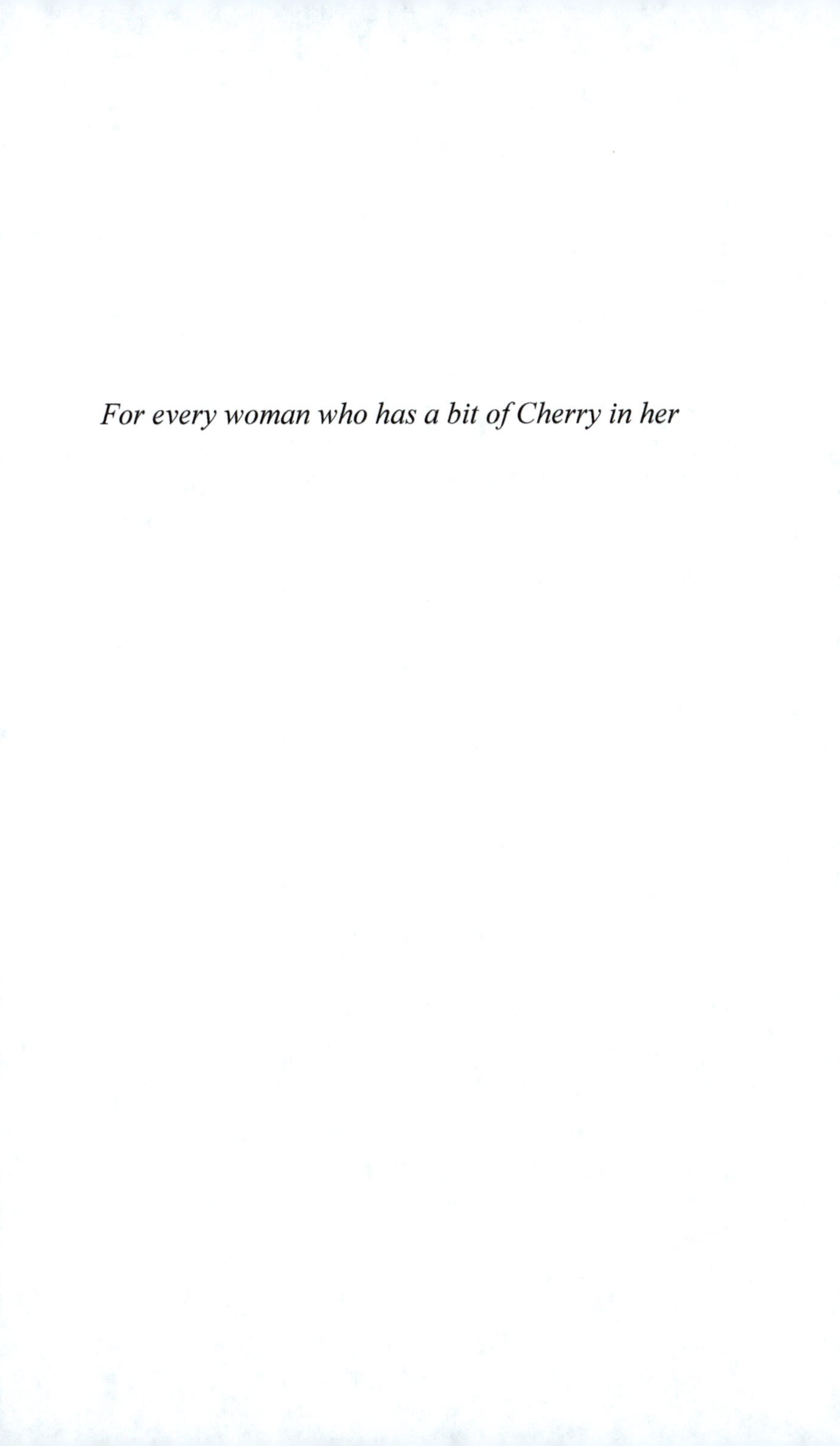

For every woman who has a bit of Cherry in her

Table of Contents

Prologue

My mom always told me not to play with my food. I try to keep that in mind.

She never told me not to let my food play with me, however, so I would let tall, dark, and handsome—with gray eyes, a brilliant smile, and killer cheekbones—flirt with me to his heart's content. Then I'd let him take me to his place.

Then I'd feed.

By the time he woke up in the morning, he'd remember having great, anonymous sex and nothing else.

That was the plan, at least. That had *always* been the plan.

Until things changed.

Chapter One

I was about to leave my apartment, when there was a knock at my door. I opened it, and Dotty, one of the second-floor tenants, burst into the room.

We weren't friends per se, but she'd occasionally pop by for some girl chat. I'd told her I worked nights and that I needed my beauty sleep, so she wouldn't disturb me during the day, but she'd never before come by after nine in the evening.

"I need your help." She gasped for breath as she turned to face me, running a hand through her short, spiky black hair.

At nearly six feet tall, on the heavy side, and with a square jaw, Dotty never seemed to need anybody's help.

"What can I do?" I secretly hoped whatever it was could wait until my stomach was full. Her outfit somehow made me doubt my hopes would be justified; she looked ready to go out.

As did I, which I prayed she'd notice.

She bit her lip, then said, "The sitter was with Mark until now, but she had to go, and my date—ummm. I invited him upstairs for a drink, and he's waiting in the car." She blushed and sucked in a gulp of air, before blurting out the actual reason for her visit. "Can Mark stay here for an hour?" When she took in my short leather skirt and bustier that left little to the imagination, she pouted. "I guess not." With a sigh, she turned for the door.

Even though she turned slowly enough that I knew she *expected* me to stop her, I felt bad. "Okay, but only for one hour," I said to her back. I'd looked after him before, and he wasn't *horrible*.

The words had barely left my mouth when she opened the door again and let Mark, her pudgy six-year-old son, inside. "I owe you big-time," she told me over her shoulder, blew Mark a kiss, and rushed out before I could change my mind.

"Why aren't you wearing pajamas?" the boy asked, tilting his head to the side. "Did you just come back, like Mommy?"

I swear he would have had a brilliant career with the Spanish Inquisition, had he been born back then. Since I always believed in treating children like adults, I opted for the truth. "Nope. I'm going out as soon as your mommy picks you up."

"Why are you going out after dark?" His thin eyebrows were furrowed, the sharp expression looking out of place in the adorable roundness of his face.

"Why not?" I asked innocently. *Ha.* I beat him at his own game.

"My daddy says only bad people go out after dark." He crossed his arms in front of his easily breakable chest and looked at me smugly.

I understood why his mother never asked her ex-husband to babysit. "Your mommy was out until now," I said with a saccharine smile. "Is *she* bad?"

He apparently took offense, because he stomped his foot. "*No.*"

"Well, then, your daddy is wrong." There. I'd had the last word. How would he beat that argument?

"But it was *day* when my mom went out." Smug again.

I was tempted to try my brainwash gaze on him but thought better of it. Instead I said, "If you don't talk again until your mom comes to get you, I'll give you ten bucks."

He squinted at me. "Twenty."

I should have started lower, but it was too late for that now. "Fifteen, and you never tell her about our deal." Hey, I said I'd looked after him a couple times; I never said I was good at it. I'd have to find another way around his questions next time, though. He was getting expensive.

Dotty wasn't late to pick him up. She was disheveled and grinning like the Cheshire cat, but not late. I grabbed my keys, stuffed them in the front of my bustier, all but tossed Mark to her, and was out of there.

****

The Gridlock was one of my favorite bars, which meant I visited it only every couple of months. It wouldn't do to be seen leaving with a different man every night, especially if said man didn't remember me the following day.

Spacious and dimly lit, the Gridlock was decorated in black and shades of red. Drapes separated a few private stalls, and the upper floor housed the supersecret VIP area. Get your minds out of the gutter; the place wasn't a sex club. The VIP area was only secret because celebrities often chose it to unwind when they needed to stay away from the public eye for a while—no orgies took place there as far as I was aware.

What added most to the bar's appeal was its patrons—young professionals, not out to get wasted. Pretty people, who took care of themselves and looked and smelled good, relaxed on leather armchairs. A smorgasbord of dining possibilities, *and* the music was to my taste.

As was the bartender, but he was off limits.

Heads turned as I entered, but I maintained my cool. The outfit I'd chosen was at odds with the surroundings, but by the time I left home, I was in a hurry, and the club I initially had in mind was too far away. I might have gone through the trouble of finding another place that suited my attire, but a phone call earlier that evening had jarred me— always, *always* change your cell number after breaking up with someone, or they can bug you for years.

I looked cheap for the place, but it was too late to do something about it. Holding my head high and keeping from swishing my butt more than necessary, I made my way inside and pretended not to notice the glares a group of businesswomen in their thirties with impeccable hair, threw my way. I was there for a reason.

I moved toward the bar with deliberately slow steps. Gaze not lingering on a face for more than a split second, I tried not to broadcast that I was looking for someone to fulfill my needs for the night.

I spotted the perfect guy within twenty-five seconds of scanning the room. I'd never seen him around before. Believe me, I'd remember if I had. A head taller than everybody else, and with shoulders as wide as my bed, he leaned casually against the bar, holding a bottle of beer. Even at a distance, I could see his eyes were the same charcoal gray as his shirt, and fringed with long, dark eyelashes. And his gaze was locked on me.

The first phase of the plan was complete—the prey had seen me and was attracted.

Phase Two consisted of me feigning disinterest until he made a move. If I took the first step, he might deem me too easy, and as I'd discovered in the past, that wasn't always enough of an ego booster to make a man take me home. Although, if I played my cards right, it might be more than enough to make him follow me into the ladies' room.

With the rent deadline approaching, I needed money tonight almost as much as I needed blood, so a quick hit wasn't an option.

Oh, the blood thing reminded me there's something I should have said earlier.

My name is Cherry, and I'm a vampire.

Sadly, since L. A. wasn't brimming with job openings for an aspiring porn star turned vampire, I often found myself in need of cash. When that happened, I looked for someone to serve as more of a sponsor, rather than a blood donor. For the day, not indefinitely.

I'd been in a couple of adult movies; I wasn't a sex-worker. Most of the guys I fed on got nothing other than the *promise* of sex. If I was into them, I might do them as I fed, but I never did it because I thought I had to. Letting someone cover my expenses in the long run would change that dynamic.

As would falling in love with someone. A *breathing* someone, with a pulse and an expiration date.

It would screw things up majorly, which was why I never slept with the same human more than once since I became part of the living dead. *The living dead.* It sounds so very ominous, but some of us are nice.

And… I'm digressing.

One of the coolest vampire powers is mind control, which some swear is the best way to a healthy relationship. Personally, I prefer not having to wipe my lover's brain clean every so often. A steady, living boyfriend from whom I'd have to hide my true nature was therefore out of the question.

As for dating a vampire? No thanks. Too many relationship issues. The way I see it, knowing you'll be around for a *very* long time can make you extremely picky as to whom you want by your side.

Also, male vampires are patronizing, controlling assholes with superiority complexes.

And they cheat.

I admit to only knowing one of them that well, so call it an educated guess.

I approached the side of the bar farthest from the guy and ordered a Bloody Mary. Silly private jokes like that give me a weird sense of accomplishment. I know; I need therapy.

Drink in hand, I tapped my foot to the rhythm of the music and observed the crowd dancing—slowly swaying, to be more precise—while I mentally counted the seconds it would take for him to approach me. When he hadn't moved any closer after a whole minute, I turned and gave him the *squint*.

The squint is a leftover from my short days as a catalog model, before I decided on a major career change and made my first of two adult films. To achieve it, you narrow your eyes enough to make your gaze look focused and promising. Overdo it, and you look myopic. Combine it with a slight pout, and you have guys eating out of your hand.

Or flashing you a smile, as was the case now.

His smile was dazzling. Straight, white teeth—I'm a *vampire*; we pay attention to teeth—and a lower lip that begged me to nibble on it. And *oh* those cheekbones...

I clenched my jaw and made a show of turning away. *You want me, buddy? You have to come and get me.*

He didn't, but a fifty-something man with alcohol-laced breath and red-rimmed eyes appeared out of nowhere and cornered me against the bar. Just my luck. There was *one* person in the establishment who hadn't bathed for a couple of weeks, and of course he decided to make a pass at me.

"Can I buy you a drink, honey?" His words were slurred, and he stood too close for comfort.

I could have ripped his head off his shoulders within seconds, but I don't generally like violence. Placing a hand on his shoulder, to keep him at arm's length, I indicated my glass. "No, thanks. I'm set." I smiled, allowing a bit of fang to show. He couldn't possibly have enough credibility to expose us.

The drunk stumbled back, hands held up in the universal giving-up sign, at the same time the yummy male specimen made his way to us. Yummy's face fell. *Aha.* Hero complex.

"I was coming to save you," he said, "but I see you handled him yourself." His voice complemented the rest of him. Deep, masculine—the voice you'd want whispering dirty things in your ear.

The ball was in my court. "Maybe you should stick around, in case I can't handle the next one." I smiled. No fangs.

His grin gave me a better look at his pearly whites. Yup, still flawless. "I'm Alex. Alex Marsden."

"Cherry." No last name for me. There was no reason.

Up close, he looked even better. I figured he was in his late twenties, thirty tops, and worked out. His fingers, which I got a good look at when he raised his beer to his mouth, were long, and I couldn't help but imagine how his big hands would feel on me.

"So, what do you do?"

His question threw me. People didn't usually care what I did when I was dressed in leather and thigh-high boots. I wondered how he'd react if I said I was a lawyer.

I took a sip from my overpriced, alcohol-laced tomato juice. "Used to model. I'm between jobs now." Had been for a long time, since my maker hadn't bothered to ask about my future plans before turning me. At first I'd been really pissed off to wake up dead while at the peak of my career.

Meh. I may as well be truthful. I hadn't been at the peak, rather at the beginning. I'd filmed two *highly* erotic movies as an extra and had just been given the starring role in a third one. And the main reason I'd been pissed off for the better part of six years was that I'd been turned before getting the lipo and boob job I'd planned on pampering myself with for my twenty-fourth birthday. Now I was doomed to go through eternity without the flat belly and double D breasts Dr. King had promised me.

Alex nodded and looked me up and down. "You look familiar, and I don't follow fashion. Have we met before?" To his credit, his gaze didn't pause anywhere but on my face during his perusal.

Classic pickup line, although he might have seen me before. I couldn't really ask him if he liked porn, so I shook my head. "What do *you* do?"

"I'm a cop. Detective." He shrugged like he was saying *nothing special*.

A detective. This could be bad. These guys have good memories as a rule, and he might have seen my missing-person report. Still, I wouldn't panic. I'd gone from blonde to redhead for *Knotting Cherry Stem*—hell, I'd changed my name for it—and had bangs now and forever. No, he wouldn't recognize me.

And *no*, I'm not telling you my real name.

"Sounds exciting," I drawled, all wide-eyed. "You should tell me more." To stress how interested I was, I ran the tips of my fingers down his bicep. Nice and firm. Yum squared.

As if he didn't notice, he began saying something about my eyes. Most guys would be all over the chance to touch me back, but not him. I could see he was the type to really take his time with a woman, and it intrigued me. Would he take his time with *everything*?

I cut him off, pointing to the speaker booming overhead. "It's too loud in here. Maybe we should go someplace quiet?"

He arched his left eyebrow but put his palm on the small of my back. The touch gave me goose bumps, and that's a real feat when talking about a dead girl. "My place is quiet." Ah, he got the hint. Smart man.

As soon as I left my drink on the bar, he caught the bartender's eye and paid for us both. I didn't offer to cover my half, but I made a mental note to thank him properly once we were alone.

"Do you have a car?" he asked as I let him lead me to the exit. "You can follow me in it, or I can drive you back here…" His voice drifted off. What would he say? What could he say? *Later? After?* His sentence was better left unfinished.

"No car. I took a cab." Not all vampires can fly, but only because some can't fathom lifting off the earth and therefore won't focus their will enough to achieve it. *I* can. I'd flown to the bar, but I couldn't tell him that.

"Are you okay with taking my car? Riding with strangers, and all?" He was so thoughtful, and I had to try not to swoon until he added, "We could go to your place, if you'd feel more comfortable."

No no no no no. No. Bad enough that I was still going through with my plan though he was a policeman—but he was *so hot*, who could blame me? Bringing him to my apartment would take *risky* to a whole new level.

"I wanna see how a cop lives." A bat of my heavily made-up eyelashes, and the deal was closed.

****

The drive to Alex's place was long enough to get me wondering if he was some psycho killer, looking for a place to have his wicked way with me. If that was the case, he was so in for a surprise that I felt bad for him. Although the possibility of that being his agenda made me feel less bad for what *my* agenda was, which in itself was weird.

I've never felt shame or guilt for feeding off unsuspecting victims. *Never ever*. It's not like I do them any harm. Nothing like the harm that was done to me, anyway.

I'd met my maker at a party.

His name was Willoughby, and he'd been gorgeous and polite. Nothing like the grabby crowd my agent usually brought me into contact with. When he'd suggested driving me home, I'd been all up for it. Maybe the mention of a limo had added to the appeal.

We never reached my home. We started making out in the car—I remember giggling too much, because of the champagne—and things got heated fast. My sequined dress, extremely short to begin with, was bunched around my waist, and he had his hand between my legs, when I felt a sharp pain at my neck. I never liked hickeys, and I'd been supposed to begin shooting *Knotting Cherry Stem* the following day so I'd tried to push him away, but to no avail.

The shooting of *Knotting Cherry Stem* had been canceled, of course. I wasn't sued for breach of contract because nobody was able to locate me. Willoughby had dumped my lifeless body in an alley.

Alex didn't seem like the kind of man to dump someone in an alley. Maybe that was why I felt a pang at the thought of using him. A *pang*, mind you, not guilt. We, creatures of the night and all, don't feel such puny emotions. Just a pang when he opened the passenger's door for me; another when he didn't try to cop a feel while grasping the gearshift; another when he asked where I was from, how old I was…

Turning sideways in my seat, I took in Alex's profile. He reminded me of a Greek god—nose a bit too large, adding a masculine tone to a face that would otherwise be too pretty with the long-lashed eyes and pouty lips, and hair just long enough to curl over the collar of his shirt. The streetlights gave the black curls a shine that tempted me to run my fingers through them.

He pulled into a driveway, and I focused on the scenery outside for the first time since we got into his car. A nice street in Monterey Hills, with single and two-story houses. Not the kind of neighborhood I'd associate with a cop.

Then again, the house the driveway led to didn't look like what I'd expected a cop's house to be.

He seemed apologetic while telling me there had been a gas leak in his city apartment. "My mom's away for a few weeks and said I could crash here until it's fixed."

His mom? He'd brought me to his *mom's*? Okay, so she was away and his place wasn't habitable at the moment, but hadn't he heard of hotels? And how would I even enter the place? "She won't mind you having company over?" I asked, trying to decide whether to stick with him and see if I could go inside, compel him to take me somewhere else, or cut my losses and find another guy to get me through the night.

"Nah. I grew up here. It's as much my home as it is hers." From where I stood at the threshold, I saw a wistful smile grace his lips. "Plus it's always tidy and with a full fridge."

It was the smile that sold me. This place was special to him, and something deep inside made me want to see it. If he turned out to be a momma's boy after all, I wouldn't stick around for it to matter. That was one problem solved.

He gave a half shrug and held the door open for me. "Come in."

I lifted my foot over the threshold and met no invisible barrier. *Phew.*

Gesturing to his right, he indicated the living room. "Make yourself at home. I'll get us something to drink."

I couldn't get comfortable with all the frilliness and floral patterns surrounding me, but I tried. I sank into the huge sofa, crossed my legs demurely at the ankles, and waited for him.

An *uh-huh* came from the kitchen, followed by, "I knew she had liquor here." Alex poked his head out of the doorway that separated the kitchen from the living room. "What'll it be?"

My turn to shrug. "Do you have beer?" I didn't feel like making him prepare me a cocktail.

"Beer?" He mock scowled. "What kind of drink is that for a lady?"

I chose to believe he was kidding, and made a show of looking around. "Lady? Where?" If that wasn't an invitation, I don't know what would be, but Alex laughed. It was a nice laugh—deep, like his voice, rich, and hearty.

"All women are ladies until proven otherwise," he said with a wink before disappearing from sight.

I could explain why that was old fashioned and a tad sexist, or I could be proven otherwise. I seriously didn't want to be a lady tonight. Other than having the serious munchies, I was more attracted to him than I'd been to anyone since I broke up with my last boyfriend almost four years ago.

Alex brought me my drink and sat in the armchair to my right. That wouldn't do.

"Why so far away?" I asked. "And aren't you drinking?"

He shook his head. "I've had enough for one night."

He didn't explain his seating choice, and I was confused. He wouldn't have brought me here unless he was attracted to me, so why wasn't he doing anything about it?

"So… are you seeing someone special?" I didn't know why, but I wanted to know the answer. And I wanted it to be *no*.

He took some time to reply. The look in his eyes made me antsy; it was too serious. Maybe he *was* seeing someone. Maybe he was married, despite the lack of a wedding band on his finger, or he lived with his girlfriend, and that was why he'd taken me to his mother's house. It would explain why he was reluctant to make a move.

It felt like forever until he spoke again. "No." He sighed. "I couldn't be more single. You?"

"I don't do relationships anymore." Not since I found Constantine in bed with his maker. Constantine, who promised to love me forever and then broke my heart.

Silence again. I hate silence sometimes. This was one of those times.

He opened his mouth, closed it again, and rubbed his temples. "I may be about to say the stupidest thing, but… I'd never pay for sex."

I looked at him, mouth agape. My first instinct was to go over our interactions and find what I'd done, to give him that impression, but I held back. It wasn't my fault he jumped to conclusions. He was an asshole, pure and simple, and the only thing that saved him from a full-on angry-vampire attack was that said angry vampire was too shocked to react.

"It's not about my job." He leaned forward, elbows on his knees. "I'm not going to arrest you or lecture you, though going after someone you know is a cop is stupid. I just thought we could talk." After a pause, he added, "I'm not paying for that, either."

I wanted to slap him, but that might end with his head flying into the wall and I'd hate to ruin the beige tapestry with bloodstains. "I don't charge," I said through gritted teeth.

"Come on, Cherry." He touched my knee in a brotherly fashion. "The clothes, the attitude…"

I hated the tears that sprang unbidden to my eyes as I jumped up and turned toward the door. "I'm leaving," I said. "You're an asshole." My taste in men seemed consistent, if nothing else.

He was fast for a human. And strong. He grabbed me by the arm and spun me to face him. "You're telling the truth." The incredulity in his voice gave my anger a fresh boost.

"A woman can't go out at night by herself to have a drink? She can't see a man she likes, and—and *want* him, without being a prostitute?" If I'd fed, I be beet red by then.

"Cherry, I'm sorry. I—all the leather and the way you came on to me… I thought—"

"What you *should* have thought was that you were about to get incredibly lucky." I shook off his hand. "Not anymore."

I kept glaring, even after he grabbed me again and lowered his lips to mine. Glared for all of a second before melting into the kiss. His lips were soft and moist and apparently magical, because while they were attached to mine, I forgot all about how he'd insulted me.

When I remembered, I pushed him back hard enough to send him flying into the chair he'd recently vacated. "Oh, now that you know it's for free, you want it?" I leaned over him and grabbed the arms of the chair, trapping him. "Well, you can't have it." I said the words slowly, my tone even. I can say with certainty that vampires can't kill with our eyes, since Alex survived the daggers thrown by mine.

"I wanted it from the start." He got in my face. "Just not the way I thought it was offered." His voice gradually lost oomph, until the last few words were whispered, his face a study in misery. "I *am* an asshole. You looked so pretty and so out of place, and I couldn't believe that you—" He ran his palm over his face. "I'm an asshole. And I'm so very sorry. Both for insulting you and for screwing this up. I'll drive you to your place, and you can forget we ever met."

There was no doubt in my mind he felt bad about what he'd thought and said, but he'd really insulted me. I should accept his apology and walk away. But maybe I shouldn't be hasty. I mean, he said he was sorry and called me *pretty*. Too pretty for him to believe I'd genuinely been into him. That had to count for something, right? Most importantly, though, I shouldn't care what he thought of me. I should feed, have fun, and get out of here.

This time *I* kissed *him*.

I wasn't in the mood for softness and hadn't been for a while. I pressed my lips against his violently and invaded his mouth with my tongue.

After his shock wore off, he took over, his languid pace lulling my sense of urgency. He cupped my face and withdrew enough that his breath merely caressed my lips.

I tried to kiss him again, and he chuckled. A mewling sound came from my throat. That snapped me out of my lustful haze long enough to push his hand away and crawl onto his lap. I wasn't the prey, I was the predator, and it was about time Alex knew that. Knees framing his thighs, I undid his belt and pulled hard enough that it came out, ripping a couple of loops in the process.

He unzipped his pants one-handed, bunching the fingers of his other hand around my thong and pulling it aside. Stretching awkwardly to reach his back pocket, he fished out a condom.

Since I couldn't explain why there was no need for it, I took it from him, ripped the packaging with my teeth, and slowly rolled it down his cock. I took my time touching and stroking his long, hard shaft, enjoying his gasps. He was hard *for me*, gasped *for me*, and that made me want him more. I had the sort of power over him that had nothing to do with physical strength or vampire thrall, and I relished it.

He grasped my wrist, stopping my movements. Time held still for a second, as our gazes locked. I could get lost in those eyes, and that was dangerous. I squeezed my eyelids shut, shifted my grip, and guided him inside me. I didn't want to look at his face; that might make this more than sex.

He closed his hands on my hips, lowering me onto him slowly. Inch by agonizing inch, he entered me, and I wanted nothing but to take all of him in. I couldn't be patient. The void inside me ached to be filled.

Alex wouldn't be rushed. "God you're beautiful. So beautiful." He caressed my hip bones with his thumbs, and I got goose bumps all over. "I want you so much. Feels so good being inside you."

His words wouldn't let me focus on the feeling of his cock. I kissed him, to shut him up. I didn't want to hear the pretty words, when he wouldn't remember saying them later. I just wanted to ride him until I saw stars.

He thrust upward, and I hissed. He was big, stretching me this side of pain.

I liked it, but it wasn't enough. "More."

He fisted his hand in my hair and pulled my head to the side, to graze my neck with his teeth. "I didn't prepare you," he whispered.

He hadn't needed to. I'd been wet since his fingers made contact with the skin of my lower back at the club. I tried to swivel my hips, to show him, but he held me still.

"There's no rush. Let me make it good for you." He pulled me backward and lowered his lips to my collarbone, his free hand fiddling with the laces of my top.

I couldn't imagine how he'd make it any better than this. Every nerve ending in my body felt exposed. His breath on me set my skin ablaze. "Fuck me." I slid a hand inside his shirt and dug my nails in his shoulder.

He bucked his hips and growled, but wouldn't move other than that. "Let me make it good for you," he said again, uncovering my breasts.

My keys fell with a happy jingling from where I'd stashed them in my cleavage; I'd left the house thinking there would be no undressing. Handbags, clutches, and the sort aren't easy to handle during an emergency takeoff.

Unaware of my self-ass-kicking, Alex fastened his lips around one nipple and rolled his hips. I could do nothing but moan as he pumped inside me slowly, his shallow thrusts synchronized with the pulls of his mouth. His tongue flicking my nipple sent a tingle down my spine, but it was his cock driving in and out of me that sent jolt after jolt of pleasure to my core.

His thrusts turned deeper, harder, stoking the fire he'd lit inside me. He turned his attention to my other breast, and his warm mouth made me shiver. I arched my back in abandon, offering more of me to his wandering mouth, his hold on my hip the only thing keeping me from falling backward.

I clawed the air, seeking purchase against his shirt and failing. The silky material evaded my fingers, until I stopped trying. I couldn't focus on anything but the pressure building between my legs.

Alex pulled me up by the shoulders and gathered me to him. The angle changed, and he rocked his hips faster, every stroke sending me higher on a seemingly endless spiral of pleasure.

His chest was sweaty against my breasts. My tender nipples throbbed as they rubbed against him. I nuzzled his neck, nibbling on the smooth skin over his pulse point. I wanted to penetrate him like he was penetrating me. I wanted to taste his blood. I wanted more of him inside me than I already had.

I ran my tongue down the column of his neck and loved the goose bumps that rose when I blew on it.

He bit me.

Blunt, human teeth dug into my shoulder at the same time he raised my hips and slammed me down on him again. His balls slapped against my ass, and I couldn't hold back under the sensations assaulting me. My body tightened, and the tension in my belly uncoiled in every direction, wiping out logic and turning me into a creature made of pure need. A scream of delight burst through my open lips, before I fastened my mouth on Alex's neck and pierced his skin with my fangs.

I tried to be gentle—if done right, a vampire bite can be painless—but his fierce thrashing under me and plunging inside me made me lose my mind. I drank and drank, drawing more of Alex inside me with every sip. Each pull on his blood made my pussy spasm and drew out my orgasm, his moans music to my ears.

For a few moments, it was like I was floating. My lips felt dry. I opened my eyes and had to blink a couple of times before my vision cleared. What had just happened was… *wow*. My fuzzy brain couldn't come up with a more appropriate word.

I licked closed the wound on Alex's neck. Then I cleaned my lips with my tongue and raised my gaze to his, getting ready for the moment that canceled the whole night— the moment to erase me from his mind.

He smiled and held me tighter, oblivious to what I'd done. His chest heaved with panted breaths. His heartbeat pounded in my ears.

I hated that I liked it.

I started to stand on leaden legs, letting his softening cock slip out of me, but his grip felt made of steel despite the blood I took from him.

"Stay," he said. Though worded as an order, it sounded like a plea.

"I can't." If I did, there might be no turning back.

He kissed me leisurely. Intimately. It was too much.

I gave in. "Only for a little while."

He shifted me sideways in his lap and gathered me to him, tucking my feet snugly between his thigh and the armchair. "I wish there was a blanket down here," he said. "Or do you want to go upstairs?"

Upstairs. Where the bedrooms had to be. Where he'd want me to stay longer. I should go. Right now.

I shook my head. "I like it here."

Laying his cheek on my head, he whispered, "I like it too."

I stayed here, cuddling with him, for longer than I should have. Unwilling to let go of his warmth, I listened to his heart rate slow to normal and his breath even out. Once he was asleep, I thought it'd be a shame to wake him and wipe his memory. Instead I watched him, until the angles of his face, the curve of his lips, and the smoothness of his brow were imprinted on my mind. I dropped my gaze to his neck. My bite mark was nothing more than a couple of dots, like pinpricks. I kissed my mark and inhaled Alex's scent, to complete my mental picture of him.

I never allowed myself to fall asleep anywhere but in my basement apartment and had to be there before dawn. The sun coming up doesn't make us narcoleptic, but it can make us nice and crispy, so I always made a point of checking the sunrise time online before going out.

Well… almost always.

I fell asleep.

Chapter Two

I awoke with a jolt. Sharp pain sliced through my right side. My arm hurt like it had been carved to the bone. I tried to lift it, see what the damage was, and had to bite back a scream. The pain became sharper, deeper, as if the flesh was peeling off.

The curtain, flimsy as it was, had blocked some of the sunlight, but not enough to keep it from burning the skin of my right shoulder and as much of that side of my back as wasn't covered by the armchair and Alex's arm. It stretched and felt about to tear open with every move I made.

I shrieked—an honest-to-God shriek I'd thought could only be accomplished by teenage drama queens—and jumped off Alex's lap to crouch between the armchair and sofa.

Alex snapped his eyes open. "What—"

"Room without a window?"

Why was he looking at me and not replying?

"*Alex.*"

His eyes cleared and became more focused after I barked out his name.

"Is there a room without a window in the house?" I hated to think of what would happen if there wasn't one. The sun was low enough now, but soon it'd be streaming in through the glass panes. Even if I managed to find a spot where it didn't directly hit me, I'd feel like I was in a furnace.

Cop instincts must have kicked in, because he stood, fully alert now, and pointed to the back of the house. "Second door to your left. Takes you to the basement."

I took off, leaving him to run after me.

"Cherry? What's wrong?" I doubted he realized he was yelling.

An unfiltered, stray beam of light found my foot when I paused to fumble with the door. My flesh sizzled, and I cried out.

Alex was by my side now, close enough to see my fangs.

Whenever vampires are threatened enough for instinct to overcome logic, our fangs pop out. It can prove immensely helpful when fighting another of our kind but is all kinds of inconvenient when dealing with the sun and a human bystander.

As I finally opened the door, I saw Alex's hand fly to his neck. Yup, this wasn't one of those times when auto-extending fangs would help. "You—you're... *What are you?*" he asked.

I slammed the heavy door in his face.

He called my name, then tried to push his way in. Yeah, good luck with that. The door locked from the inside, but even if I hadn't pressed in the lock button, all I had to do was sit on the steps behind it and lean my back against it, and it wouldn't budge an inch.

"What the fuck is happening, Cherry?" Kicking now.

I tried to check my shoulder burn but couldn't. Not because of the darkness—every story you've heard about vampires having night vision is true—but because of the position of the damage. It didn't matter; I knew it'd be healing. I'd fed well, and my constitution was good even without that. "Nothing. Don't worry," I yelled back. Well, that was convincing.

He grumbled something about his gun and a lock. Then silence.

Sadly it didn't last. His voice, calmer now, drifted to my ears. "Come on, Cherry. Open the door. I don't know what's wrong, but we'll figure it out." A pause. "Please." The word didn't sound like one he had much practice saying.

I haven't needed air in years, yet I still inhale all the time. Like at that moment, when I decided lying wouldn't help me. I took a deep breath. "I can't come out. The sun burns me."

"Are you photophobic?" It made sense for that to be his first thought.

It was my way out, and I should take it. I didn't. I respected him too much to lie—or maybe I'm the kind of woman who loses her mind when a gorgeous man offers her mind-blowing sex and then cuddles her until morning. "That too," I said. Before I chickened out, I added, "I'm a vampire."

The reaction I'd expect from someone after such a revelation would be to burst into laughter. Alex sighed. "A vampire?" He cleared his throat. "Seriously? Tell me more about it."

Wow. That was open-mindedness I didn't see coming. "Well, not much to tell." He didn't doubt me. He wanted to get to know me better. I tried to put my thoughts in order. "I need blood to sur—" Realization dawned. "*You don't believe me.*"

He tapped his fingers on the door, an impatient sound. "I'm sorry, it's… No. No, I don't."

What an ass. Instead of letting him think I was crazy, I decided to prove I was telling the truth. "Move away from the door," I said.

"Why?"

"Can you please just do that?"

I heard him take a step back, and I opened the door enough to show my face and slide my unscathed arm through the opening. I waved at him, then bit my lip and put my hand straight in the sunlight's path.

The burn was tolerable for a split second but soon made my eyes water. My flesh felt about to fall off.

Alex stared wide-eyed at my blistering knuckles, then my face. I clenched my jaw against the pain and lifted the corners of my mouth in a forced smile, letting my canines elongate.

He jumped away, knocked over a lamp that looked too expensive to be on such a tiny table, and fell on his ass.

I snatched my hand back and held it to my chest before closing the door again. "Let me stay in here until sundown," I yelled. "I promise I'll leave as soon as possible, and you'll never have to see me again." This time I was lying. He would see me one more time, so I could return his state of blissful ignorance by taking away his memory of the last few hours.

Nothing.

I listened. Surely I'd have caught the sound of feet running to the nearest exit. Unless he hit his head when he fell…

I was about to open the door again, when he said, "So it's Bram Stoker more than Stephenie Meyer?"

I couldn't contain a very eloquent, "Huh?"

"Your hand." As if that explained everything. "Stoker had the vampire thing down better than Meyer, right?" He sounded like he really wanted to know the answer.

Only a dead *and* buried person would have missed the buzz the latter's works had caused, and the former was a legend. "Stoker's definitely closer. I mean, sparkling? Seriously? Neither is completely right, though."

"What is he wrong about?"

I sighed. I shouldn't be telling him anything about my kind, but I'd buy some time by keeping him talking. He was a cop; his word had gravity. If he decided to tell people about me, someone might check his story out. I couldn't have that, so I had to keep him within reach until I could wipe him, and the best way I saw to do that was to convince him I wasn't a monster. I'd stall till sunset, leave the basement, and wipe his memories of me with the least amount of trouble.

Plus I hadn't really *talked* to someone in a long while.

"Um, where to start? We don't turn into wolves, bats, or mist—not to my knowledge—and we don't have a thing against God or anything religion related."

His gasp pissed me off. Here I was, trying to keep things between us civil, and he was upset one of the ways of hurting me was off the table. "Yeah, you can't use a cross on me." My tongue dripped venom—not literally; we don't do that either. "Pity, huh?"

"Don't be stupid," he said, adding to my ire. "Vampires seem to be repelled by crosses in most books and movies. I was surprised that, of all things, the religion part is a lie."

Were we really having a theoretical discussion about my vampireness? I shrugged it off and picked at the scab forming on my foot. "Also, we don't feel compelled to follow the orders of any head vamp." I thought that over again. "Well, there's a council that issues laws, but they don't micromanage."

"Hmmm." Typical can't-think-of-anything-to-say reaction.

"Yeah…" Typical reaction to can't-think-of-anything-to-say reaction.

Five, ten, *twenty* seconds went by, and then he said, "Do you kill people?"

"No."

"But don't you—"

"I've never taken a life."

I expected some expression of relief on his part, but he shot his next question. It wasn't an easy one. "Do you have mind-control powers?"

Unfortunately our superhuman speed does not include speed of thought. I could hear the wheels in my head turn as I tried to find the safest way to respond.

I must have taken too long, because his next words came out in a high-pitched voice I couldn't quite associate with his husky tones until then. "Did you… *hypnotize* me? Is that why I brought someone I thought was a prostitute to my mother's?"

He had no sense of danger; I could snap his neck, and if he kept accusing me of things, I probably would.

I don't use my mojo to get a guy to take me home. I've never needed to do more than swish my hips and smile lasciviously, or stretch and let my boobs do the flirting. His gall was incredible.

"No, *Einstein*. That was all you, wanting to *talk*. I didn't need thrall, to get in your pants."

"How do I know you're being honest with me?"

I couldn't believe we were having such a stupid dialogue. He couldn't know. And I had no reason to keep being honest. But being me got lonely from time to time, and since we were talking anyway, I wanted to be real. "Because if I'd used thrall, we wouldn't be talking about it at all."

"But you bit me." There went the upper hand. I'd lost it. Buh-bye, upper hand.

Begrudgingly I muttered, "Yes. Had to feed." Why was I hanging my head? I really did have to feed. "I tried not to hurt you." That was the closest thing to an apology any of my donors had ever gotten.

"You didn't." His voice lost some of its edge. "I thought it was a"—he cleared his throat—"an expression of passion."

I ghosted my fingers over the door in the wish-it-were-my-guy-instead-of-the-wooden-surface rom-com way. For a second, I allowed myself to believe he wanted it to be just that, and maybe I'd get a chance for a do-over.

"*But I was a snack.*"

I got defensive, though his tone hadn't been angry. "I *chose* you, okay? I *slept* with you." I jabbed the air with my index finger, like he could see me. "I don't fucking do that." I barely resisted punching the wall to stress my point.

"Am I going to become like you now?"

"No." Maybe I should open the door and use my mind trick after all. Nothing else seemed likely to get him off that interrogation line.

"How do I know that?"

Again with the stupid questions. "It doesn't work like that. There's more to turning someone, and I'm not allowed to do it, anyway."

"Why?"

I didn't have to keep answering but decided to stick with it. "I was the last person to be turned before the new regime banned turning altogether." I was also the reason for the banning, since my asshole of a maker didn't realize I was sort of recognizable and had a family, unlike most people chosen for turning, so there was the possibility my resurrection wouldn't go unnoticed.

"You're the youngest vampire?" He huffed. "When were you made?"

"*Turned*," I said. "Six years ago."

"That makes you what? Thirty?"

"No." I added *dumbass* in my head. "It makes me twenty-four, forever."

I caught a buzzing sound, and soon he was on the phone. I didn't bother listening to both sides of the conversation—it's good that we can tune our senses up or down depending on our needs, or the abundance of stimuli would drive every last one of us crazy. My relief when I heard him say, "I'm coming over now," was indescribable.

He hung up and told me he had to go see a contact and then run by the police station. I found the fact that he explained both odd and endearing.

"I shouldn't trust you with the place," he said, "but I guess I don't have a choice."

My day just got better, except for one thing. "Will you tell people about me?" I hated how small and worried my voice sounded.

"Of course I will. Nothing says *captain material* more than a cop claiming he has a vampire locked in his basement."

"You know, you were a lot nicer before I put out." That shut him up as expected, so I continued refusing to acknowledge the fact that his attitude had changed after my revelation, and not after the sex.

Just before the front door slammed shut, I heard him mutter, "You better be here when I get back. This isn't over."

This couldn't have been *more* over, but I said nothing. When he got home, I'd wipe him and fly out of there, never to be seen by Alex Marsden again.

Chapter Three

"You've been missing for six years." That was the greeting Alex gave me when he returned to the house.

I could say *duh* or say nothing. I opted for the latter. It sure took him long enough to get back. At least I took a nap while he was gone. Nice of his mom to have a comfy sofa in the basement.

"I found your file, Cherry. Or should I call you—"

"No, you definitely shouldn't call me that." Bad enough that he'd found out my real name. I didn't want to hear it again. It belonged to someone who died, who had a family and a future. Still, I couldn't help but feel a little flattered that he'd searched for me, especially since it had to be hard without knowing my real name when he went looking.

"Okay, but I don't get why. It's a nice na—"

"Never. I'm not her anymore. And how'd you find that file?"

"Looked for models who went missing six years ago. You don't look like your picture." Conversational tone, calm voice—maybe we were done with the drama for the day.

"I better not, if it's the picture my mom put in the paper when she was looking for me. I've lost seventeen pounds since that was taken." I missed Mom every day that went by, and the thought of her brought tears to my eyes. I wiped at them furiously, mentally thanking God that sunset was near. I could feel it in my bones.

"I don't know. I think you looked adorable. Blonde, green-eyed, round cheek—the poster child for healthy upbringing."

Alex sounded—dare I say it—flirty, but I couldn't respond in kind. I *had* been brought up perfectly, by loving parents who wanted the best for me. I'd been a rebel, though, and left home for a life in the big city. And here I was, in the City of Angels, but with no life to talk about and no way of getting back to the people I loved without risking their lives.

The tears began flowing freely, and I couldn't contain a sob.

"Cherry? Are you all right?" Concern colored his voice, and I wondered what had happened to bring that about. He seemed to despise me when he left the house hours earlier.

I sniffled. I wasn't all right. Not even close. I was alone, and that wasn't likely to change. "I miss my mom, okay? The big bad vampire misses her mom. And my dad…" My dad, who'd supported me in everything—who acted as a peacekeeper when Mom and I had one of our stupid yelling matches over something menial—thought I was dead. I was only a couple of hours away from him, but I'd never again get one of his bear hugs. Unable to put my emotions into words, I thudded my head against the door.

"Can I… Is there some way I can help?" Alex asked.

"Don't worry. I'll get over it."

"Want to open the door? We can talk about it. I can hold you."

It sounded so tempting that I reached for the knob, but I stopped myself. I didn't want him to make me feel better. I didn't want to need him or anyone. I didn't want to be weak and sad.

"Why do you care, anyway? I bet you just want me to open the door so you can see what vampire flambé looks like." Under my breath but loud enough for him to hear, I added, "Jerk."

"I'm not that attached to the door. I could break it in and watch you burn if that was what I wanted."

Don't be reasonable, for fuck's sake; work with me. "Then what? You want a second round? I'm a good lay, huh?" The words tasted bitter. I was being unfair and unreasonable, but I needed some distraction from my reality.

"I'm sorry," he said, effectively silencing me. "I freaked out this morning. I was scared, I guess. I shouldn't have acted the way I did. I'm so—"

"*I'm* sorry." It was becoming a trend, him apologizing, and this time it felt wrong. He'd come back offering an olive branch, and I'd been nothing but bitchy.

"I'm sorry I bit you, too. I just don't know of another way to stay alive; I need blood." The truth, pure and simple.

"Did you only wanna fuck so you could feed?"

"I wanted to *have sex* with you because I liked you. I didn't mean to spend the night, and I'm sorry I fell asleep." I really was. More sorry that spending the night in his arms had felt like the most *right* thing I ever did.

"You liked me?"

I snapped, thinking he was after some ego stroking. "Yeah, I liked you. You're hot. Satisfied?"

"You don't anymore?"

I felt like screaming. What did he want from me? That morning I'd been something he couldn't wait to get rid of, and now…

As if he read my thoughts, he said, "When I found your file, you became more real. You were once again the woman I spent the night with, not a vampire." Pause. "I liked you too. Still do."

Ah crap. "Well, that's a bummer." We were not supposed to like each other. We were supposed to fight and yell. And I wasn't supposed to want to kiss him again.

"Tell me about it. Hottest woman I've met in a while, and I don't know if I can trust her not to eat me." I could tell he wasn't exactly joking.

Though justified, his lack of trust stung. At least it solved my lust problem. I no longer thought about kissing him. He was attracted to me, but he feared me, and because of that, nothing could happen between us again.

I was trying to find something to say to lighten the mood when the sound of wood breaking reached my ears.

"What was—"

"What the—" Something cut off the rest of Alex's words and made him grunt in pain.

I burst out of the basement without a second thought. I had to save Alex from whatever harmed him.

As he told me later, the sun was already down when he returned. So much for vampire instincts—go, me. At the time, however, I wasn't thinking that I might be in danger—and just when my previous burns had healed.

A man in a black ski mask held Alex by the neck against the living room wall, his grasp not loosening despite Alex's struggles. I ran toward them, but a second masked intruder flew into me before I reached them.

He had no pulse.

The discovery shocked me enough that he managed to elbow me in the face and flip me on my back. I listened for the other burglar's heartbeat but got nothing other than the erratic thudding coming from Alex.

I tried to get up, but the guy straddled my thighs. I had to get him off me. I thrashed and kicked but only made him cackle. *Cackle*. Like a cartoon villain.

"Stop that, Cherry," he said, "or Mr. Marsden will get to watch me do naughty things to you." The lack of profanity and his matter-of-fact tone scared me, but not as much as his knowing my name did.

I forced myself to relax and tried to think. He knew who Alex and I were, so it wasn't a random burglary.

"There's a nice girl." The scary vamp on top of me caressed my cheek. I'd heard his faint British accent before.

Out of the corner of my eye, I saw the second vampire relax his hold on Alex, who panted for air. Before relief could sink in, the guy shook Alex like a rag doll.

Alex's head hit the wall with a sickening *thud*, and he slumped to the floor, his heartbeat weak but steady.

I went from scared to furious.

A small table lay on its side next to me.

I squirmed underneath the heavy man. I didn't try to throw him off. On the contrary, I rubbed my body against his. "If you know me, you know what I can do."

He closed his fingers around my neck and pulled me closer. "Haven't seen you in action, but I wouldn't mind a private showing." He slid his knee between my thighs. Gag.

I reached out and closed my fingers around one leg of the table. There was no way I could break it without him noticing, but wood doesn't need to be sharpened, to be lethal. Not if you use enough force.

I arched upward and rubbed my cheek against my attacker's neck. He roamed my body with his free hand, and I made an effort not to flinch away from his repulsive touch. "I have something in mind for you," I said.

"Oh, I'll get what I want. Don't worry." He raised his head to look at me, and I went for the throat.

I closed my jaws over his jugular, locking him in place. Before he could react, I brought the entire table up. Hoping I my aim was good, I plunged the leg through his back with all the strength I could muster. Flesh ripped and ribs cracked under the force of my blow. The next moment, my mouth filled with ashes. I'd heard staking led to instant death, but I couldn't imagine that a person could be there one moment and simply *not* there the next—nothing but a thin layer of white powder.

I didn't have time to pull back before the end of the leg hit my chest. Sputtering and blinking hard against the dust that was everywhere, I rolled to my side and looked around.

The second male vampire snarled and lunged at me. I was on my feet and swinging the table in no time. It caught him on the head and stopped him in his tracks.

"*You bitch.*" He took a couple of steps back. "I should have killed you after all."

That voice I knew. "Willoughby?" Impossible. He met the sun half-a-dozen years ago.

Before I could move, he was out the door, promising we'd meet again. "And the next time, I'll make things right."

Vampires can't faint, but I was as close to that as physically possible. I went to Alex on legs as sturdy as noodles, and let out a sigh of relief when he inhaled. I picked him up and carried him to the armchair we'd spent the night in. "Alex?"

To my relief, he opened those beautiful gray eyes of his. "Cherry?" His lips moved slowly. "Who were—? What—? *What?*" He let his head drop back and squeezed his eyes shut again. "Were they vampires?"

"Yes. I dusted one of them, but the other escaped." I took his hand between mine, and my heart clenched when he pulled away. I tried to keep my voice from wavering. "Are you all right?"

He looked at me with a rueful smile. "I'll survive." His voice was hoarse.

"You'd better." What was it with me and crying today? Tears filled my eyes again, making my vision blurry. Still, I made out the narrowing of his eyes as he studied my face.

"These are real tears?" When I nodded, he muttered, "I thought they'd be blood."

"I'm so sorry I dragged you into this. The guy who escaped was my maker. He was supposed to be dead. *Dead* dead. He must have been after me, and you were in their way." I shouldn't have spent the night. I shouldn't have—

"What's done is done." He touched the back of his head gingerly and winced. "Why did you help me instead of running?"

"Oh, I dunno. Because they attacked you?"

His eyebrow quirked, one corner of his mouth twitching before he elaborated. "They're your people. You should be on their side."

"That's not how it works. We're not a pack." He'd offered to hold me and keep the sadness at bay, before the attack. For that reason alone, I wouldn't lose my patience and bite him to shut him up.

"So what?"

"Do you help criminals out, 'cause they're human?"

He shook his head.

"I didn't think so. Besides, I like you more than I do them. Plus it's my fault they were here. They must have followed me to the club and waited until it was dark again, to make their move." My theory had enough holes to be used as a fishing net, but the gist of the matter was that I was to blame.

"I don't think they were after you," Alex said.

I reached for his hand again. He didn't avoid my touch this time, and I gave him a gentle squeeze. "What do you mean?"

"Can vampires enter someone's home uninvited?" He coughed like his lungs were on fire, and I wondered if he'd taken a punch or two before I came out of the basement.

I patted his back. "No. They have to be asked in by the owner. Unless the owner is dead, of course, in which case…" The horror of what I said made me numb.

Alex searched his pockets like crazy. "My phone."

I spotted the cordless lying on the floor and rushed to get it for him.

He snatched it from my outstretched hand, punched in the buttons, and brought it to his ear. His body relaxed after a couple of seconds. Not wanting to intrude on a family moment, I pretended to be preoccupied with my nails but watched him for signs of discomfort.

"Hey, Mom. The house is fine." He blushed and lowered his voice. "Yeah, I'm eating right. Mom, I'm thirty-two. I live by myself; I know how to… Yeah, okay." He nodded a couple of times. Rubbed his throat. "I promise. See you soon." A grin split his face. "Say *hi* from me too, and he better be taking care of you."

I didn't look at him until he caressed my knuckles with his thumb.

"She's fine," I said with a smile. His mother was unharmed, and he was being all chummy with the back of my hand. Things were looking up.

He cleared his throat and nodded. "Which proves my suspicion. They've been here before."

Another coughing bout took him over. I went to the kitchen, filled one of the glasses on the drying block with tap water, and rushed back. He took it with a shaky hand and a mumbled *thank you*, and downed the water greedily. Choking on the second gulp forced him to take it a bit slower, but he still finished the whole glass.

Reverting to cop mode happened instantly, in front of my very eyes. The line of his mouth hardened, his face becoming a stone mask. He was scary in a way that turned me on beyond words. "We've never met before last night, have we? You haven't…" He waved a hand by his head.

"No. Of course not."

"Then I was right. They were after me."

The idea seemed preposterous. "Why?" I didn't mean for it to sound like I didn't find him significant enough, but he scowled.

"I'm a *cop*, Cherry." The scowling lost its oomph by the way he rubbed his chest, as if in pain. He waved off my worry when I asked if he was all right, and said, "I go after bad guys. Most of the time, I piss them off."

I rolled my eyes and sat on the armrest, one foot tucked under my butt. "Supernatural bad guys? You couldn't piss off the normal mafia kind?"

His laughter caught me unawares. "It seems the supernatural is attracted to me these days." He was still chuckling when he cupped the back of my head and pulled me in for a kiss. Brief and casual, it felt like something I could get used to—if I weren't a vampire or he weren't a human.

He seemed to no longer resent my nature, and he was still attracted to me, but I couldn't allow myself to get comfortable with that idea. "Any clue why they'd be after you?" I tried to pull away, but he didn't let me.

"Been looking into a series of disappearances lately. Girls in their twenties. Beautiful, sociable, no direct family. They go to a club or a party, then nobody hears from them again."

I pushed against his chest and straightened up. "Willoughby—my maker—he turned me after a party. If he's part of it…"

"You think he's turning them?" His voice was flat, no emotion coloring it.

"I think you should look for them in Dumpsters."

"He's killing them?"

"That was his plan for me." Making my voice gruffer, I said, "*I should have killed you, bitch.* His words, not mine."

Alex narrowed his eyes and furrowed his brow. "We haven't found any bodies."

"Oh my God, I knew the other guy too. The one I offed? He lied the first time we met. He hasn't seen me."

Alex looked perplexed. Of course Alex looked perplexed. Alex didn't know, and I didn't make any sense.

"I was in a couple of films. Of the adult variety." Biting my lip, I turned away. "It was a long time ago."

It was the perfect time for him to say something, but he was quiet, even the wheezing gone from his breath.

"A long, *long* time ago." I needed to know he was fine with it. "Never mind. Forget about it. The point is the guy whose remains I'm now wearing was the one who found me after my turning. His name was Ted. Back then, he said he recognized me. That he was a fan." Alex was watching me, expressionless. I wanted to slap him. "Tonight he said he'd never seen me in action, which means he lied before. Also—hey—he was here with my maker. Isn't it too much of a coincidence?"

For the first time, I thought maybe my situation hadn't been an accident. *Maybe* I was supposed to have been found. "I remember waking up, hungry and disoriented. I'd just found my footing when Ted appeared. He made a big fuss about how he loved my work, and insisted he take me to the council. If he and Willoughby are a team now, they could have been one back then too."

My maker's insistence on leaving the party early also made sense with that scenario. Newly turned vampires don't rise until the next evening, if their turning is less than a few hours from dawn. My rising had to be the same night as my death, or Willoughby would have risked someone else finding me first, and my awakening taking place in the morgue.

"Are you sure it was him? Ted?" Nice. Alex would pretend he didn't hear the porn-related part.

"Yes. I knew his voice when he spoke, but I couldn't place it till now."

"Hmmm." He motioned for me to lean closer, and I did. He was hurt. Perhaps he needed me to help him up. He smirked. "Can I get my hands on either one of those films?"

I matched his expression. "If you beg, maybe." He licked his lips. He was about to kiss me again. Badness lay that way. Flirty territory was too shaky under the circumstances. I got back to the subject we should be concerned with. "We have to do something."

He grimaced. "I know. I finally have a lead, thanks to you, but I can't tell my lieutenant that *vampires* did it." He pulled me sideways onto his lap. "Any clue where we can find that guy?"

"I told you, I thought he was dead. Executed for turning someone recognizable." I loved how soothing his hands felt, caressing my back, yet I had to wonder how we got where we were.

His acceptance of my undeadness had to be due to my fighting on his side, but could we pick up where we'd left off the night before? A question for another time.

"A huge mess was stirred when I was found," I said. "The existing council at the time was overthrown. My turning was the reason for the ruling against any but the oldest of vampires turning people, and even they must have a special permit."

"Maybe you should start at the beginning." His chuckle sounded forced. "My head is spinning with all the random data."

I offered what I saw as a good alternative. "I can do better than that. I can make you forget that I—that *we*—exist."

He pushed me back. Not hard. Not a shove. He just grasped my shoulders and made me sit up, my upper body away from him. "No. You don't mess with my head. Don't even think about it."

I felt the need to explain, if not defend myself. "It won't be messing. I won't take away anything you need, just the—"

"*No*. You will take away nothing." He threw his arms in the air. "*God*." Upset as he sounded, he didn't make me get off his lap.

"I'm only trying to help." Maybe, just *maybe*, I was sulking.

"Help?" He widened his eyes. "How? By making me forget important info about a case that may never be solved otherwise? By making me forget one of the best nights of—"

He clumped his mouth shut midsentence, but what I heard was enough to make me stop sulking. I got the point. And I liked it. Not that I could show my improved mood, with him scowling the way he was.

"I'll pretend you never offered to do that," he said, only slightly mellower. "Now tell me what I need to know about all this."

What *did* he need to know? "I guess I'll take it from the start." I bit the inside of my cheek. "I mean, I was sort of a celeb, I got bitten by a guy I met at a party, and until now I thought he left me for dead." Alex's gray-eyed gaze was locked on mine, making it exceedingly hard for me to remember what I meant to say next.

I can proudly say I managed, nevertheless. "Ted—vamp who went poof—found me, said he recognized me from my films, and took me to the council to record my turning."

"The council. You mentioned it before. What is it exactly? How does it work?"

I took an unnecessary breath, then let the air rush out noisily between my lips. "It more or less comes up with rules to be followed. And of course with the repercussions for not following those rules." Like for spilling my guts about our kind to a human. But it wasn't like he'd tell anyone while I was around, and I'd make him forget about us when I said *goodbye*, whether he wanted me to or not.

Alex looked at me, waiting for the interesting part, I guess. Too bad there wasn't such a part coming. "There are five council members. Used to be the oldest vampires that ran things, but after"—I pointed at myself—"well, most of the ones who overthrew them are younger."

"Why was the council overthrown over something an errant vamp did?"

That was a great question, actually. Why didn't I wonder about that before? Oh, right—I didn't bother with logic. What I cared about at the time was that I'd never have the perfect abs, that I was hungry, and that my career would never take off. "The story was that the old council should have come up with rules against random turning earlier, and that by not having done so they betrayed the ones they were appointed to protect."

"And the new council cares more?" he asked.

"I don't know. The services that took me in were established when vampires were first organized, but they're no longer necessary, since we don't have more fledglings, so they were… discontinued. That's the only change I know of."

"*Services?*" He tilted his head to the right and cocked an eyebrow. It was unsettling that I considered the movement a trademark of his, like I'd known him for a long time and not just twenty-four hours. "Like *social* services?"

I could see the idea of a vampire society with an infrastructure similar to that of humans amused him. "Yup." I popped the *p*. "*Vampire* Social Services. We called them VSS. They took in new vamps and taught us what we needed in order to survive." I paused. "There were also leaflets and a handbook to be memorized and destroyed before we left."

Alex gave me a full-blown grin, and I swatted his shoulder. "Don't mock, sir. It was helpful. I wouldn't have learned how to control the thirst or fend for myself without it. I'm not sure I'd have even wanted to." Constantine had helped me practice what I'd read, but it wasn't the time to mention him.

He caressed my back, his long fingers drawing soothing circles that drove the stress away. "In that case, I'm glad you had it." He leaned closer to me.

I wanted to kiss him, but there were things to be discussed. "I think I should talk to the council about tonight."

He sucked in his lower lip. I wished I were the one doing the sucking.

"Sounds good." His fingers crawled up my neck and began massaging my scalp. "And I should keep looking at what the missing girls had in common other than their age and looks. They didn't even all vanish from the same place."

The massage relaxed me, and soon I felt my eyelids drifting shut. "Can I take a look at their pictures? I know people. I could ask around, see if they heard anything about new fledglings.”

“I can get you their files, but I don’t want you to take any risks. He already saw you with me. If he finds out you’re looking into this…” He stilled his movements and narrowed his eyes. “If he hurts you—”

That was another sentence he didn’t get to finish, this time because I sealed his lips with mine. It was a spontaneous reaction. He was worried for me. Wanted to protect me.

“Where did that come from?” He didn’t seem to mind.

I shrugged, unable to meet his gaze. “Felt like it.”

With his index finger, he tucked my hair behind my ear. “I’m glad you did.” His thumb brushed my chin, lingering at the corner of my lips.

There was too much tension, too much *something* I didn’t want to identify between us. I wouldn’t be able to handle it if he kept being so nice, so cute, so…

I looked around. The place wasn’t wrecked, but we had stuff to do. Thank God for small favors. The smashed coffee table lay by a broken lamp, the overhead light reflecting off the scattered shards of glass and sprinkling tiny dots of light onto the upturned couch. Dust covered a doily I was sure had been handmade. The table I used as a weapon was remarkably unscathed—more than could be said for the curtains, one side of which had been ripped off the rail.

“Let’s clean up.” I hopped off Alex’s lap.

He got up after me. "The front door lock is busted. I'll have to go buy a new one." He stood so close, I felt the heat of his body like we were still touching.

I nodded. Casually putting some distance between us, I picked up the doily and shook it, in an effort to get dusted vamp off it.

Alex turned the couch upright and replaced the cushions on it. "The bolt wasn't on, so I can use that to keep the door closed, but I can't lock from outside."

I studied the ruins of the coffee table, our glasses from the previous night miraculously intact on the floor. I tried hard not to stare at how his dress pants stretched over the curve of his ass when he bent down for the last throw pillow. I needed to get the vacuum and mop from the basement. Anything to keep from jumping him.

"Can you stick around until I'm back?" he asked.

I raised my gaze to him. Why did he have to look so adorable, looking at the floor, his hands deep in his pockets?

"Alex—" I wanted to say how bad an idea that would be.

"You know—so nobody robs the place? Of course, I won't be able to put in the new lock till morning. I'll need better light." He looked like the cat that swallowed the canary. The porch light was probably as bright as the sun. "You could spend the night. Stay here for backup if Willoughby returns. And we can talk about the case. See how to proceed with it."

Bad, *bad* idea, but I couldn't think of why. I wasn't wiping him yet, and he already knew we existed, so one more night wouldn't be a problem.

"Sure." I tried to sound disinterested, though the thought of being with him a bit longer made me giddy. "I'll crash in the basement."

"Good. That couch turns into a double bed, so we can both sleep there."

I was torn between feeling stupid for not figuring that out, or giddy because he was suggesting we spend the rest of the night in bed together.

"You can—" He cleared his throat. "You can drink from me again if you need to."

As if his initial offer wasn't alluring enough. My mouth watered.

"I don't have to go in tomorrow, so we can stay here during the day too." He rubbed his chin. A day's stubble gave him a more rugged look.

Okay, okay—I was sold. "You'll have to get me something to wear. I'm not sleeping in leather again," I said, trying not to sound suggestive.

"I'm on it." Waggling his eyebrows, he moved toward the door. "I'll be right back. Feel free to start tidying up," he said over his shoulder as he crossed the threshold.

I called his name, but he ignored me. I hoped he'd be careful and stay safe. Willoughby wouldn't be going after him again so soon—not without backup, since he knew Alex had me to help him—but caution is always a good thing.

A door was shut between us once more, and I hadn't been the one doing the shutting. Still, I felt oddly optimistic as I skipped down the steps to the basement, to get the vacuum cleaner. I'd met an extremely hot man with whom I'd had incredible sex, and he hadn't wanted me out of his life the moment he found out I was undead. For the first time since Constantine, I felt warm inside.

Vampires are not supposed to feel warm.

Chapter Four

Alex took a bit more than an hour to get back, which left me with plenty of time to kill, after the fifteen minutes it took me to clean up in vamp speed. Impressed? If the vacuum sucked harder, it'd take even less.

I was in the shower but clearly made out his footsteps on the stairs, even under the running water.

"Honey, I'm home," he called out.

I knew he was joking, yet the relentless romantic hidden deep inside me let out a *woot*. I opened the glass pane so he'd hear me. "I'm in here."

I didn't get to tell him I'd be right out, because he came right in. He wore the clothes he had on since last night, shirt untucked, and he was barefoot. He had beautiful feet, I noticed. Big, *male* feet with long, straight toes.

I had to get a grip.

Hiding my body seemed silly after we had sex, so I didn't. Not that he looked.

He dropped a duffel bag by the sink. "Thought you'd want clean clothes as soon as you were dry. Got a couple tees and sweatpants from my place. They'll be too big for you, but the pants have drawstrings. Should be good for the night."

Then he pulled his shirt over his head.

If I were human, the water filling my mouth and clogging my throat while I gaped at him would have drowned me. As things were, I was grateful I'd opened the shower stall door and could enjoy the view.

Most people look better when they're dressed than when they're out of their clothes. There are always flaws. Something that needs covering up—a jutting stomach, love handles, scars, pimples. *Something.*

To me, Alex was perfect.

I ran my fingers down his chest and abs last night, but seeing the smooth, flawless skin stretch over rippling muscle made me ache to caress it. His shoulders were wide. I knew that already, but the way they rounded, leading to his flexing biceps, was a sight to behold. And that was what I did. I *beheld*, wishing he was closer, so I could press my breasts against his chest and see goose bumps rise.

I'd have kept staring at his six-pack for much longer if his fingers hadn't gotten in the way. Splayed across his abdomen and ghosting their way down to the front of his pants, they touched what I longed for. I wanted to lick my way along the trail of fine hair beneath his navel that disappeared inside his waistband. I sucked in a breath when he undid the button and another when he lowered the zipper to allow his slacks to fall to the teal tiled floor.

I followed them with my gaze, until he stepped out of the pooled fabric and toward the shower stall.

Toward me.

I bit my lip, barely registering the pain as I took in the muscled calves, the strong thighs, and finally his magnificent cock. He was inside me last night, but our hurry and my position above him didn't allow me to fully appreciate his… assets.

I did now. Springing from a nest of trimmed black curls, hard, darker than the rest of his body, long and thick and slightly curved to the right, Alex's cock beckoned with every step he took.

I was more than ready to respond to its beckoning when he joined me under the water jet.

Like staying here again became a good idea and telling Alex about vampires seemed preferable to making him forget he ever met one, having sex with him one more time now struck me as the only viable scenario.

I didn't care how he'd take me; he could press my face against the glass door, my back against the tiles, or have me on all fours. I just wanted him inside me. I tried to wrap my arms around his neck, but he got hold of my wrists, stopping me.

My face must have shown my confusion, because he smiled. "The water is cold," he said.

"Don't like it much hotter than this." Ignore what you read in most books. Vampire body temperature makes us sensitive to heat, not cold. For him, I turned the faucet a bit to the left.

He turned the water off altogether. "That's better."

I watched, mesmerized, while he took his time uncapping the shower gel, pouring some of it in his palm, and capping the bottle again.

He put it back in its place and rubbed his hands together until they were covered in foam. "Turn around. I'll do you first."

Oh, the innuendo in that last sentence.

Uncaring that I'd lathered and rinsed, I turned my back to him.

"Pull your hair up," he said.

I twirled my red tresses into one thick curl and tucked it at the side of my neck.

It wasn't enough. "Hold it up with both hands and don't let go." His voice brooked no argument, and I was more than excited with his take-control attitude.

I did what he asked, trembling only slightly when he closed big, strong hands over my shoulders and massaged the lather onto my skin. He pressed his thumbs against the back of my neck, digging his fingers rhythmically into the muscle and releasing knots I didn't know were there.

Moaning my approval, I let my head fall forward. His hands went to my shoulder blades, spreading the foam there before moving to my back. He followed the line of my spine, his palms and knuckles taking turns in working my flesh. I barely kept my footing as he slowly stroked his way down to my ass before kneeling behind me.

He ran a finger between my ass cheeks and chuckled when I reflexively clenched. He pressed a finger lightly against my asshole. "Don't worry. I'm not going here—today."

I wanted to come up with some smart retort, but he began massaging my inner thighs. His thumbs almost touched my pussy. I jerked back toward him, trying to rub against them. I craved his touch a bit higher. Just a bit…

Argh. He moved on to the backs of my knees, which nearly buckled, and then to my calves. I was wet, and not just from the shower. His touch set my skin on fire, and I squeezed my thighs together, needing friction to ease my need. It wasn't enough. It felt like nothing but Alex would be enough ever again.

When I couldn't take more teasing, he stood and ordered me to face him. His voice sounded husky and strained. Thinking I would finally get what I wanted, I complied eagerly.

Alex had something else in mind.

He prepared more lather and rubbed my throat. The pressure from his hand combined with the silkiness of the foam to make me light-headed. He was so close, his breath warmed my skin. I tried to lower my arms and grab him—wanted to smash my lips against his, climb him and impale myself on him—but a shake of his head told me not to.

"Trust me," he said.

"Why should I?" Despite my flippant answer, I knew that frighteningly, inexplicably, I did. I would angst over that later, once I was satisfied and had the luxury to worry about my budding feelings for a mere mortal.

"Because I know how to make your body sing." Cocky, but a proven fact. "Now no more talking."

Nodding sapped my strength. My entire being felt tense, not from the strain he chased away with his magic touch, but with anticipation of what would happen next. Where would his hands go after my collarbone? I couldn't believe I stood there while he made my body react any way he pleased. It had been a long time since I granted anyone control over me, and I found it hard to do so now. Then again, it was so long since anyone evoked such lust in me, since I enjoyed anyone's attentions like I did Alex's, that I couldn't find it in me to be anything except passive.

That would change if he took much longer.

He feathered the heels of his palms over my nipples, making them rise in hardened peaks.

I arched my back, pressing my breasts against his palms, and reveled when I realized his hands trembled. His heart thundered, and his jaw was clenched. It took as much effort on his side as it did on mine, to maintain the slow pace he'd imposed.

Good.

Gaze on mine, he cupped my breasts and kneaded them. He rolled the nipples between his fingers. His breathing sounded labored, but his movements weren't rushed. He lowered his hands to my stomach and got on his knees once more, this time in front of me, to soap my belly and thighs.

I pushed my hips forward, craving his touch on my pussy. He didn't disappoint. He snaked his hand between my legs and glided it back and forth. His touch didn't linger, but it didn't have to. Each stroke raised my temperature and made me rub against him. My legs trembled. I felt empty. I needed him to fill me and soothe the ache in me.

He massaged my clit with his thumb and slid it inside me, but not deep enough. I let go of my hair and placed both hands on his head, trying to stay upright, as well as hoping he'd use more than his fingers on me. Instead he withdrew and finished lathering the front of my legs. Then he rose and reached behind me for the shampoo.

"You shouldn't have let go of your hair," he said. "Now it needs washing too."

He kept his lower body away from mine till now, not letting me feel him. When his hard cock brushed my stomach, I hissed. He seemed unaffected, fully focused on making lather of the jasmine-scented liquid.

He proceeded to work the shampoo into my hair, and I couldn't help but look down at him. Our bodies touched, his length rubbing against me at the same time his arms moved so he could massage my scalp. I wanted to drop down onto my knees and take him in my mouth.

Too suddenly, he stopped and took a step back. "My turn."

I thought he meant I should treat him to the same pampering he treated me to. Wrong again. When he held me at arm's length and poured shower gel down his body, frustration made me see red.

He washed himself fast, with not even half the care with which he'd washed me, yet his hands caressing all of him was the most erotic thing I'd ever seen. Tan skin gleamed against white foam and made me lick my lips.

He closed his fist around his shaft. In a circular motion, he coiled it from the tip to the base of his cock once, twice, before returning to his abdomen. A groan escaped me.

I think it was what finally made him break. Or maybe it was his plan from the start to do things the way he did next. He turned the water on, folded one arm around my waist, and cupped my neck with his other hand, to bring me to him. I stumbled and clung to his biceps, to keep my balance. They were made of steel. Once I was flush against him under the jet, he lowered his face to mine for a kiss.

His posture held such urgency, I expected him to devour my mouth, yet his kiss was gentle. Almost timid. He brushed his lips against mine with tenderness, before tracing their seam with his tongue. I opened for him, meaning to deepen the kiss, but he wouldn't be hurried. Suds and water cascaded down my face, getting in my eyes and mouth, but I couldn't have cared less. Alex gasped for breath, but he wouldn't stop kissing me. He leisurely explored my mouth until I felt like my feet didn't touch the ground.

And then they no longer did.

Alex lifted me in his arms and turned the water off with a nudge of his elbow. I don't know what he was about to do next, but I didn't wait to find out. As he maneuvered me in his arms, I lifted my legs, wrapped them around his hips, and let myself sink on his dick.

"Cherry—" He lost his footing but regained his balance and turned so I was pressed between him and the glass wall. "You really shouldn't have done that." His eyes glinted with mischief.

"Um, if it's about the condom thing, can't get pregnant and not carrying any nasty germs." I moved against him.

He chuckled and grabbed my ass with both hands, stilling me. "I thought we could use a bed this time."

I tightened my inner muscles' grip on his shaft. "Beds are overrated."

His body tensed, his grip on my ass becoming punishing. I must have made some sound, because he relaxed his hands and whispered an apology before claiming my lips. This time his kiss was hungry, demanding. He bit my lips like he was trying to devour me, and began driving his cock in and out of me.

Water didn't make for the best lubricant, but I liked the friction. I loved being sandwiched between a hot man and a cool glass pane and being thoroughly fucked.

Only it didn't feel like mere fucking.

Alex was rambling. I wasn't sure he knew what came out of his mouth, but I heard it all. I was beautiful, perfect to him. He never wanted to hurt me. The openness and honesty of his face, the awe in his eyes as he sank and withdrew from my body was overwhelming. For the second time in as many days, he offered me much more than just sex. He offered me companionship. Comfort. He promised me a tomorrow.

I wasn't sure I deserved it.

I knew I couldn't handle it.

I leaned my head back and cried.

There were no sobs, only tears falling down my cheeks, pooling at my neck. Tears that seemed to cleanse me of all the bad that had accumulated inside through the years.

He noticed, despite my already wet skin, and ceased his movements. He caressed my cheek and asked if something was wrong. I wanted to ease the worry in his voice but could do nothing other than shake my head and rock my pelvis, urging him on. I couldn't tell him he'd touched me deeper than anyone else. I didn't know why I was crying. I only knew I was happy and terrified at the same time.

He took my hint and started fucking—no, *making love* to—me again. He lifted one of my legs higher and plunged inside me faster. His mouth found mine, and he swallowed the choked mewls that escaped my lips.

He was deeper than before, but that wasn't enough. "More."

My wet back made funny sounds against the glass, but the only sound I cared about was Alex's heartbeat.

He panted into my mouth, slamming his hips against mine. He hit all the right places with every move of his pelvis. That was all that mattered.

"Come for me, baby," he whispered. His breath quickened.

I was close. All I needed was…

Not losing a beat, he slid his hand down the length of my body, all the way to where we were joined. "Come for me," he said again, pressing down on my clit with his thumb. "*Now*, Cherry."

The earth-shattering pleasure seemed to short-circuit my brain, white fire bursting through my veins. I locked him in place with arms and legs while I rode out my orgasm. My legs shook and my hands trembled, while my body convulsed against him. Stars blossomed behind my closed eyelids, as rapture washed over me.

His thrusts, rhythmic until then, became erratic, jerky, when he gave in and let go. He came inside me, the heat of his cum making me shudder one last time, but he didn't stop moving until his cock was half erect and his heartbeat had slowed to normal.

I have no clue where he found the strength to remain standing, but he toed the stall's door open and carried me out of the bathroom and into the next room, where a large double bed took up most of the space. The rest held a desk and a bookshelf in one corner, the latter decorated with pictures of a young boy. *Alex.* "Your old room."

He nodded and laid me gently on the bed before collapsing next to me. "Gimme twenty minutes, and we'll show this room things it never saw before."

My lips were too numb to form a coherent reply. I giggled.

Swallowing a gulp of air, he looked at me, head tilted to one side. "Something funny?"

I shrugged, still laughing.

His eyes glinted. He shook his head. "As soon as I regain feeling in my legs, I'll show you it's not nice to laugh at people."

I silenced him with kisses. Tried to, at least.

Before dawn, he carried me to the basement, where we spent more time exploring each other's bodies. I fed, but only after he reminded me I hadn't in more than twenty-four hours. He insisted he'd had something to eat while he'd been out.

When I drifted off this time, I knew I was safe in Alex's arms, the rise and fall of his chest soothing against my back.

I also knew another thing—I was falling hard.

For a human.

Hopefully, I wouldn't come to regret it.

Chapter Five

I was just done relooping the laces through my bustier's tiny eyelets, when the bedside light was switched on.

"What's with the leather again?" Alex lay on his side, propped up on one elbow, his cheek cradled in his palm. "I brought you clothes. You can wear those around the house."

I pursed my lips, thinking of the contents of the bag he'd brought. Not the most flattering fit. A dazzling smile blossomed on his lips, and I had to smile back.

"Or you could wear nothing." He waggled his eyebrows.

I looked away. If I spent a couple more seconds looking at the curve of his hip, his white teeth nibbling at his lower lip, or the way he invitingly caressed the sheet in front of him, I'd forget what I had to do, and jump back under the covers with him. "I have to go." My traitorous gaze returned to him.

He turned on his back and pulled the sheet up all the way to his chest in a gesture so prudish it'd be funny if I didn't want to rip the covers off him. "To the council?"

I shook my head. "No. Someone else first. I want to see if he can arrange a meeting." I'd showered again but hadn't paid enough attention to towel drying, and it was a bitch putting my boots on, which worked out fine since fighting to pull them up meant I didn't have to look at him.

"*He?*" Out of the corner of my eye, I saw him run a hand through his hair. "Should I be jealous?"

My worry that maybe he should be, that my meeting Constantine was a horrible idea, was what made me snap at him. "You have no right to be jealous." I shouldn't feel bad for saying that; he wasn't my boyfriend.

Ha. The boots were finally in place. I trained my gaze on him.

Alex nodded.

Right. So I felt bad. And I'd pop by my place to change into something less sexy before visiting my ex. "Will you be okay?" I expected him to say I had no right to ask that.

He surprised me. "It depends. Will you be back?" He wasn't facing me, but I made out the muscle ticking in his jaw. I liked knowing it took effort for him to be so calm and civil—and God, did that make me a horrible person.

I should keep my distance. Especially after the way I felt last night. I should go see Constantine, have a quickie for old times' sake, and only contact Alex when I knew something about the case. "Don't you plan on going home at some point? Oversee the repairmen?"

Why did he have to have that boyish grin? "Nope. No need to. Gas company guys know what they're doing." He shrugged. "And I have everything I need here." The look he threw me indicated he was referring to much more than groceries. "So will you be back?"

"Yeah. It won't take long." Not if my brain still worked after seeing Constantine for the first time since I broke up with him.

Alex held out a hand to me. I closed the distance to the bed, took it, and leaned over so I could kiss him goodbye.

****

Constantine's human butler, Wesley, opened the heavy mahogany door. There was no sign of recognition on his ancient face even after I gave him my name. It stung that he didn't remember me—not like he'd seen me almost daily for two years.

He let me in and told me Constantine was waiting for me in his *boudoir*. His smile when I groaned at the thought of meeting my ex in his bedroom took twenty years off his wrinkled face. "I suggested the parlor, but when Master Constantine is set on something, there is no talking him out of it," he said.

Tell me about it. I'd been yelling at the stubborn ass to leave me alone for four years now. Constantine didn't relent one bit in his pursuit and still called me at least twice a week, to see how I was doing and ask if I'd reconsidered.

I followed the human inside with a nod, trying not to scoff at *parlor*. Why would a vampire need one unless he was a pretentious bastard? Never mind, I got my answer right there. I scratched out the thought that I'd considered his flashiness part of his charm when we were together. I'd been too smitten to be objective.

Not staring at the blatant expressions of wealth along the corridor that led to the stairway took a lot of effort. The tapestry was embroidered with what I knew was real gold. I couldn't help but compare my ex's lifestyle with Alex's. It both relieved and scared me that in my mind, Alex won, hands down.

The thick carpet enveloped our feet, drowning out the sounds of our footsteps as we took the stairs down.

Constantine heard us, nevertheless. "Come in, darling," he called from behind the closed door of his bedroom. "We won't be needing you, Wesley."

The old man reached for the doorknob, but I placed my hand on it and shook my head. "I got it."

I expected him to insist, but he gave me a small bow, his joints creaking, and disappeared up the stairs faster than I considered possible.

I so didn't want to open that door.

The knob felt cold under my palm, uninviting. I turned it and pushed anyway, to reveal a sight that would have taken my breath away, if I had any.

I'd called before dropping by, in hopes Constantine would be decent by the time I went to his mansion. I ought to have known better. The light of at least ten dozen candles showered a room twice as big as my apartment, in the center of which stood a bed double the width and length of a king-size. The deep-purple silken duvet matched the color of the walls and made stark contrast with Constantine's naked upper body.

He was waiting for me *in bed.*

Fortunately he was covered from the waist down. His long legs were bent at the knees, and he had one arm folded behind his head, the other lying loosely at his side. His hair, long and golden, framed his head, making him look like an angel. I knew no angel would be as wicked as he was or have as perfect a body.

His height—I confess, I like my men tall—and absurd sexiness were the only similarities between him and Alex. Alex's well-built body and short, wavy hair, that perfectly black that even the best colorist wouldn't be able to duplicate, brought to mind a Greek god. Constantine's lean and sinewy frame, his long blond hair, and blue eyes made me think of a Norse deity. One that pillaged and made love for hours.

That was definitely not how I should be thinking of him.

I couldn't move. Couldn't enter the room or back out of it and run like I wanted to.

He reached out, much like Alex had when I left him earlier that evening, and beckoned me to him with his index finger.

For a moment, seeing his bare skin gleam in the candlelight, I forgot everything. I forgot how he crushed my heart underfoot after I gave it to him. I forgot that he was a cheater and that he filled me with insecurities even before I knew he was sleeping with someone else. I shut the door and stepped closer.

His beautiful, sexy, promising smile was what snapped me out of it. It was too self-satisfied for my taste. That lift of his sensual lips said, *I knew you'd come to me.* Once upon a time, that would have been enough for me to strip and jump him. Now I was glad I'd taken the time to go by my apartment and change into a pair of blue jeans, a hoodie, and sneakers. It was a small victory that I hadn't dressed up for him.

I stopped at the foot of the bed and said, "We have to talk."

He pouted, and I felt like a loser for wanting to pull his jutting lower lip between my own. "Do we have to?" he asked.

Why would he still have an accent? He'd been in the States for a couple of centuries, long enough to speak like he was born here. Was he keeping it only to make me want him?

"Yes. We do." Go me, for sounding so sure.

"Can't we kiss *hello*, first? That's what my people do."

"You're not Italian, Constantine." That wasn't even his real name, not that I could talk. He'd changed his name when he moved here, going for something more sophisticated. "Your people probably decapitated one another as a greeting." Okay, I was being stupid, but all that hotness put me on my defensive mode.

He laughed, and the sound felt like a caress. He used to laugh like that when he reduced me to a pile of goo after hours and hours of amazing sex. *Gah.* Could I stop thinking about that, please? I hadn't been the only one he liked goo-ifying.

"How about a kiss because you want to, then?"

I scowled. I didn't want to kiss him, did I?

"I guess that's a *no*." He raised his arms in defeat. "Fine. We'll talk, then." I was about to sigh in relief, when he folded the quilt back from his legs and slid out of bed.

He was naked.

And hard.

And walking toward me.

Telling him to put something on took all the self-control I possessed, and I was drained by the time he draped a dark-blue robe over his shoulders. It didn't hide anything, but if I opened my mouth to tell him that, I'd drool.

There was nothing in the room we could sit on except the bed, so I reluctantly parked my butt at its edge. I had to hop a bit to manage that, but I did so as gracefully as possible and locked gazes with him. Big mistake. He was the only vampire I knew whose eyes changed color according to his mood. Their current violet meant he was hungry. And not for blood.

That was the way his eyes had looked every time his lips sought mine. Every time I took him inside me.

That was the way his eyes had looked the day I found him balls-deep inside the woman who'd created him.

I didn't need the visual that came to mind uninvited. The she-devil had been on her knees, facing the door, and he was slamming inside her, making her breasts bounce. She'd seen me first, smirked, and urged him on, which he had no objection to until he noticed me. Even then, when he'd frozen, she kept fucking herself onto his cock.

I had to focus on what was important, not the way he'd had his face buried in her golden mane. "I need you to arrange a meeting with the council."

"I need you too." He covered my hand with his and brought it to his chest, over his heart. "This almost beat when I was with you." He sounded sincere, which was unsettling.

What was more unsettling was that I cared. I tried to speak, but nothing came out of my mouth. Unless you count that mewling sound I wished I could take back.

"This is serious, Constantine." This time I formed words, but my voice lacked conviction.

"This is serious too." He moved between my legs and guided my hand down his front, to his cock.

I pulled away like I'd been burned. "No. *That*"—I pointed to his groin—"is *stupid*. You don't want me. You just hate having lost me."

"I hate having lost you *because* I want you."

"To complete your collection?" Why was I letting him pull me into that talk? We'd had it over the phone, more times than I could count.

"Because I can't live without you."

"You're already dead. It doesn't matter."

"I made a mistake, Cherry. I've apologized a million times, and I will apologize a million more. It meant nothing."

Yeah, sure. It meant nothing. According to him, that was why it had happened often—because it meant nothing. "*Vampires are overly sexual beings*," he kept telling me, back when we were together. "*We are driven by our passions and our lust.*" When I said that made us animals, he countered that it made us superhuman; the way we let our wants dictate our actions held us above society's rules and conventions.

I'd said that was bullshit, and he'd said I was too young to know better. I'd wanted him to be monogamous, something rare in our kind. He'd made an effort for me, which was why he'd only been fucking Ádísa. *Because it meant nothing.*

Well, it meant a lot to me, and I said so now, as I had then.

He grabbed my wrist, and when I moved to slap him with my free hand, managed to trap that too. "I love that you're so stubborn."

Then the asshole kissed me.

It was nothing like the kisses Alex and I exchanged the last two days, although it did have the same bone-jellifying effect. It was dominant and possessive, and I didn't want it.

For four years, I'd avoided meeting him, despite calls and letters that begged me to do so, because I'd been afraid I'd give in to the passion he always ignited in me. And before Alex, I probably would have. After Alex, however, hot and irresistible as Constantine might be, it was only my body that wanted him. The body has its own memory. It remembers how a touch made it shiver once—remembers how it felt to be taken by an experienced lover.

Sadly for my ex, those memories weren't enough to overcome the memory of his betrayal, or the memory of another lover, a considerate one, waiting for me.

I freed my hands and shoved him back so hard, he'd have flown across the room if he were human. As it was, he barely saved himself the embarrassment of falling on his ass.

"You don't get to kiss me." I stabbed the air with my index finger. "You don't get to touch me and make me want you. We've been over this."

"I love—"

"You don't get to do *that*, either. You'd convinced me I was nothing without you, and you hate that I know better now."

His face hardened, and I had the niggling suspicion I wasn't entirely right on that account. Not that I cared. I didn't. *Wouldn't.* Even if part of me wanted to hug him and hold him close.

"You're not getting me back, Constantine. Ever." I hated that he squeezed his eyes shut with something akin to pain at my words. I hated that I cared.

He tightened his robe around him. "I'll let you know when I've spoken to the council."

I nodded. "Thank you."

"They may ask what it's about." He turned his back to me and walked to the door. I reassessed my earlier reflection on similarities between him and Alex and added one. They both swaggered with a feline grace that made me feel like a klutz.

I followed, happy my legs were steady. "I think there is a rogue out there."

His step faltered for a split second.

He opened the door and held it for me. "If you change your mind—*ever*—I will be waiting."

"I won't." I couldn't do more than whisper, but I was reasonably confident that I meant what I said.

He bobbed his head once. "I will be here, regardless."

I cupped his chin, allowing myself to take in the lines of his face, his cheekbones, his high brow, his square jaw. "Thank you."

I was halfway up the stairs when he said, "Please be careful."

****

I was too stressed to fly after leaving Constantine's place, so I took a stroll, let the night air calm my nerves.

The way things had been going the past couple of days, it made sense that my little walk would end up frazzling me even further.

The conversation with my ex went well, all in all. I felt bad for causing him pain, but at the same time, I felt vindicated. Besides, I'd hurt him less than he hurt me. At the end of the day, we'd been mostly civilized, had long-overdue closure, and he would talk to the council for me. I hoped they'd agree to see me, and that they weren't the grudge-holding type.

When the new council was first formed, they asked me to voice my approval of them when interacting with other vampires. I didn't refuse, but I didn't socialize with any vampires other than Constantine, so it's not like I really helped them. I hoped the former lack of active support on my part wouldn't make them think twice about helping me now.

I flared my nostrils as a car drove slowly by. The driver, fortunately alone, was drunk but extremely polite when he stopped and asked if I needed a lift. I locked gazes with him, declined, and ordered him to go straight home and never again drive inebriated.

The alcohol on his breath and the smells of the night—trees, flowers, a cat or two, the earth itself—made me think of another smell. Blood. The emotional roller coaster seeing Constantine put me through had me on edge, and I needed to feed.

A couple turned the corner, coming my way. They were holding hands, and the boy, who couldn't be older than seventeen, with saggy hair and baggy clothes, leaned to whisper something in the girl's ear. She laughed, her earrings jingling, and turned to him for a kiss, her auburn hair catching the streetlight and showing red streaks.

Red.

Blood.

I could have a quick snack on the spot and be on my way without either of them remembering what had happened. Their throbbing pulse called for me to do just that. I didn't even have to go for the neck. A nibble on the bend of the arm would be more than fine.

No. Even if they didn't remember the violation of a happy, carefree moment, I would. I didn't want to burst their bubble. They had a few more years ahead, before they absolutely had to face the cruelty of the world. My stomach protested my altruism, but I ignored it.

They smiled when they passed me by, and I returned the smile, fully meaning it. I

I'm a really scary vampire, aren't I? But they were so cute and so obviously in love.

Love. Love is something beautiful, something that should be treasured, and something not all people find in a lifetime. Many take it for granted, failing to recognize its magnificence. I am not one of them. I know love needs nurturing to thrive, and at that moment, I felt too scattered to focus on that nurturing. If I let myself go, what I felt for Alex would become deep enough, but I doubted I'd be able to handle it. Perhaps once I had my shit together, if he was interested in something more than sex and could wait that long…

Time was something I had in spades, barring an impromptu staking, decapitation, or burning, but Alex was mortal. Even if he fell head over heels for me, he would one day want more—a family, someone to grow old with. I would never grow old with anyone.

Thinking of Alex made my head hurt. It wasn't just my future that turned complicated when I tried to factor him in, but my present too. Would I drink from him again? Another rumble from my belly reminded me I should drink from someone, and soon. The thing was, I couldn't wrap my mind around going to a bar or club and hitting on anyone other than Alex. Sinking my fangs into someone else's throat and sucking wasn't appetizing at all, for some reason.

Some reason? Ah, how I love my denial. Still, I couldn't feed on Alex for a third time in a row. Could I? Especially when I wanted to keep whatever was between us casual?

Most importantly, would anyone see me if I started smacking my forehead repeatedly?

I decided to go with the third, least appealing option where dinner was concerned, and say *no* to my hand's urge to meet my temple. I glanced backward, to make sure the couple was out of sight, and took off.

****

Once the VSS had deemed that I was able to take care of myself, I'd been given a nest egg and the boot. The nest egg hadn't been enough for me to re-rent my old apartment, but that wasn't why I'd had to move. The guidelines say returning to our previous life is frowned upon, and *frowned upon* usually leads to staking in our crowd.

The money had, however, been enough to pay the first four months of rent for this underground studio with no kitchen. I'd bought a microwave oven for reheating the occasional cup of packaged blood, placed it on my bedside table, and I'd covered my culinary needs.

I got a bag of blood from my emergency stash in the teeny-tiny freezer that came with the teeny-tiny apartment, and warmed it. By the way, reheating frozen blood doesn't make the stuff tasty, just bearable.

I could have asked Constantine for a sip or two. Feeding from another vampire keeps us going for at least two or three days. It makes no sense, considering dead man's blood is poison to us, but it's true. And Constantine had been my donor many times in the past, so technically it would have been wrong to ask him. If I had no conscience.

Then again, I doubted he would have been very giving, without demanding something in return. I lifted my mug to my lips and took a mouthful. *Bleah.* I'd forgotten how bad frozen food tasted. Pinching my nose, I gulped the rest of the liquid down and went to the closet-sized bathroom to rinse my cup.

Deciding what to do next was hard. I could stay home and watch reruns, or I could keep my word and go to Alex, as I promised. Alex, who was waiting for me. Alex, who seemed unfazed by the weirdness that was my reality, and who treated me like I was special. Alex, with whom I'd spent the whole day in bed, going through pictures from his childhood, laughing, and making love. Alex, on whom I was developing a crush, though I tried hard not to.

Alex, with whom I couldn't be for more than a few measly decade—far too short a time for someone destined to live forever like I was—before his body betrayed him and he inevitably passed away, as all mortals do.

I couldn't do that to myself. Crush or not, I had to get out as soon as possible. As soon as we figured out his case.

But I promised.

I checked my cell phone. No missed calls. Nobody sought me out in the two days it lay under my bed, where I'd thrown it. It didn't surprise me. I shoved it in my back pocket. Constantine would call to let me know what he'd arranged. I grabbed my backpack, stuffed some clothes in, pulled my hair into a ponytail, took a deep, unnecessary breath, and opened the door.

I couldn't spend the rest of Alex's life with him, but there was no danger in enjoying his company for a few more days.

Plus there's safety in numbers, and two is a bigger number than one.

And I promised.

****

It was odd, seeing Alex in the kitchen. I hadn't associated him with that room. I'd thought he'd be more at ease in a luxurious bedroom, with dark colors and lavish fabrics. No, I didn't have a specific one in mind.

Nevertheless, he seemed comfortable among the spotless white countertops, flipping an omelet in the air when I walked in. So comfortable, in fact, that he was doing so wearing only an apron. What was it with naked men today?

"Does your mother know you wear her clothes?" I lifted one corner of my lips in appreciation of the view.

He threw me a smoldering look over his shoulder and wiggled his ass. "I like how airy this thing is."

We managed to keep a straight face for only a second or two, before cracking up.

I placed a kiss on his shoulder, hung my pack on the back of a chair, and hopped on the kitchen counter. "Saw you fixed the front door. You might consider locking it too. Anyone could walk in."

"I'll lock up tonight, so we can sleep without worrying about burglars." He added grated cheese to the omelet, and I watched it melt.

"So I'm staying tonight too?" I asked. Don't judge; I was there already.

"Unquestionably." He slid the omelet out of the pan and onto a plate he'd set to the side. Switching the cooker off, he turned fully to me and captured my lips with his.

"Good." I returned his kiss, internally thanking whoever was listening that Alex didn't have a vampire's sense of smell. Constantine's scent lingered on me, and we hadn't even had that much contact.

Alex looked at the plate, which gave out a divine aroma, and then back at me. "I forgot to ask if you can eat. Food. Solid food?" His perfect teeth trapped his lower lip.

I tore off a bit of fried egg with my fingers, dropped it in my mouth, and made a show of chewing and swallowing it. "It does nothing to sustain me, but I can have it." I ran my tongue over my front teeth. "It needs a bit more pepper." I like spicy food.

"It does not." He mock glared. "I make a mean omelet, and you'd better get your butt in a chair if you wanna have any more of it." He pointed at the table, which was set for two, a candle in the middle. "I'll make a salad and be right with you."

The whole thing was bizarrely cozy and sweet. I did as he said, making myself comfortable at the table and crossing my legs at the ankles, all prim and proper. Was that how being with him would be? Would he always remain so very wonderful? And why was I torturing myself? Vampires don't get to share *always* with humans.

"I like you," I blurted.

He furrowed his brow. "I thought we'd established that."

I nodded. "Felt like saying it." Oh God, I was sixteen again.

Looking at me meant he wasn't watching the knife, which missed the tomato and found the pad of his thumb instead. "*Ouch.*"

I was beside him before he got to the *ch*.

"It's nothing," he said, raising his hand toward his mouth.

I was faster. I took hold of his palm and lead his thumb between my lips. I licked the wound, sealing it, but he didn't pull his hand away. When I looked up at him, I was stricken by the way he watched me; it was intense and warm and full of something more than lust—which was utterly, indisputably *wrong*.

He averted his gaze, and I let his thumb go with a *pop*. "The omelet is getting cold. We should eat." If I sounded any cheerier, I'd barf.

"Yeah. Better forget the salad and dig in." He took the omelet to the table and pulled out a chair for me.

"Naw, I'll finish it. You sit." I was done with the tomato and chopped the lettuce by the time he began protesting. He gave in and took the seat across from mine.

Finding a bowl for the salad took a rather long time, because Alex stared at me with a hint of a smile instead of telling me which cupboard to look into. I scraped the salad from the chopping block into the bowl, snatched the pepper mill, and batted my eyelashes at him.

He chuckled as he served his creation to our plates. "Have at it."

I sank back in my seat and twisted the mill over my plate until one more speckle of pepper would make me sneeze. Then I tried the eggs. I may be exaggerating a bit, but that omelet was the best I'd ever tasted. We shared it while playing footsie under the table. Yup, I was sixteen, all right. And loving it.

Until things turned sour, as they almost invariably do.

Washing a sizeable bite down with cola, Alex asked, "How come you only stopped the blood?"

I had no idea what he was getting at, and it must have shown on my face.

"Aren't you hungry? You haven't eaten since late last night."

I worried he'd want me to drink from him again if I mentioned the frozen blood. I didn't want to get used to his taste, when I wouldn't have it for long. "I can take it a bit longer. And you need to build up your strength." Hoping I sounded blasé enough, I stuffed a forkful of salad in my mouth. "This is filling, as well as yummy." All that was missing from my performance was a satisfied tummy rub.

His fork clanked against the plate, where he let it drop. "You're lying. I see it in your eyes." His lips were quirked in a smile, but his tone was serious.

I turned the double-crossing things to the table. "Am not."

"The question is *why*."

Sighing in resignation, I took his hand in mine. "When I went to pack, I had a bite. Frozen stuff."

"You can have more of mine later if you want." He caressed my knuckles with his thumb, seeming relieved. "How did the meeting go?"

I shrugged one shoulder, focused on chasing a piece of lettuce around my plate. "It was fine. He'll call me when he hears from them."

"So do I get to know who he is?"

My hesitation indicated guilt, and I wasn't guilty, damn it. "My ex. His name is Constantine." Eh, I felt guilty.

"I see." Alex didn't speak again, switching his attention to his food. When his plate was squeaky clean, he pushed his chair back, stood, and left the room.

It took a couple of seconds for me to make up my mind on whether to follow him or not. If I didn't, he might think I didn't care. If I did, he might feel suffocated. Rock, meet hard place.

While evaluating my options, I factored in a very significant parameter—I was stronger and faster than he was. If he tried to pick a fight or leave the house, I could easily hold him still until he shut up and listened to me. Though why I had to explain myself, I really couldn't say. It wasn't like we were an item.

My chair screeched against the floor, the sound a million times more annoying to my ears than to a human's. Then I was on my feet, walking slowly to the living room. I'm talking real slow, not slow for a vampire. I dragged my feet because, although I'd done nothing wrong that night, I didn't want to talk about Constantine. Nothing good could come out of it. What was more, I didn't want to lie.

Alex sat in *our* armchair—funny that I felt we had shared custody of the thing—rubbing his face with his palm.

"Do you wanna—"

"My last girlfriend broke up with me eight months ago," he said to the wall behind me. "My life was too *adventurous* for her. We'd been together for a year and a half, and I was gonna ask her to marry me. Letting go of her was the hardest thing I've ever done." Amazing how a man his size seemed small at that moment.

The sadness in his voice made my throat constrict. I moved farther inside the room and leaned my thigh against the side of the couch, crossing my arms in front of my chest. I wanted to tell him I was sorry to hear that, yet I said nothing. *Sorry* wouldn't cover the extreme dislike I felt for the woman who'd wounded him, though I'd never met her. Still, it wasn't up to me to help him heal; I was nothing but a passerby in his life.

He shrugged, but his face had clouded. His nonchalance was an act. "She said she'd never be able to keep up. That she was leaving me for my own good. She said she was sorry and that it hurt her too. I didn't believe her. I couldn't get how the fuck she could leave me if it hurt her to do it."

I didn't want him to finish that story saying that he finally understood what she'd been talking about, that now he knew what being with someone too fast for him felt like. The conclusion was unavoidable though. He was only telling me about her as a preface to calling things off with me. What other reason could he have? In all my deep contemplation of the future, I'd failed to take one thing into consideration—

delayed freakout. Alex had been fine so far because the goings-on hadn't sunk in. Until now.

I let my head fall back. At least I wouldn't have to worry about leaving him; he was making my choice for me. I should be feeling relief instead of that numbness spreading from my fingertips toward my chest.

"She broke my heart to the point I thought it'd never mend again. I didn't even go on a date until I met you," Alex said.

I felt the need to interject, delay the inevitable. "It's not like we're dating." Good job, Cherry. *Great* job.

He might as well not have heard me. "The thing is"—

I dug in my biceps. Despite *knowing* we could be nothing to each other, I didn't want to hear what *the thing* was. Couldn't we forget *the thing* for the time being?

—"I want us to."

Okay. Rewind. Let's talk about *the thing*. "Huh?"

"I want us to date, Cherry. I want to take you out and come back home with you, but"—

Ah, the *but*. I should have known it was coming. *But* he couldn't handle it. *But* we weren't good for each other. *But* it wouldn't go anywhere, so we ought to save us both the trouble.

— "I'm not going to let another woman in, just so she can eventually hurt me. I want to know where you stand. How available you are, emotionally." He rolled his eyes and let his hand land heavily on the arm of the chair. "Fuck. I sound like a chick." At last he turned to me. "No offense."

"None taken," I said without thinking about it. I hadn't had time to take offense anyway. My mind was too busy trying to become pliable enough to bend around the unfathomable idea that Alex wanted to see more of me.

"What I'm saying is that there's something here." He wagged his index finger between us. "But I don't want to make more of it than it really is. I mean, if there's someone else…"

"I see." He wasn't saying we couldn't be together. I wanted to bounce. I refrained because really, we couldn't. But he wanted us to give it a try—and wasn't this a wonderful *but*?

"And?" He drew out the question, staring at me. Why was he staring? Had I done something wrong?

"And?" I batted my eyelashes, trying to buy some time. It was up to me to define what we had. Oh God. I *suck* at definitions. Doubly so when the definition I feel like giving is completely inappropriate.

"And would you like to say something?" His eyebrows shot for his hairline, his face such a contrast to the apron, I'd giggle if he hadn't just opened his heart up to me.

There was no one else, but that wouldn't be enough of an answer. I started at the beginning. "I met Constantine shortly after I was turned. He was my sponsor." The blank look from Alex made me elaborate. "He was the one in charge of me. He taught me how to choose my prey; how to deal with missing my family; how to not let the thirst take me over." And I fell so in love with him, he became my whole world—which Alex didn't need to know.

"Constantine made me stop hating what I'd become. He was there for anything I needed. He showed me fighting moves and made me read. Reading was what distinguished us from savages, he said. We became lovers." We had been more than that. He'd made me happy, and in return I'd let him suck me into his whirlwind of an existence.

Alex's mouth twitched almost imperceptibly, his eyes darkening a shade.

I shouldn't linger on that subject. "We were together for a couple of years, until I walked in on him with another woman. We hadn't seen each other since, until tonight." That didn't feel entirely honest. "We spoke on the phone lots, though."

Alex still stared at me. I hadn't answered his question. "It was weird seeing him," I heard myself say. *Weird* was an understatement. "But I'm okay. And nothing happened." That was as much as I could say about my emotional availability. I wanted Alex, and yes, I was over Constantine. Mostly.

No, I wasn't in the best place for a relationship. Yes, I wanted to give it a try anyway. No, I couldn't do what I wanted. There were repercussions for me to consider.

"Can you see yourself with him in the future?" There was cop face again, only this time his worry seeped through the mask's cracks.

"I… No. I don't think so." I hated the doubt in my voice. "I'm not in love with him anymore, but he's important to me. I'd like for this to be something, Alex. *Us.* I just don't think I can be what you need." There. Full honesty. My cards were spread on the table.

The room was so silent once I stopped talking, I tapped my foot to make sure I hadn't gone deaf. I wasn't what Alex needed. He had the chance to make a family with a human who'd grow old with him. Nevertheless, I wanted him not to let that stop him. Hey, I'm dead, but I'm still a woman.

He leaned forward, hands on his knees. "I'll go by the office in the morning. Get you the pictures." That was a change of subject if I ever heard one—or so I thought, until he spoke again. "We'll talk about this more once we've solved the case. Fucking will tide us over till then." He winked.

If any other man spoke to me like that a couple days after we met, no matter how carnal his knowledge of me might be, I'd snap at him. Instead I laughed. Alex tone showed he didn't mean it as a slight, and it was nice laughing with him—easy, pleasant. He made it possible for me to be carefree, when my head was filled with problems to be solved.

"Was that a *no*?" He gave me a lopsided smile.

I licked my lower lip and walked to him, swishing my hips with every step. "It was a most definite *yes*."

The future was so very far away that moment.

Chapter Six

My knight in shining armor, Alex brought the portable television downstairs before leaving for work, but daytime TV wasn't enough to keep my mind busy. My thoughts returned to my current situation despite my efforts. As a last resort, I started counting the bricks in the room.

I was halfway through the third wall, when I heard a car pull up and soon steps rushed along the driveway. Friend or foe?

I knew it was Alex when I heard the key in the lock. Willoughby would have no qualms busting through another door.

If it weren't for the evil sun, I'd have flown up the stairs to meet Alex and thank him for saving me from my boredom. As it was, I jumped out of bed when he switched on the light, planning on smooching the breath out of him as soon as he set foot on the landing.

His grim expression stopped me in my tracks. "We had another disappearance last night." He kissed my forehead and passed me by to drop an armful of folders on the bed.

I looked at my feet with their ever-perfect red toenails, ashamed that my worst crisis last night had been which hot male to sleep with.

"She doesn't fit the pattern. A bit older and rather… Well, she isn't a match, physically." He hastened to add, "Not that she's ugly."

"Maybe her disappearance is not related?" I tucked a strand of hair behind my ear and blew my bangs up off my eyes—really inconvenient hairstyle to carry indefinitely.

Shaking his head, he sat on the bed and patted the mattress next to him. I sank down by his side, rubbing his neck with one hand while he opened the first folder.

"She disappeared from a nightclub." He didn't find what he was searching for, so he checked the second one and let out a huff before tossing that aside too.

His shoulders were full of knots, so I slid behind him, legs outside his, and used both hands to massage him. "Maybe she wanted a change of scenery and will show up eventually?"

"She has a kid. She wouldn't have left him willingly," he said in a low voice, shuffling through more papers. I was about to point out that there are some horrible mothers in this world when he cursed under his breath. "Finally."

An uneasy feeling in the pit of my stomach made me stop what I was doing and glance over his shoulder at what he held up. It was a passport picture, and not a recent one.

"Theodora Williams," Alex said. He didn't have to.

I knew the big, earnest eyes looking out at me from the face with the prominent angles. Her hair was longer than she'd worn it since I first met her, her cheekbones sharper, her neck slimmer. Still, there was no doubt in my mind. Even in a photograph taken something like ten years earlier, I recognized the girl.

Dotty.

Alex was still talking, but I wasn't listening. His voice was background noise, lost as I was inside my thoughts. Was Dotty randomly targeted, or did my maker know where I lived? Who my friends were? Doubt and self-recrimination were circling in my mind like sharks in a tank, and in these circumstances, I wasn't a good swimmer.

"I know her," I said after several long moments. "She lives in my building. We're friends. Sorta." It couldn't be a coincidence.

He turned, trying to meet my gaze. When he couldn't, he rose and sat again, this time facing me. "I'm sorry, Cherry. We'll do everything we can." He reached for my hand, and I let him take it but couldn't accept the solace he was offered.

"Mark. Where is Mark?" I couldn't believe I hadn't asked that sooner.

"With his dad. Dad went to drop the kid off, and there was no sign of Dotty. They waited, but she didn't show. The boy said she was out with a guy she'd been seeing, but we have no name or description."

"Can't you find him from her phone records?"

"We're waiting for the judge to sign the subpoena."

Waiting. I wasn't good at waiting. I pulled away from his touch. "We have to do something. I think it's because of me. 'Cause we're looking into this case."

His other hand found my shoulder and squeezed reassuringly. "Don't do that. She was unlucky. We'll—"

"No." The word came out so harsh, it reverberated off the walls and came back to me like the snap of a whip. "This has nothing to do with luck, bad or otherwise. She doesn't fit the profile. You said so yourself. She isn't young enough and has family. If she was indeed taken by Willoughby, it can't be for the same reason. It's to get to me, like breaking in here was to get to you."

"But we don't know why the others were taken." There he went with the sense-making again. "We still don't know why *you* were turned."

"You think my turning is connected?" I was already half-convinced it wasn't random, but six years had passed since. What he was suggesting was…

"I do." He drew circles on the back of my hand with his thumb. "And I'm going to find out how."

I stood so quickly that I'd have felt dizzy if I were alive. "We can do that later. We will. First we have to find Dotty." I itched to sink my teeth in the throats of those responsible for it all.

"*We* will do nothing until it's dark outside." Alex headed toward the stairs.

"Where are you going?"

"Gotta make some phone calls."

I wondered what good it would do but said nothing. I paced while waiting for him to come back down. I couldn't shake the feeling that I was the reason Dotty was in danger, and I was restless with the need to act. Wouldn't stupid dusk ever come?

"…one of you can come in." Alex got in my way, snapping me out of my internal musings.

"What?" I had no clue what he was talking about or when he'd returned to the basement. Vampiric senses, my ass.

"I said, at least we know only one of you can come in."

"Where?"

"In the house," he said. "*This* house. Only one vampire can come in—other than you. My mother said two guys came by a few days before she left. They were selling cable service. She's had no other visitors that she didn't know."

I was perplexed. As was becoming a habit, he read my facial expression all too well. "I told her there was a burglary in the neighborhood," he said. "Asked if she'd seen any strangers around."

I nodded. "Is she sure?"

"A hundred percent. She's a hell of a gossip. The cable guys refused to say anything about themselves, and it struck her as odd. They were also very insistent about coming inside the house but didn't stay for more than five minutes once she invited them in." He ghosted his knuckles down my cheek. "Are you okay?"

"No. I want to go by Dotty's, see if I can find anything out."

"We've already spoken to her son and her ex-husband."

Of course they had, but I could find out more than Alex's colleagues had. "Mark said she was out with the same guy she'd been seeing for a couple of weeks." I should have asked her about that guy last time she wanted me to babysit. "Sure none of our neighbors has seen him?"

To his credit, Alex didn't look upset that I more or less questioned how he did his job. He shook his cell phone in the air. "Called Lieutenant Roebuck again. Nothing yet. We'll keep asking around, but there's not much to go on. Guy might as well be a ghost."

"I have to go, Alex."

"No, you don't. What's more, you can't. Her place is filled with cops. They're talking to her neighbors. If you show up, they'll ask questions, and if they need to talk to you for hours, they won't be understanding of your sun allergy." His voice rose gradually. "Let us handle it, all right?"

"No. It's not all right. I *need* to do something about it, and you can't stop me."

"Cherry." His tone was pleading now. "Please try to understand. It's our job."

"Well, you're not very good at it, are you? Those girls can attest to that." I regretted the words the moment they were out of my mouth.

His face fell and closed up at the same time. He was still looking at me but with narrowed eyes.

"I'm sorry," I whispered. "That was cruel."

"You think?"

"I'm sorry." I leaned my forehead against his broad chest. "I hate being unable to help her."

He wrapped his arms around me. "I know the feeling. I promise my guys are doing their best. They're gonna turn the place upside down, to find clues about her guy."

The calmness that washed over me when he embraced me was unsettling. I couldn't let myself lean on him like that, when he wouldn't be around for long. "I still believe I can do more," I said, trying to pull away. "I know her. Your guys don't. And poor Mark must be scared to death."

"He's with his dad." He wouldn't let go.

"His dad is a first-class jerk, Alex. Please let me go."

He sighed so deeply, my head rose and fell against his chest. "Can you get in and out of her apartment unnoticed? The kid may tell you more than he did the officers, but he's not alone."

"I can make others not notice me." I hung my head and looked up at him through lowered eyelashes. He'd made his thoughts on mind control clear.

He surprised me by kissing the crown of my head. "You're not going to hurt anyone." It wasn't a question or a demand, more a statement of fact, yet I felt the need to reassure him.

I met his gaze and gave him a weak smile. "I'll… *compel* them to look elsewhere. No harm, no foul."

He chuckled. "Fine. You can *compel* away. Just don't get into trouble."

"I won't. Honest."

****

The uniform in front of my building was in his mid to late thirties and impeccably groomed. He leaned against the glass door, obviously bored. I could relate. I'd twiddled my thumbs most of the day too, waiting for it to be dark outside.

He snapped his head my way when I started up the steps. Huh. He wasn't as out of it as I initially thought.

I caught his gaze. "I'm not here," I said. "You never saw me."

His eyes went blank. "I never saw you."

I nudged him aside and crossed the threshold.

The two cops outside Dotty's apartment were equally easy to get off my case, as was Mark's dad, a short, tubby man with beady eyes and thin lips—I don't know what Dotty ever saw in him.

Finally certain my presence wouldn't be remembered, I walked to the boy's bedroom.

Mark rushed me and wrapped his arms around my waist the moment I opened the door. Gone was the snotty brat whose ass I wanted to kick every time I babysat him. He was just a lost little kid now, and I was the only adult he felt close to. He buried his face in my belly and let out a choked sob that broke my heart.

"It's okay, big guy. We'll get your mom back." I caressed his hair. "We will. And she'll be fine. You'll see."

"Will the scary man let her go?"

I wouldn't have made out his question without my enhanced hearing. What did he know? "What man, Mark?" I wanted to see his face, but he might find it easier to talk without facing me.

"He came to my window earlier. Said—" Another sob, and then he wouldn't talk despite my urging him.

Only a vampire could have appeared at his second-story window, and I bet my bottom dollar I knew who it had been. "Did the man have big, pointy teeth?"

Mark sniffled.

I decided to resort to extreme measures. "Look into my eyes, sweetie."

He did, his face open and full of trust. The hope mirrored there made me feel guilty, but not enough to stop me from using my abilities on him. "Tell me exactly what the man said."

His eyes glazed over. "You're a good boy, Mark, and that's why I won't kill your mom. But you have to do something for me too. Tell Cherry to get her boyfriend off my case. If you tell anyone else you saw me, I'll come back for you." The voice that came out of his mouth was his, but deeper, like he was imitating an adult.

I knew beyond the shadow of a doubt whose disdainful tone I heard.

Willoughby.

Mark trembled like a leaf, and I clutched him to me harder. I would find the stupid vampire who thought he could mess with me and mine, and I'd turn him to dust, like I did with his buddy.

"You *are* a good boy, and I'll get your mom back to you." I slid down to kneel before Mark, never tearing my gaze from his. "You must believe me and not be sad."

He smiled—not the cocky grin that resembled his dad's, but a sweet tilt of the lips that was a hundred percent Dotty. "I believe you."

I kissed his cheek and told him not to tell anyone he saw me. I trusted him not to, though I'd stopped the gaze lock by that point.

He grabbed my shirt before I could go. "Dad wants me to stay with Gran for a while. What if Mom comes home and doesn't find me?"

Dotty had mentioned her mother-in-law lived in Bakersfield, far enough for Mark to be relatively safe. "I'll tell your mom where to find you. Don't worry."

He wiped his nose on the back of his hand and nodded.

****

I rang Alex's doorbell and waited. My phone vibrated in my back pocket. I pressed the little green button and brought it to my ear.

"Constantine." I said his name flatly, instead of a greeting. *Hey* or *whazzup* wouldn't cut it.

"Cherry." It sounded more like *Chérie*. It pissed me off without real reason.

"Did they say yes?" There was no need for niceties; we both knew why he called.

Alex opened the door, and I motioned for him to be quiet as I walked inside and let him close it behind me.

"Indeed." Constantine sighed. "Where are you?"

I ignored his question. "When?"

"Now." I detected impatience in his voice. "Where are you?"

"Not your business. Where?" The council's private meeting chambers have always been hush-hush. They hold hearings in safe houses, but never without an appointment and never at the same place twice. Last I'd seen them, they'd been in an old warehouse.

Only a handful of people knew how to contact them, something I found at odds with their purpose. Rulers are supposed to know their subjects. Also, I hate being considered anyone's subject. That said, I assumed their agreeing to meet me meant I was in the inner circle. Sort of.

"Come by the mansion. I'll take you to them," Constantine said. So no inner circle for me.

Alex frowned, and I turned my back to him to whisper into the phone. "I don't want you there, Constantine. Thank you for arranging it, but I don't need you to cover my ass."

He tutted. "First off, I prefer your ass naked. Secondly, *they* requested I be there."

Bullshit. It wasn't a *they* that wanted him at the meeting; it was a *she*. A bitch, who happened to be one of the council members. *Ádísa.*

"I'll be right there."

Chapter Seven

As it turned out, I wasn't the only one to grumble.

Alex insisted on coming with me, but I couldn't very well present him to the council and say, *Hey, peeps. This human knows all about us, but it's cool*. Not if I liked my head where it was—and it just so happened my shoulders were kind of partial to it.

"Are you sure it's safe?" He stood at the open door, blocking my way out of his mom's ground-floor bathroom. Arms stretched over his head, he held the door frame and rolled his shoulders and neck. His heartbeat betrayed that he wasn't half as relaxed as he appeared.

"Yes"—an endearment was about to roll off my tongue, but we weren't there yet—"Alex. It's safe. They're the council. The good guys."

He snorted, the sound carrying more snark than any nonverbal response should. "What about the warning?"

The thought had bugged me since I left Mark behind. "The warning was about *you* backing off, which you said you would. Plus, I don't see how he'd find out I'm meeting the council."

"You do realize I'm not officially withdrawing from the case, right? Just lying low?" He sounded concerned. "That doesn't mean the department is going to drop it. There are people looking into this as we speak."

"I know," I said. "And it's not like you and I are gonna sit on our hands in the meantime. We're just going to be more subtle."

"Still, maybe going with him—"

"Isn't a good idea," I finished his sentence. I had no time for jealousy and territory marking now, although I might enjoy Alex and Constantine comparing their machismo at a less panicky time. "The council asked for him, and they will know what to do." I wholeheartedly hoped they would. If they couldn't help, Dotty wouldn't be Willoughby's last victim.

"Fine. If you want to go, go." There went the cool act, right out the window. He didn't raise his voice, but there was an edge to it. "If you're not back by dawn, I'm coming after you."

"I'm going, and I'll be back way before dawn." Not that he'd know where to begin looking. I rummaged through my bag, for a bobby pin. My nowhere-near-natural, bright-red hair color was damaging enough for my credibility in front of the vampire ruling body. I had to at least pull the bangs back.

Ah, there it was.

"Fine," Alex barked once more

I had the pin in my mouth and was trying to hold the front of my hair up, to secure it. "Fine," I spat back around the hairpin. I finally got my bangs where I wanted them and tried to pin them in place. No luck. My hair isn't great at staying in place unless copious amounts of hairspray are involved.

Alex plucked the thing out of my grasp and shoved it in my hair so hard that, at a steeper angle, it would have gone through my scalp.

"Ow." I ducked away and turned to glare at him.

"Sorry." No, he wasn't. The corners of his mouth lifted. A smiling Alex was a good thing, so I wouldn't hold this against him.

I pinched his ass and begrudgingly returned the hug and peck he gave me. They felt too much like *goodbye* and made me want to burrow into his embrace and forget about the meeting.

I couldn't. "I'll be back soon."

"I'll be here. Told Roebuck I'm following a lead, so I won't have to go by the department until we know something about the case. And I've got research to do." He pointed to the folders strewn all over the coffee table. "So I'm clear, though, I don't like this."

As I walked out the door, I couldn't help but wonder how much harder letting him go for good would be, if leaving him for a short time felt so bad.

****

Constantine waited for me at the door, dressed this time. Can't say I wasn't a bit disappointed over the lack of bare flesh, but most of me was relieved to see him in his black dress pants, designer black shirt, and purple tie. A vampire dressed in black and purple. *Stereotypes-R-Us.*

He looked scrumptious, dressed up—don't get me wrong—and with clothes covering his body, I had less trouble focusing on his face.

I tugged at the end of his ponytail. "My, my, aren't we all spiffy for the meeting." I wasn't jealous that he'd spent time becoming even more gorgeous than usual because he'd see Ádísa. Wasn't jealous at all.

He narrowed his eyes and looked at me top to bottom and up again. He didn't seem pleased, and I instinctively ran my hands down my blouse. It was a nicer top than the one he last saw me in, but the jeans and sneakers were the same. When he clucked his tongue, I wished I'd bothered to wear something fancier.

"Does your human keep you too busy to clean up properly?"

I be offended, if his tone didn't hold a hint of covetousness. *Touché.* Er…I mean, I won. He was jealous, *and I wasn't.* "What human?" I asked with an innocent smile.

"The one I can smell all over you." He flared his nostrils, and *damn*, that was too sexy to be legal.

Mega-oops—I didn't shower after this morning's sexcapades with Alex. The council would smell him too. Not that they'd care, but I hated the idea of them knowing what I did earlier today.

I batted my eyelashes at Constantine. "Are we driving? If we're flying, you'll have to tell me where we're going." I'm so smooth when I want to be. *Not.*

He didn't fall for my attempt at changing the subject. "Last time… He pursed his lips, then closed his eyes. "I didn't realize he was more than food." When he opened them again, he looked at me like he saw right through me.

His irises had turned nearly black, a color I hadn't seen them before. They were mesmerizing. His expression changed—no distinct movement, just the barest tensing of muscle. I can't explain it, but it was the most vulnerable I'd seen him. A knot formed in my stomach. I did whatever this was to him.

"Constantine…" What was there to say?

He pinched the bridge of his nose, and when he withdrew his hand, there was a smirk that didn't reach his eyes. "We're flying."

I had no time to react when he pulled me to him and cupped the back of my head. For a moment, I was sure he was about to kiss me—and not sure at all that I'd stop him.

Instead he pressed my face to his chest. "You're not allowed to see where we're going."

Why all the secrecy? Not like the council would be visiting the place again. Snuggled in his arms, with the night air swishing around us, I didn't voice my thoughts. I leaned against his body and trusted him to lead me to our destination.

In retrospect, that might not have been my best idea ever. I hadn't felt dizzy after a flight since my first takeoff as a vampire, but I was light-headed by the time we landed. It might be the flight, or I could blame it on Constantine drawing circles on the small of my back with his thumb and moving his lips against my hair, like he'd been whispering a secret.

The flight it was, if I wanted to get any sleep that day.

My knees buckled when Constantine let go—the way knees do because of uncontrolled landings, and nothing else—and he grabbed my shoulders hard enough to leave bruises. Good thing bruises fade fast on us.

I found my footing and pulled away, but his grip lingered. "I'm not letting go," he whispered.

He wasn't talking about my shoulders. "It'll be hard for us to walk this way." Keeping my voice steady and my tone light took a lot of concentration.

"But it will be fun." He ghosted one hand up my neck and traced my jawline with his thumb, stopping a hairbreadth from my lower lip.

I turned my cheek to him, doing my best to gather my wits and figure out where we were. We stood on what seemed to be the runway of a deserted airport.

"We'll be late," I said to the tarmac, refusing to meet Constantine's gaze.

****

The good news was I was too rattled by the moment I shared with my former lover to let the idea of facing the five vampires whose word was law frighten me. Plus they were supposed to be on my side.

Mostly.

That last word flashed bright neon in my head, as soon as the first of the council members walked inside the cold room, in the middle of which a tiny scrap of a human man had seated Constantine and me.

Ádísa glanced at me, a smirk on her full, red lips. She would have headed the council if the job description depended on age. Legend had it she was a Valkyrie, a *chooser of the slain,* who'd escaped Odin and renounced Valhalla, the Old Norse version of warrior heaven. I was convinced she'd created that legend herself because she loved being the center of attention.

With her long blonde hair braided at the sides of her neck, and her barely-there leather getup, she looked the part as she regarded Constantine with a small smile. Her breasts were too firm to spill over her bra-like top, even if they looked like they were about to do just that. Whether because of awesome genes or Odin's favor, she'd never curse herself for not getting a boob job in time.

In her wake came Gheorghios. Second oldest of the council members, he'd for a while followed the arch-bitch's example and tried to convince people he was *the* Saint George, who'd slain the dragon. Even one-day-old newbies knew he'd pulled that out of his ass, yet nobody would dare say so in his presence. Unlike his story about his past, his viciousness and quick temper were never disputed.

His hawkish gaze landed on me like an actual physical weight, and I strove not to show my discomfort. I couldn't smile; he might take it as insolence. So I met his gaze with the best combination of respect and earnestness I could muster. I guess I did well enough, because he nodded at me and my escort and took a step back, to stand on Ádísa's right. The way they lined up made me think of a beauty pageant. *And now, our next contestant, in dark 'n' gloomy wear.* I shushed the thought. This wasn't the time to giggle.

The urge to squirm was overwhelming. I wasn't there to get judged, but I felt every part the naughty schoolgirl, appearing before the school board—an extremely strict school board, with a propensity for bloodshed.

I calmed down a little when the third of the five we were to meet strutted our way and graced me with a full grin and a wink. He shook hands with Constantine and took his place at Gheorghios's side. John—Johnny Boy to his friends—had been turned in his late teens and dressed as if he was still in them. His jeans were faded and ripped, his boots heavy and with metal fronts, his T-shirt snug. Barely a century undead, he'd accumulated a great following and had gained the respect of friends and enemies, despite being known as a pacifist—something not guaranteed to gain you status among our kind.

I'd spoken to him once before. He was the one who approached me for that spokesperson deal in the past, and he was as mellow as vampires come, in spite of the bad-boy exterior.

Hui Zhong, following close behind, was the exact opposite. Her china-doll appearance, complete with a silk robe—which I'd called just that and had been glared at, 'cause "*it's a* hanfu"—belied her bloodthirsty nature.

She'd been turned in China in the late 1800s, and her kills during her fledgling days rivaled the number of deaths from the plague epidemic, which had conveniently covered said kills.

She didn't smile, frown, or even look at us. A demure bow, aimed at nobody in particular, was all the acknowledgment we received. I found the act too much, like the outfit, but I resisted the eye roll I felt coming. I'd heard she carried a sword under that robe—hey, it's my head, and I say it's a *robe*—and I didn't care to find out for sure.

The last vampire to walk in before the door was bolted on the outside was Benjamin. He was a paradox, in that he'd been turned in his sixties and had been one of us for only seventeen years. There was a theory that he'd been recruited for the council to appeal to a different demographic. Hui Zhong was supposedly there for the same reason—diversity. The new council advocated it, and that was the basis of its power. One look into Benjamin's flat eyes, however, and one could see the cold calculation and single-minded determination that gained him his position.

He'd been the instigator of the coup that ended the old council, and the first to dust one of them. One moment he'd been one of those present at the hearing about my irresponsible turning, the next he'd been yelling that the council was inadequate and driving a wooden stake through the oldest vampire's heart in the ensuing melee.

He scared me shitless.

With Benjamin in place, a semicircle was formed around me and Constantine. A black semicircle, with the exception of Hui Zhong's colorful attire. A shiver ran down my spine. Constantine found and squeezed my fingers. I squeezed back. There was no reason for worry. They were scary-ass, all right, and I had to tell them something they wouldn't like, but they wouldn't turn their wrath for the rogue against us.

Right?

"State your name, please." The man who'd told us to sit was now between us and the council. He looked at me expectantly and waved a pen over a pad. He didn't seem nervous enough for being in the presence of so many of us. I certainly felt more apprehensive than he looked.

"Your name?" he asked again when I took a whole entire second to reply.

"Cherry Stem."

Someone snorted; I'm not sure whether it was at my screen name or because of what I'd done on said screen. Either way my money was on Ádísa having made the rude sound, but I didn't glance her way. The secretary, or whatever Little Man was, squinted at me before jotting down my name.

"Is your reason for requesting an audience political, ethical, or personal?"

I'd rocked multiple-choice quizzes in high school and was about to say that, when Constantine nudged me with the heel of his shoe. "I am not sure," I said. "It affects all of us, but it's not political."

The guy narrowed his eyes again. "Ethical, then?"

I shrugged. "Sure."

The pen scratched the pad once more. "And who vouches for Ms. Stem?"

Umm, what was that?

Before I could say I had no clue someone was supposed to vouch for me, or what said vouching was about, Constantine spoke up. "I do."

"Are you sure?" I muttered the question under my breath without looking at him, but the council members no doubt heard it.

He wasn't perturbed, of course. "Yes. They needed someone to vouch that you had a valid reason for asking to see them. I did. They know and trust me."

I tried not to dwell on the fact that, last time I checked, only *one* of the members knew him well enough.

I smiled at the human, who cleared his throat to get our attention. "Yup, he's the voucher, all right." By his frown I assumed a bit more formality wouldn't hurt. I beamed a smile at him, grateful I didn't have a pulse. If I did, it would be racing now.

Constantine's name was noted down—he didn't give his real name, either—and we were done with the formalities. The human moved to the side and sat behind a little desk.

I turned to the standing vampires, studying each face briefly. They all looked at me in expectation. *Don't waste their time*, I told myself, yet my brain froze. How was I to start?

I wet my lips and went for it. "I have reason to believe a rogue vampire is turning young women." There. Like pulling off a bandage.

I expected some reaction to my statement—a widening of the eyes at minimum, maybe a gasp—but all I got were blank looks.

I hate blank looks. "A woman in my apartment building went missing, and I overheard the police talk about how that fits a series of other disappearances."

They still not said nothing. They didn't even blink. John gave me an almost imperceptible nod, so I went on. "The thing is, the day before the disappearance, I was attacked by one of us. He was masked, but I recognized him as Willoughby. My maker. I thought he was dead."

Benjamin spoke. "Willoughby? That's highly improbable." His frown made him look even scarier than before.

"It was him. He said he should have killed me."

"But your attacker was masked." Hui Zhong's voice was light, like a chirp, and neutral.

"And I'm sure more than one of us has thought about killing you." Ádísa was friendly as always.

I huffed. I had to tell them the whole story, or a version of it that would keep me out of trouble. The lie I'd decided on wouldn't cut it. "I was with a man. A human." Constantine tensed beside me, but I couldn't do this *and* spare his feelings. Besides, he and I weren't together. "I was at his place for… dinner, when Willoughby broke in. He attacked us both."

I should have told them about Ted too, but I didn't want to admit to dusting him. "I didn't realize who he was at first," I said, "but then I recognized his voice. The man I was with turned out to be the detective investigating the disappearances. See? It all makes sense. Willoughby must have planned the attack. He must have gotten a member of the family to invite him in the house earlier on, or he wouldn't be able to enter."

The synchronized bobbing of heads with matching skeptical expressions was a funny sight, but I didn't feel like laughing. "I wiped the human. After." I sounded convincing enough. "I don't understand how Willoughby is still around, how he escaped when we all thought he was executed, but I think he's out there killing or turning women, and—"

"Thank you for bringing this to our notice, Cherry. We'll look into it." John smiled at me, eyes twinkling, and the knot in my stomach loosened. I had at least one ally in a high place.

"*If* there's something to look into," Gheorghios added, and Hui Zhong raised an eyebrow—the first expression I'd seen on her face so far. Benjamin was frowning. The lines of his face deepened, and the result was disconcerting.

I hesitated. Should I tell them about Dotty's son getting a visit from the kidnapper? My instincts told me not to. As far as I knew, said kidnapper wasn't aware his message was delivered, and that might keep Mark safe for a bit longer. "Could you let me know if you find my neighbor? Her son needs her." I was asking for a lot, but I liked Dotty.

"We're done here. You may go now." Ádísa, ever helpful, waved one hand toward the exit.

I was about to object—beg, if I had to—when John said, "We'll keep you posted."

It was more than I could have hoped for, although I was still planning on looking deeper into Dotty's disappearance.

Ádísa stressed her dismissal by folding an arm behind her head, arching her back, and yawning.

I never had illusions concerning my appearance, nor did I have any complexes. I'm not a stunner, but I'm pretty and can turn heads with little effort. And makeup. All in all, I have confidence in my looks, despite my handful or two of extra pounds. When Ádísa stretched, that confidence wavered.

Seeing her exhibit how much I was boring her should be insulting. She probably meant it that way. The only thought that crossed my mind, however, was that *I* would probably cheat on me with her. Toned abs, high cheekbones, bee-stung lips, golden mane—and we've covered the boobs, right? Her curves looked preordered, and knowing they weren't pissed me off to no end. I pinched the inside of Constantine's bicep, just because he'd let her seduce him.

Since I was pinching, I kept my hold on him as I rose to leave. Constantine stood next to me and gave the council a little bow, before placing his hand at the small of my back and guiding us toward the exit.

"Not you, darling." She even *sounded* gorgeous, damn it, her voice throaty and melodic.

Constantine turned to her. "Pardon?"

I took a couple of steps forward, fully aware ignoring her was impolite, yet not caring.

Then she said, "I thought maybe you'd like to see me home," and my feet ceased moving.

To his credit, Constantine didn't jump at the suggestion. "It isn't gentlemanly to let the lady I'm escorting return home alone."

"We're not in the eighteen hundreds anymore." She laughed. "I'm sure your little friend can find her way home."

Little friend? Grrr!

"She can't, Ádísa. She doesn't know where we are, nor should she find out." Nice. He'd pretend to be protecting the council? He lacked the balls to tell her he didn't want to go anywhere with her?

Unless he did.

Constantine must have sensed my irritation, because he reached over the distance between us and put a hand on my shoulder. It had a calming effect. I realized he was protecting me by trying not to piss her off. I was happy my back was still to them. I doubted she'd appreciate my face-splitting grin. And it was face splitting. It made my jaw hurt.

"Rowland can drive her, then." There was such finality in her tone, Constantine argued no more.

The human all but ran to my side. A peek over my shoulder showed me the others had left. The sneaky bastards hadn't made a sound. Ádísa held out her arms for Constantine. She met my gaze and blew me a kiss.

Bitch.

****

Constantine was safe and would probably enjoy himself, if he wasn't already. I'd be safe too, despite having been blindfolded as soon as I stepped out of the building.

Still, refraining from bitching took all the energy I had. The council hadn't shown interest in what I told them. I was tired, hungry, and my hot ex, with whom I had unresolved issues, was practically vamp-napped by your stereotypical femme fatale.

The latter wasn't my worry; it just annoyed me.

The ride was quiet and uneventful. Rowland wasn't the world's best conversationalist, but he was nice enough to offer me a reheated bottle of blood when I mentioned I hadn't eaten in more than twenty-four hours. I needed to feed so badly, the packaged meal didn't taste half bad.

When I entered the house, Alex was sprawled on the couch, his bare feet propped on the armrest. The lower half of his face was hidden by the folder he'd been working on when sleep overtook him, and he was snoring lightly. Seeing him made me forget all about Constantine as a wave of affection washed over me. Coming back to Alex was like coming home.

My heart expanded at the thought of doing that on a daily basis, and I shook my head to get rid of that mental image. Neither the time nor the subject matter was right for daydreaming. I plucked the folder from his fingers and left it on the floor so I could lean over him, to touch my lips to his.

He smiled without opening his eyes. Just a quirk of the lips. He was still asleep; I could tell by his breathing.

"Want to come to bed?" I whispered in his ear. My tongue trailing along it was just an accident, honestly.

The response I got was an adorable furrowing of his brow and an even more adorable scrunching of his nose.

"Alex?" I caressed his stomach, first over his shirt and then under it, loving the feel of his heat and smoothness. "Come to bed with me?"

He fluttered his lids and stirred a bit. Snaking an arm around my waist, he pulled me to him. "No," he mumbled, burying his face at the crook of my neck.

Being held bent over wasn't the most comfortable thing in the world, even for an immortal, so I draped a leg across his hips and crawled on top of him. "I'll carry you if you don't get up."

Idle threat—I could pick him up and carry him but had no intention to—yet it worked. Alex blinked at me drowsily. "You'd better be joking." He found my waistband, bunched his fingers around the loop at the back, and gave it a playful yank.

I giggled. "Only one way to find out." I started to get off him, but his hold on me didn't budge.

He caressed my cheek tenderly with his free hand. "You okay?" His eyes were serious and completely awake when I looked up at him.

I nodded, nuzzling his palm.

"Will they help?" He pulled the hair band from my ponytail and ran his fingers through my hair again and again.

"Uh-huh." Too tired to elaborate on the meeting's result, I let my head drop on his chest and melted into his touch. I'd fill in the blanks in the morning, since he didn't have to go in. Whoever kept tabs on us should take that to mean Alex was off the case, and Dotty would be safe until we got her back.

"Good." He trailed his thumb under my chin, so he could lift my face to him. When his finger feathered over my mouth, I wrapped my lips around it and sucked it in, like I had the previous night.

This time there was no omelet going cold, and I'd let no doubts hold me back. One more night wasn't forever, but it was one more night. For all I knew, it was all we had.

My jeans weren't accommodating for impromptu romps on the couch, especially with Alex obviously unwilling to move and me unwilling to lose touch with him long enough to stand and get rid of them. I had to work around them.

I squirmed in his lap, feeling him hard and thick between my legs. He drove his slim hips against mine, making me wish it was his cock I was sucking instead of his thumb. His gaze was fixed on my lips, his tongue all but lolling out of his mouth. The desperate moan he let out, a sound I'd heard men make before but which didn't touch me so deeply in the past, made up my mind for me. Without a word, Alex had conveyed such urgency that I decided to let his need come before mine.

I let go of his thumb and placed a kiss on the inside of his palm. Then I took hold of his other wrist and raised both his hands over his head. "Hold on and don't let go," I said with a wink, closing his fingers around the armrest. "It will be a bumpy ride."

He bucked beneath me. "This bumpy?"

"You don't know the half of it." I caressed his cheek. His stubble pricked at my fingertips. I used both hands to trace the sides of his face and continue down his neck to his smooth chest. I wanted to bury my face in the crook of his neck and inhale his deep, masculine scent until I got light-headed. Instead I bunched his T-shirt in both hands. "How attached are you to this?"

He barely had time to say, "Not very," before I pulled. The fabric shredded with a ripping sound and exposed his toned abs. He sucked in a breath, the muscles of his stomach clenching and becoming even more lickable. He strained not to move, his biceps bulging inside the short sleeves, and looked at me under hooded eyelids—all male, and all mine.

Maybe I could take my jeans off really, really fast?

Nah. I leaned forward and trailed my tongue down his throat. His skin was salty. A clean taste that made me want to savor more of him. He shivered and craned his neck to the side, spurring me to close my teeth over his jugular and nip lightly.

Alex groaned and rocked his hips. Finding and pinching his nipple, I pressed down on him, the seam of my jeans at just the right spot to make the friction pleasurable. We both hissed—okay, maybe I was louder than he was— and I moved back a little so I could lick his stomach without spraining my neck.

I blew air over the wet trail my mouth had left. The change in his breathing and heart rate would have made *snapping* my neck worth it. His chest rose and fell rapidly, and I realized I instinctively matched his intakes of air. By the time I undid his buttons and kissed below his navel, he was trembling. I looked up at him. His eyes were narrowed with concentration, and veins popped in his arms.

I'd had men want me before. As a human, I'd been in those circles where getting ahead meant giving head, and as a vampire, I'd had my share of conquests. Men had tried to charm, con, blackmail, or buy their way into my panties, but none of them had wanted me as badly as I could feel Alex did at that very moment. Not even Constantine, who'd been an experienced and considerate lover, and who I knew had loved me.

I shooed my former lover's memory out of my head. It was easy to do, with Alex's long and hard cock so close to my mouth. I wanted to wrap my lips around him and feel his silkiness on my tongue, feel his pulse throbbing in my mouth. I wanted to taste him when he lost control.

But I wanted him to beg first.

Alex had been the one doing the exploring during the few days we'd been together, and I thoroughly loved seeing how he responded to my touches now that it was my turn to play. I crawled between his legs and pulled his jeans as far down as they could go. It wasn't enough to expose all of him. I nibbled at the soft, smooth spot above his hip bone, and he mumbled something that sounded like *fuck*. I liked that, so I treated his other hip bone the same way, taking the opportunity to inhale his distinctive *Alex* scent under that of his shower gel.

He swayed his hips, and his cock nudged my cheek. Ignoring him, I placed an openmouthed kiss right next to his shaft, where it lay partially constricted on his lower abdomen. I trailed my fingernails over his length, and he tried to push against my palm, but I was faster, withdrawing it.

"Cherry, come on." He panted, his voice raspy. He raised his legs, bending them at the knees, and pressed his feet to the cushion.

"What?" I flicked his erection once with the tip of my tongue.

"You know what." His lower body jerked up from the couch when I did it again, and he said, "*Evil.*"

Stroking his inner thigh over the denim, I nodded. "I *so* am."

His muscles were tense, stretching the fabric and making me want to rip his pants off too. He amazed me by not releasing his grip on the couch when I licked along his cock. Though he did threaten me with revenge, unless I sucked him off immediately.

"I didn't hear the magic word." I sat back on my haunches, a silly giddiness overtaking me. "Without the magic word, you don't get a thing." I smirked, pleased with myself, and tickled his stomach with my nails. "Say the magic word."

"*Now?*" He growled, trying to move his legs.

I held on to them. "That's not the magic word." Since I was being childish anyway, I tickled his side when he stopped thrashing.

His eyes were the darkest gray I'd seen them so far, but he seemed as amused as I was. "Then what is?"

"*Please*," I said smugly. That was my mistake.

"Well, since you're asking for it nicely." His hand flew to my hair and fisted in it. He used his grip to press my face to his cock.

I laughed. I'd never laughed during sex before I met Alex. I was usually too busy being the sultry seductress or the eager student. The latter was with Constantine, who'd always been teaching me, both in and out of bed. With Alex, it was different. He felt lighter, for lack of a better word.

He laughed too, stopping only when I closed my lips around the head of his dick and licked a single, salty drop of precum from its tip.

Not needing to breathe is a major asset when it comes to going down on a man. Nevertheless I couldn't do much with his jeans in the way. I made a valiant effort to take all of his cock in my mouth, but the angle was wrong.

As I was getting frustrated, Alex whispered, "Not attached to the jeans, either." I tugged on them sharply, and they were out of the way, framing his thighs with their front torn.

I took his cock down my throat and sucked. His balls were heavy. I cupped and rolled them in my palm. Both his hands were in my hair now, fingers tangled and tugging. I loved the illusion that I couldn't break free from his grasp.

He used his feet to propel his thrusts in and out of my mouth. He didn't hold back, but then, he didn't need to. I welcomed his frenzy. The sounds he made while his dick, slick with my saliva, slid forcefully between my lips filled me with a sense of power that had nothing to do with physical strength. This strong, assertive man was reduced to meaningless cries of ecstasy because of what I was doing to him. Holding him still, I sucked harder, withdrawing enough to circle his cockhead with my tongue.

His grasp on my hair intensified, and I thought he meant to push back in, but he didn't. Instead he pulled me up and gave me a fierce kiss. "Turn around," he said.

I was so lost in enjoying his pleasure that I didn't understand what he was talking about.

"On your knees. Face the other way."

Ah. I turned and braced myself on the opposite arm of the couch with one hand, undoing my fly with the other.

He yanked my waistband halfway down my thighs, and in a single thrust buried his cock inside me. He didn't pause when I cried out at the suddenness of his intrusion—not that I wanted him to. He fucked me with almost punishing force, my position making the friction between us more intense, despite how wet my pussy was. He gripped the back of my neck and pressed my face down against the cushion.

The change in angle of penetration added to the pressure building in my lower belly. The couch's fabric scratched against my skin, but only heightened my pleasure, as did Alex's roughness. I reached down to stroke my clit. Each move of his hips, each touch of his fingertips, each thrust of his cock made a claim over my body. I was his to take, his to fuck, his to please, and I wouldn't have it any other way.

I loved this dominating side of Alex as much as I loved his easygoing one. And I wouldn't linger on the *love* part.

"Who's fucking you, Cherry? Who are you going to come for?"

"You, only y—*oh God.*" A crushing wave of pleasure bowed my back and made my head light. The tension inside me finally broke. It felt like a vial of adrenaline was poured in my veins. Without warning, my senses became more acute, my hold on them gone. Alex's scent filled my nostrils, and the drumming of his heart thundered in my ears. I could make out the slightest change in pressure, where he dug his fingers into the back of my neck. The hairs on his legs tickled the oversensitized skin of my thighs. My pussy pulsated. My stomach tightened.

The force of my orgasm made my body shake. I tried to look at Alex over my shoulder, but all strength had been sapped out of me. My vision blurred. I squeezed my eyes shut and bit the cushion, trying to stay grounded. It didn't work. I expanded and expanded until I was nothing but light and color. I flew and I fell, my limbs light as feathers and made of lead.

Alex slammed his hips against me once, twice, three times, and then spilled himself in me, hot cum dripping down my inner thighs.

We slumped down and stayed there, until I could feel my legs again. He wrapped an arm around my waist, gathered me to him, and lay back, peppering kisses on my shoulder. I wanted to roll over and face him, but his hold wouldn't budge even after his cock slipped out of me. He hadn't been at his chattiest after sex so far, but there was now a tension in him I didn't like.

He spoke before I could ask if something was wrong. "That last part… I don't know where it came from." He interlaced my fingers with his, brought them to his mouth, and brushed his lips over the knuckles.

"It's okay. I liked it." I let the *l* roll on my tongue for emphasis.

"I'm lying." He sighed, stroking my stomach.

I sucked it in—not my sexiest body part. "What about?" Post-coital Cherry brain doesn't work at full capacity.

"I do know where that came from." The words, though whispered, were crystal clear. "You and your ex. You saw him, then came here all frisky. I guess I was jealous." Before I could respond, he went on. "And don't tell me I have no right to be. I want you, damn it, and I can be patient, but I won't be left here again while you're out there with him."

I should have been offended by how little faith in me that statement indicated. I knew how it felt to have been betrayed, however. It made people more guarded. It took something from them.

Dropping the pretense that I couldn't break free, I used my vampire agility to flip on my stomach. What I said right then and there could make or break what we had. "Alex"—I waited until he looked at me—"I was frisky for you. I'm not going to screw around." It wasn't possible for us to be in a relationship, but whatever we had was for two players only. He opened his mouth, and I silenced him with my index finger on his lips. "I know what we have is… Well, it's a wait-and-see thing, but I'm only waiting to see things out with you."

His smile shone on his face for a moment, and then he was kissing me again.

We barely made it to the basement before sunrise.

Chapter Eight

I needed to sleep. My brain was fuzzy, and my body felt too exhausted to keep my head up while Alex talked. I found the perfect solution in confiscating his pillow and placing it on top of mine to hold my head propped up as I lay on my side. My mind didn't benefit from the more upright position. It still wanted to shut down.

Alex nudged my shin with his foot. "*Hey.* I didn't sleep while you were telling me about your meeting."

"Mmm."

He'd been a good little trouper and paid attention while I'd described how my night had gone, and he'd had all the right reactions, including a disgusted face when I'd mentioned Ádísa's behavior after explaining who she was. It was by all means my turn to listen. And I tried to. Honestly.

"Tell me." I turned my face to the pillow to hide my yawn.

"Like I said, I got a call. Your friend's case has another thing different than the rest."

I blinked drowsily. "What's that?" He'd better tell me soon.

"She left her cell phone behind. Not on purpose, most probably. It was found under the couch at the club where she was last seen. They're working on locating her boyfriend and checked her calls. No outgoing calls after noon, but her last incoming one was from a private number. They're working on tracing that. Meantime she had a missed call that night. Apparently from a modeling agency."

That woke me up. He was sitting up, and I had to crane my neck to look at him. "A modeling agency? I didn't know Dotty modeled."

I was ashamed that I didn't think she could model. Like Alex had said, she wasn't ugly, not by a long shot, but she wasn't extraordinary looks-wise, either. My shame deepened when I realized my train of thought assumed I'd been something special during my modeling days.

"Weird that she didn't mention it. You said she's your friend. Anyway, I'll be checking that out first thing in the morning." He touched his lips to my cheek and slid under the covers, facing me.

"This *is* the morning," I mumbled.

Chuckling, he glanced at his watch. "Yeah, but I doubt Sheena's Models is open at six thirty."

"Sheena's Models?" It came out squeaky.

Alex arched both eyebrows. "That's the agency. Why?"

"Sheena was my agent."

I've never believed in coincidences.

****

Alex promised not to go see Sheena by himself before sunset, and I slept like the—wouldn't you know it?—dead.

What interrupted my slumber was a curse coming from the floor above. I sprang upright and instinctively reached for Alex. After the first few seconds of disorientation, I realized he wasn't in bed. As a matter of fact, he was the one who'd done the cursing. I could hear nobody else upstairs. Maybe he'd jabbed a toe or something, while making me breakfast. The thought of him cooking for me made me smile.

"It's the only way," Alex said.

So he *was* talking to someone. I tried not to listen in, but his next words piqued my curiosity.

"If you don't suspend me, I'm leaving the force."

Resisting my natural instincts was futile. I settled my head back on the downy pillow and eavesdropped.

"You know you owe me," Alex said. "I was in a bad place, and it worked out well for you. This is *my* case. Let me work it the way I know how."

I couldn't make out the other side of the conversation.

"Just do it, okay? I'll deal." Pause. "Thanks." The last word was whispered.

The next sound was of footsteps approaching.

I kept my eyes closed when Alex sneaked back into bed. I didn't know how extensive his detective training had been, but even if he was trained to recognize when a human faked being asleep, I had no breathing he could listen to, in order to call my bluff.

He snuggled behind me and buried his face in my hair. I couldn't tell if the sigh he let out was of contentment or frustration.

I pushed my body against his with a *mmm* sound, and he pulled me closer. I mmmed again when he kissed my shoulder. He cupped my breast, and I shifted so he could catch a glimpse of my face. Scrunching my nose, I asked, "What time is it?" My voice came out thee right amount of groggy.

"Eleven thirty. You can sleep some more." His hand roaming my body indicated he wouldn't mind if I didn't.

"Are you going to work?" *Come on, buddy. Fess up. Don't lie to me.* The latter became a chant in my head for the brief moments until he replied.

"No. I'll nod off too." As if to prove he had every intention of doing so, he stopped caressing me.

I was aware of the irony of wanting him to come clean, when I was deceiving him, but it was about self-preservation. My first priority was making sure I didn't trust someone else who'd lie to me. I'd have time later to feel bad about it. "Right. You're not going in. Following a lead..." There was his opening, and I hoped he took it.

He didn't. "Yeah." The single whispered word sounded regretful.

With any guy before Alex, I'd have let them go on, dig a bigger hole for when I dumped their asses into it. Since Constantine made me trust him and then duped me, I regard men lying as the norm. I expect to be lied to; it fits into my world theory. For Alex, however, I did something out of character. I gave up my efforts toward an Oscar-winning performance. "I heard you. On the phone."

I expected him to make an excuse or be upset I eavesdropped. I couldn't blame him if he was, but I was relieved when instead he said, "I didn't want you to have to worry about me too, with everything else happening. Wanted you to believe I had things under control."

I turned within his embrace. "I only heard what you said. Wanna talk about it?"

"Roebuck wouldn't let me investigate what I found out unless I let him in on it. I said I had a source I couldn't reveal—that it's big and lives are at stake if the department is involved—but he's stubborn. He offered to come by and talk about it. I can't drag more people into this." He cupped my cheek and tucked my hair behind my ear with his fingertips. "Thought about asking for a leave, but I can't take days off in the middle of a case. Finally asked him to suspend me, so I could do what I wanted."

"But he wouldn't." I walked my index and middle finger up his torso, then along his collarbone. It wasn't a sexual touch, more an *I'm here* one. If my touch afforded him half the comfort his afforded me, it would help him open up.

He shook his head and closed his hand around mine, stopping me. "He refused to. Said they needed me. So I had to play dirty. First I threatened to quit, and then I reminded him he owed me. It was a low blow." He rubbed his face with his free hand. "I can't believe I did that. I'm such a prick."

"You're not." I kissed his cheek.

He turned away. "I shouldn't have said what I did. It's not even true."

I didn't ask. Going against my nature, I remained silent until he began talking again.

"Roebuck was my partner. I was going through my dark phase when promotions were up. It was too soon after my breakup with Marion." I assumed that was the ex. "Anyway." He sighed and wet his lips.

My gaze was drawn to his mouth before I returned it to his eyes, feeling guilty for thinking naughty thoughts at a time like that.

"We scored close enough on the test, but my performance had taken a plunge. Roebuck got the promotion to lieutenant and deserved it, but he's felt bad about it since. And now, like the asshole I am, I rubbed it in."

I couldn't watch his self-kicking any longer. "You did it for him. If he got involved—if *anyone* got involved—there'd be more people missing. Dying."

"I'm still an asshole."

I batted his shoulder. "That's irrelevant."

His lips twitched, and then he did what I was hoping for. He smiled. "You always know the right thing to say, huh?" Before I could come up with a self-satisfied reply, he tickled me and kept tickling until I squealed.

****

Alex brought Mexican food, which was spicy as hell, and I took immense pleasure in his terrified response when I offered to blow him after stuffing my mouth with what seemed like my body weight in jalapenos.

Those moments of intimacy that had more to do with enjoying each other's company and wit than with sex were when I knew beyond the shadow of a doubt that I was half in love with him already. I loved the tiny little wrinkles that showed around his eyes when he smiled. I loved the long lashes that shaded his prominent cheekbones. I loved how he lowered his eyelids coyly before saying something raunchy that would make me blush if I had blood circulation. I loved the way he spoke with his entire upper body, his shoulders, arms, and long fingers stressing his points as eloquently as his deep voice.

Those moments made me want to cry. The way I felt about him was why I should leave him. I couldn't stand watching him grow closer to death every day, and the idea of turning him was preposterous. Alex's humanity was part of him. To take that away, together his chance of fathering children that would turn out as wonderful as he was, was something only a monster would do.

So I focused on the *now* and the time we had together until the case was solved, but as the hours passed, I felt him become antsy. Strangely enough, I also loved that his mind never veered far from the case. His sense of honor wouldn't allow him to have fun at the expense of people in danger. Spending time with me while waiting for a clue was one thing. Wasting time with me once a clue had landed in our laps was another. After a point, he began taking trips upstairs to check if the sun had gone down, as if he couldn't trust the Internet any more than he could my inner clock.

I, on the other hand, was in no hurry for dusk to come.

I was in no hurry to hear Sheena admit she had something to do with my turning. I'd trusted her. She was the first person to be genuinely nice to me when I moved to the city. She'd found me the apartment I lived in before I died, and booked my jobs both as a model and in the… other industry I tried to make a name for myself in. For a long time, I felt bad about not telling her I was still around, and now I found out she might have been involved in what had happened to me. I didn't want to face her, but I couldn't let Alex deal with her alone. It might be dangerous.

"It's dark outside," Alex yelled from the top of the stairs.

I barely groused on my way up.

To his credit, he was holding the door for me when I got there.

****

"I can fly us over, you know." As much as I dreaded meeting my old agent and friend, a forty-five-minute drive would only fray my nerves more.

Alex, who was locking the front door, froze mid key-turn. "You can fly?"

"I didn't mention that, did I?"

He finished locking and looked at me. "No, you didn't. How?"

"I don't know the mechanics. No sprouting bat wings or anything. I just want to take off, and I do. An open mind is essential, the handbook said."

"I see. While that sinks in, let's drive there." He pressed the button on his car key, and the car's lights flashed twice. "I don't like flying," he said, getting the car door for me. That he admitted it, instead of coming up with a lame excuse, gained him extra brownie points but still wasn't enough for me to admit I was afraid of what we might find out. I folded all of my five-feet-four into the passenger seat, and he shut the door.

We hit traffic almost immediately. Insert frustrated groan.

Stillness isn't something that comes naturally for me. I know, I know—vampires are supposed to have perfected stillness. I think it's something paranormal romance writers came up with, to add mysterious allure to their heroes and heroines. Or maybe the notion came from someone who's met Constantine. Either way I don't do still; I'm a fidgeter. I play with my hair, the hem of my top, the belt loop of my jeans, my jewelry, and occasionally tap my foot and/or fingers on the nearest available surface, which, at present, was the casing of the car window.

My nails aren't long, but they're always manicured—yay to having been turned right after full-body pampering—and they're noisy.

Disturbing was the word Alex used.

"Sorry. Didn't mean to get on your nerves." I stopped tapping my fingers, but soon began twitching my foot, and from time to time, connecting with the middle column.

"Okay, what's wrong?" Alex peeked at me before returning his attention to the road. "It's the first time I've seen you so jittery."

"Yeah, well, you haven't seen all that much of me, have you?" *Nice, Cherry.* I gave him a sheepish look. "I'm sorry. I'm being a bitch."

"That's irrelevant."

"Smooth, Marsden." Still, I felt more relaxed with his attempt at humor.

At the traffic light, he put his hand on my thigh, his warmth doing nothing for the cold I felt inside. "Seriously, what's the matter?" he asked.

Closing my eyes, I let my head roll to the side until my forehead leaned against the cool glass.

I was done with my shift at the bakery and was helping myself to a doughnut with extra glaze on it, when a woman behind me said, "I'd enjoy the fuck out of that if I were you, honey. If you're to work for me—which you are, and are going to love—that's the last of those babies you're gonna have in a long while."

I turned to bitch slap whoever dared come between me and my dessert, but the smile on her lips stopped me in my tracks.

"I bet you want to be a model, don't you?" she asked. "Or an actress? Isn't that why you came to the city?"

Mara, the bitchy waif who had the evening shift, snorted. That made my decision for me. I took a big bite of my doughnut. "What can you offer me?" I asked.

The woman's smile widened. "The world, darling. And I'll start with a ride away from this place."

I opened my eyes again and focused on the *here* and *now*. "Sheena. If she handed me to them… It hurts." I blew out my breath noisily, fogging the window. "I know it's silly. It's been so long, but—" At least she'd let me keep having doughnuts for a while.

"I get it." He squeezed my leg, and I knew he wasn't just saying that. He got me.

A look at him, and I was back in swooning mode, the knot in my stomach temporarily forgotten. Even if Sheena betrayed me, Alex wouldn't. He *got* me.

But for how long?

Chapter Nine

For all my anticipation and dread, reaching the modeling agency proved anticlimactic.

I'd imagined Alex ringing the doorbell and moving to the side, allowing me to step forward. Sheena would open the door, dressed in a possibly purple pantsuit, professional smile in place. When she saw me, that smile would waver until it was replaced by a look of shock and fear. She might try to slam the door in my face, but I'd be faster. Sticking my foot into the opening of the door, I'd say, "Hello, darling," my voice cool as a cucumber.

I should have let Alex in on my fantasy confrontation. Since I didn't, he got it wrong from the start, ringing the bell but not budging an inch, so I had to stand on tiptoe, for the top of my head to be visible over his shoulder. The door was thrown open by a blonde I'd never seen before, a distinct expression of disinterest on her face. "Can I help you?"

Yup. Anticlimactic.

I mean, don't get me wrong—the sight of Alex flashing his badge at the girl and telling her we had some questions was a thrill in and of itself. He ought to have turned the badge and his weapon in, but he was being naughty about it, and I didn't mind that naughtiness at all. I wished we were alone. Seeing him like that, jaw clenched, shoulders squared, body posture imposing, I wanted him to take me right there, on Sheena's Models' doorstep. Or I could jump him.

Nah. I couldn't. I was introduced as a consultant, and sexually assaulting a detective wouldn't be very consultanty.

The blonde said her name was Barbara Greg, and she was Sheena's assistant. She invited us in and asked if we'd like a beverage. We followed her to the waiting area but politely refused her offer of coffee or tea.

"We would like to speak to Ms. Herring," Alex said.

"I'm sorry. She isn't in."

Alex brought a notepad and pen out of his jacket's inner pocket. "Do you know when she will be coming in or where we might find her?"

She shrugged. "Well, she left two days ago and said she'd be gone indefinitely, so no."

I felt like a balloon someone punched a hole in. All the mental and emotional prep work I'd given myself on the ride was sucked out of me, leaving behind a sizeable gap and a sense of floating—not as in being joyful and weightless, but rather like having no anchor or purpose. It was a sickening feeling, and I wanted to punch the wall. Irrelevant to my personal history with her, Sheena was our best lead so far, our greatest chance to find Dotty and the other girls. I couldn't believe she wasn't here.

"Are you aware of her current whereabouts? Where did she go?" Alex tapped his pen on his notepad, while I stood against the wall, playing not-here cop. A slight twitch of his eye was the only indication that Sheena's absence bothered him too.

"She said she'd visit family, out of town. I don't know where," Barbara said nasally, pouring herself some coffee. The smell of hazelnut wafted to my nostrils. I'd have loved some but saw enough cop shows to know accepting something to eat or drink from someone you were questioning seemed unprofessional. "I haven't been working for her long enough to ask for details." She shrugged again, her breasts threatening to pop out over her constricting top.

"How long is *not long enough*?" Alex smiled, and I leaned carefully to one side, to see what he was looking at. Her eyes, not her cleavage. I caught myself nodding in approval. Good man. The ludicrousness of concerning myself with petty jealousy when so much was at risk didn't escape me.

"Almost three months now." The blonde turned to me, and I straightened as fast as I could. "What is this about?" Worry was drawn on her pretty yet overly made-up face.

Alex ignored her query. "Ms. Herring went on a vacation, leaving behind an employee with less than three months of experience?" His voice was gentle, coaxing, rather than prodding. *Amaze me with how good and deserving an employee you are*, it said.

She frowned. "I'm excellent at my job, Detective Marsden. I don't need to defend my employer's choices."

"I don't doubt your abilities, Ms. Greg." Alex smiled reassuringly. I tried not to harrumph.

"It's *Miss* Greg." She smiled back. "Better yet, call me Barbie, Detective."

Barbie, for fuck's sake.

"Miss Greg, then." Alex produced a pack of pictures from the same pocket as the notebook. "Have you seen any of these girls before? Maybe one of them has worked with your agency in the past."

Barbie barely glanced at Dotty's picture before she put it down and looked at the second missing girl's photograph. My heart sank when she showed no signs of recognition. My ears didn't pick up the slightest change in her heart rate. She wasn't acting. Second girl got a *no* too, but we sort of had a winner with the third one.

"Her." Barbie's lacquered, one-inch nail—how could she type with those things?—tapped the picture of a stunning girl with short raven locks and prominent eyebrows that brought out the green specks in her hazel eyes. "Liza Mills. She was here… a month ago? Let me check my appointment book."

She opened her top drawer and brought out a humongous folder, holding a pack of letter-size sheets. Each page had a mug shot stapled on it.

Barbie noticed me looking at the photos. "Sheena insists on candid shots of everyone we interview."

I knew that. I was just wondering if my picture was still here somewhere.

I begrudgingly admitted Barbie might be better at her work than I pegged her for. She found the girl immediately. The only info under her shot was a cell-phone number.

"Here she is."

"This contact number is all you have?" Alex reached out, and Barbie placed the open folder in his hands with a nod.

He flipped through pages, and I tried to be inconspicuous while stretching my neck to see the photos attached to them. "The other forms are filled in completely, as far as I can see," he said. He hadn't looked through everything, though. Maybe there were other girls with just their numbers jotted down, girls who hadn't disappeared yet and could be saved.

She wrinkled her nose. "I book the appointments and fill these in when the girls come. I was on my day off when Sheena met with her, though, and when she gave me the form to file it, she said not to bother with anything else."

"Do you mind if we hold on to this for a couple of days?" He graced her with that smile that made me want to be his slave. "I could get a warrant, but I see no reason to."

"I have it all in electronic form. Even scanned the pictures. I'll print you a copy." Barbie preened. "I keep telling Sheena we're in the age of technology."

Well, that was easy.

While the printer worked its little mechanical heart out, making a sound that bore an eerie similarity to grunting, Barbie looked at the other missing girls' photos and ruled out everyone else.

I started moving toward the front door, when Alex asked, "What's your work schedule, Miss Greg? Do you work Saturdays, for example?"

Why did he want to know that?

Her grin was big enough to show her gums. "I'm here every Saturday and most Sundays, but I have the afternoon off one week from today." Her face fell, which gave me an odd sense of joy. "But I can't leave the office—not with Sheena gone."

"Is it a fixed weekend every month or did you need that time off for a specific reason?"

"No reason. Sheena gives me an afternoon off each week. This week it was day before yesterday, when I last saw her."

When anyone last saw Dotty.

"And you haven't heard from her since." It was a mixture of a statement and a question. Pen poised over pad once more, Alex waited.

"She called me about half an hour before you showed. Asked if anyone had been by looking for her." And she hadn't thought to mention that so far. Finally she asked the million-dollar question. "Is she in trouble?"

She would be, when I found her. Before I did something stupid like say that out loud, Alex asked, "Does your phone show caller ID?"

****

The area code of the last incoming call was proof positive that Sheena had lied about going out of town. She had to know her assistant wasn't the sharpest tool in the box too, since she hadn't bothered calling from a private number. Still, it would have taken us a while to trace the call if I hadn't seen that number on my cell phone's screen enough times to know it by heart.

Sheena had called from her *house*. She had a private office there, with its own line, which was in her ex-husband's name. She only used that for nefarious purposes, such as organizing the shooting of adult films without her name showing anywhere. I ought to know; I'd been involved in said nefarious purposes.

Once again we were in Alex's car, but this time there was no traffic delaying us. The scenery was no longer urban, buildings having given their place to trees that appeared to run by my window at full speed. The colors changed too, from gray to green, to yellow, orange, and red. I knew Alex couldn't see the hues as well as I could in the darkness, and for a moment I grew wistful. There was an entire world he couldn't be a part of, just as I couldn't completely belong in his. The thoughts I'd tried to drive away for the finite time we had together resurfaced in my mind. We weren't meant to be. He thrived in the sun, while I could only live under the moon. The sooner his case was over, the better. We could both get back to reality.

His hand brushed my thigh when he closed his fingers around the gearshift. He flashed a brief smile my way, and I wouldn't trade that smile for the world, not even to save myself sorrow in the future.

I would if it was to save *him* sorrow in the future, though. Just as I'd go against his wishes and take away his memories of me if he refused to let go when the time came.

****

My agitation rose with every step Alex and I took on the cobbled walkway that led to Sheena's front door. I could have sworn that walkway was a lot shorter the last time I visited. Now it felt like years passed before we stood on the red, bow-shaped welcome mat.

I remembered that mat. Sheena had told me my hair matched it, once I'd changed its color for the never-shot movie I was to star in. In the darkness, I saw the vibrant hue clearly, and it made me want to rip it to shreds. In some irrational way, it was another reminder of how she'd betrayed me.

Oblivious to my train of thought, Alex wiped his feet meticulously.

I snorted. "You couldn't have stepped in some mud? Dog poo, even better."

"Sorry?"

I wasn't sure if he wanted me to explain my demand-like question or if he was apologizing. I shrugged. "It's okay."

He put his hand on the small of my back, and like the first time we met, electricity flowed between us. This time, it had a different result than to raise my lust for him. His touch now was soothing, comforting. I melted against his side.

"Is it?" He gave me a questioning look, wrapping his arm around me, to press me to him. "Are *you*? I don't need you for this. You can wait in the car. You should, officially."

I rubbed my face against his shoulder, then nodded. "Yeah, well, you shouldn't be here, officially. Let's get this over with."

He let go, gave me a peck on the lips, and rang the doorbell.

I allowed my hearing to expand to its vampiric limit and easily made out the ring reverberating throughout the house. Then I heard scuffling.

"Someone's moving inside," I whispered. My phone vibrated in my back pocket, startling me. Whoever it was could wait.

"Ms. Herring? Open the door, please. Police." Alex sounded very police-y, indeed.

There was the scuffling again, like feet dragging. Like someone being sneaky on the wooden floor. The sound wasn't coming toward us. "Back door," I blurted and took off. Not literally. I didn't have to fly, to round the house faster than a human could cross it. I was waiting outside the glass door of the kitchen when the door pulled open.

Sheena burst out and straight into my waiting arms. I grabbed her waist. She dropped the backpack and laptop case she was holding and fought me blindly. I didn't let go of my grip on her waist.

With her eyes squeezed shut, she screeched like a banshee. I lifted her off the ground to subdue her, and she did her best to lodge her pointed shoes inside my shins. Why on earth would a woman try to escape while wearing high heels? *Vanity before safety.*

Then she kneed me on the hip.

I adjusted my grip and moved behind her. That way she couldn't get me with her hands and knees. Still, she wouldn't stop trying to claw at me over her shoulder or get me with her heels.

Alex approached, gun in hand. I shook my head, and he halted but kept his weapon pointed at her.

Sheena shrieked and bucked. Her long nails found my face, and one of them gouged my cheek. It stung enough to make my eyes tear up, but I held on even as her fuchsia jacket ripped.

"Ms. Herring, I have a gun pointed at you. We just want to ask you some questions." Alex's voice of reason wasn't working. Sheena didn't cease her thrashing.

"Sheena, cut that out. You're not going anywhere until you talk to us." My fangs had come out, and my *s*'s were kind of whistly, but I sounded menacing, nonetheless. The scent of my own blood made me moodier than before.

"*Let me go.*" She stomped on my foot with her heel.

The jolt of pain was sharp but not debilitating. I held her at arm's length. "Why did you hand me to Willoughby?" I shook her before spinning her to face me. "Why?" I was certain I was yelling, but the last reached my ears as a whine. "I thought you were my friend."

She stopped fighting, and her body sagged. Easing one eye open, she said, "Cherry?"

"Yeah." I could have said something wittier, but for the second time that day, my expectations had little to do with reality.

Like I said, I expected shock and fear when Sheena laid eyes on me. Now I saw shock there, all right, but no fear.

She reached for me again, yet not to hurt me. She touched my face. My shoulders. My hair. I didn't know how to react. She wasn't trying to wound me or defend herself.

Finally she squeezed me to her. "Oh thank God, you're okay."

****

Sheena's living room hadn't changed since I'd last been there. Every piece of furniture, as well as the walls and carpeting, still made a statement—the owner had a loud personality.

Then again, the owner herself was a testament to that.

Sheena had on a pair of fuchsia pants and a matching jacket which now lacked two buttons, with a fuchsia and lime-green silk top. The set might have looked appropriate for Halloween on me, but it complemented her mocha-colored skin perfectly. Her matching makeup was messed up, mascara-tinged tears making tracks on her blush.

She'd asked if we wanted coffee or something stronger but we'd both refused anything, so she was the only person in the room with a drink in hand. Scotch. Straight up.

"I'm so glad you're okay," she said for the millionth time, reaching across the couch to pat my knee.

I traced the scratch already healing on my cheek but didn't respond. I was still so gobsmacked, I could only stare. If Alex hadn't pulled me inside the house by the hand, I'd have probably still been out in the garden, trying to figure out why Sheena acted happy to see me.

Alex, my knight in shining armor, took it upon himself to point out the mistake in her statement. "She's far from okay, Ms. Herring. She's dead." His glare was anything but professional.

Sheena sniffed. "She's walking and talking. It's more than I thought she was. Ergo, she's okay."

Ergo. Leave it to her to find the oddest time to use a pretentious word. I shook my head. Alex was right. I wasn't okay. I'd spent years alone. Even when I was with Constantine, I had no friends, nobody to be silly with, no shoulder to cry on. I couldn't see my family. Couldn't let them know I was still around, still the same person they'd brought up, except for the undead thing. I never wanted kids before I was turned, but knowing the choice had been taken away from me made me long for the possibility of one at times.

I could have been worse off, I guess. Could have been gone forever. But so much had happened to me because of her.

I looked at Alex and felt a smile tug at the corners of my lips. Some of those happenings hadn't been bad.

I no longer felt like killing Sheena. "Why did you do it?" It was the thing I needed to find out first.

"I didn't know I was doing something." The words came out soft as a breath. "That guy asked to meet you.

Nothing bad was supposed to happen to you." That she didn't knowingly lead me to my death loosened the knot in my stomach the tiniest bit.

"Something did happen, though." I thought Alex meant to urge her to say more, but a glance at his face showed me he was still beyond pissed off. "Of course, you thought you were just whoring her out." He spared her none of the formal courtesy he'd offered her assistant. This wasn't an investigation any longer; it was as personal to him as it was to me.

Sheena hung her head. "Willoughby was good looking, well mannered, *rich*. I thought he'd be good for her."

How could she have thought a guy named *Willoughby* could be good for anyone?

Alex sat on the armrest next to me, gun lying on his thigh. He hadn't even let go of it to hand Sheena her bag and laptop before we'd come inside. I squeezed his free hand.

"Why didn't you do something when you heard I disappeared?" I asked Sheena. I wanted to believe she'd initially acted with my best interest at heart, but there was no excuse for the rest. "Why did you give him more girls?"

"I didn't *hear* you disappeared." Her voice was louder, exasperated, and she was still not looking at me. "He came here and he said what happened to you would happen to me if I didn't help them or I went to the cops. He—he *bit* me." Her free hand twitched on her lap.

I didn't want to feel sorry for her, but until recently I'd thought of her as a friend. I couldn't just delete that. Instead of trying to figure out my feelings, I focused on how her words answered one of my upcoming questions. She knew about vampires. "And you let him do it to others?"

"He promised me they'd be kept happy. That he'd offer them things." I could tell she was trying to convince herself more than us. "There were some who didn't have much of a future on the runway, or at all." I remembered the entry with just a picture and number that her assistant gave us. "Others that he'd specifically suggested I approach. He'd call and tell me what he had in mind. I arranged the meetings."

"Knowing they'd die?" It was possible I could still find it in me to snap her neck. Deep down I wanted not to have found out about her involvement, even if that shot down our chances of recovering the young women.

"Knowing they'd live forever," she yelled, raising her gaze to me. "They'd stay pretty forever. They wouldn't get a single wrinkle, and they'd be rich. Nobody would miss them. I was helping them."

"What about Dorothea Williams?" Alex's question fell heavily in the quiet that had followed Sheena's outburst. "She has a son." I was grateful the wrath etched on his face wasn't aimed at me. He was mortal, and therefore physically weaker than me, but seeing him like that, I knew he'd be lethal if he chose to.

Sheena's complexion turned ashen, and her lower lip trembled. "I didn't want to give him Dotty. I wouldn't have signed her if he hadn't made me. He told me where I could bump into her. I had to make it seem like my idea. He couldn't approach her on his own, because she was cautious of going out with strangers, being a mom and all. After I met her—she was so nice. He said she'd be the last one. That it had to be her. I introduced them about a month ago, and they went out a few times. When nothing happened on their first date, I hoped he wouldn't… You know."

I motioned for her to continue, but my mind reeled. If Willoughby was the guy Dotty had been seeing for a month, then he'd selected her before finding out about me and Alex. Before there *was* a me and Alex. Willoughby had been keeping tabs on me. But why? The question was drowned out by a flood of guilt. Whatever the reason, it was *my* fault Dotty was gone.

"When he called and demanded a new girl for next week, I told him I wouldn't do it anymore. That he'd promised I wouldn't have to. I asked him about Dotty. He wouldn't talk about her, but I knew if he wanted a new girl, it meant Dotty—" Her voice, high-pitched by that point, broke, and her next words were muttered under her breath. "She was so nice."

Hearing Sheena say *was* twice drove a sharp spear of cold fear through my heart. "She's dead?"

"I tried to call her, to get her to break things off with him, but she didn't answer. I thought I was too late. Isn't that why you're here?"

I didn't realize I was almost crushing Alex's hand until he cleared his throat and tried to pry it away. I let go. "We just know she's missing. Do you know anything about where he might be taking the girls?"

"No. I swear. I was too afraid to ask for details, and he never told me anything." She downed the rest of her drink, and her hand trembled when she leaned forward to leave the glass on the coffee table.

"Have you seen anybody else with him?"

"No. Never." She chewed on her lip, and flakes of the supposed color-stay lipstick peeled off on her teeth.

"Do you have his number? Any way to contact him?" Alex produced his notepad, but Sheena shook her head.

"He always called me, and from a private number. Set the time and place, and asked for what he had in mind. He'd meet them at clubs or parties. The names the girls were to ask for were different every time."

Made-up names. I wondered if they were worse than *Willoughby*, though that had to be his real name. Or at least what he went by in the vampire circles. It was what they'd called him during my trial.

Alex asked for her phone. "Maybe he'll call again," he said. She gave it to him immediately.

He didn't ask her to specify the names Willoughby had given her on occasion. It made sense; we had no use for them. We were back to square one.

I rose, and Alex followed my lead. Nothing more to do here.

Sheena pushed herself off the couch with both hands, wavered, and finally managed to stand. "What about me? What are you going to do with me?"

Alex looked at me, and in that moment, I knew beyond the shadow of a doubt that he'd be fine with shooting her and burying her in the backyard if I asked him to.

A small part of me would be fine with it too. Sheena had pulled the world out from under my feet, and I couldn't forgive her for that. Before that, however, she'd made my world a better place for a while. "Get out of town," I said. "For real this time. If I see you again, I'll kill you." I wouldn't. I'm not a killer. But I'd do my best to make her miserable.

She nodded. "For what little it's worth, I'm really sorry. I didn't want any of this."

I believed her, but I didn't care.

****

My phone buzzed again on the drive back, and once more I let it go to voicemail. I curled up in my seat and let the rocking motion of the car lull me to sleep.

I awoke briefly when Alex was getting me out of the car. He said something about taking care of me. He was human and fragile despite his size, and I was a vampire and basically immortal. Still, his words made me feel safe. Alex's strength came from within, and it could move mountains.

Nothing bad would happen to me again as long as he held me.

Chapter Ten

Lying naked in bed, pressed against a hard male body, provided the best distraction from depressing thoughts. The body being Alex's, chiseled to perfection and warm to the touch, added an extra reason for me not to want to get out from under the covers to retrieve my buzzing phone.

It was still in my jeans pocket, where Alex left it when he'd undressed me to put me in bed, and the jeans were folded on a chair, a few feet from where we were. The distance seemed vast when crossing it entailed disentangling myself from Alex.

"You're not gonna get that?" His breath caressed the back of my neck, making me itch to leave the blasted call alone.

I let out a puff of air and brought his palm to my lips, so I could place a kiss on it. "You heard it?"

"You don't need enhanced hearing for that. I think I put your keys in the same pocket. They're jingling." He caressed my cheek with his thumb.

"I don't want to get up." The words were drawn out and nasal.

Alex ignored my whining. "I heard it earlier too. May be an emergency."

I doubted that. The caller hadn't been persistent enough; they'd let hours go by between tries. I should have checked my missed calls, but I'd honestly forgotten about them till then. "The only people who have that number are Sheena, Constantine, Dotty, and the council." Ignoring Alex's grumbling that he ought to have it too, I went on. "It's too early for any of the vampires to be calling me, and Sheena wouldn't dare to."

I was out of bed as soon as the last word left my mouth.

Dotty. Dotty or her kidnapper—I refused to think of him as her killer—could be trying to contact me. I grabbed my jeans. My fingers might as well have been sausages, the way they refused to be agile and pluck the stupid phone out of the stupid denim. The buzzing stopped.

I finally found the phone, when it started vibrating again. I let out a surprised squeal and looked at the name blipping on the screen.

My mood plummeted. *Constantine.*

There went the possibility of crawling back next to Alex and having me some early-day sex. Unless I ignored the phone. If it was urgent, he'd text me when he saw he couldn't reach me. I pressed the little red button and sent him a ready-made excuse message. *Can't talk. Text in case of emergency*. Then I turned and smiled at Alex, who was sitting up and looking at me intently. "Nobody important." A glance at the unanswered-calls list showed it had been him earlier too, but I had no voicemail alert.

Alex's features hardened, his deduction as to the caller's identity so obvious, I might as well have heard it click into place.

I put my phone back and did my best seductive prowl up the bed, but he seemed preoccupied. When I straddled him and lowered my face to his, he said, "I've been thinking…"

Shit. Nothing good ever followed that line. Sitting back on his thighs, I looked at him with a pout. "If this is about Constantine, I told you—"

"Nothing to do with him." Yeah, right. That was why he spat out *him* like the word was drenched in lemon juice. "We've been going about this all wrong."

"Huh? Like how?" I scowled hard enough to almost put my eyebrows in my line of sight. How could we have been doing the sex wrong?

"We've been looking for clues, when we don't have a theory." So it really had nothing to do with Constantine. "We have to take this from the start."

Did I mention I was straddling him naked? And he wanted to talk shop?

I slid off his body and covered myself with the sheet. "So let's." Suppressing my sulking took some effort, but being upset that he could disregard my blatant pass at him was stupid when he wanted to discuss something about the case.

"First off, you were turned—we assume by accident—and left for dead. A vampire who *happened* to be your fan *happened* to come by and spot you. Right so far?"

"Right." Where was he going with it? We knew Willoughby and Ted had been working together.

"Okay, so the question is *why*? Turning you, dumping you, and supposedly discovering you was too big a mess. Why would they do that? What did they hope to accomplish?" He might have been directing the questions to himself, his voice was so low.

"A law against turning people was established?"

Alex arched an eyebrow, his look saying what his mouth wouldn't dare to—I was an idiot to believe that. "I doubt that was what they were after, since they're still turning people."

I crossed my arms, trapping the sheet against my breasts. I wished the cloth could protect more than my nonexistent modesty and warm more than my skin. The ice-cold fingers gripping my still heart showed no intention of melting, however. That I was warm and safe mere moments ago compounded my sense of dread. Things were so fucking volatile. "We don't know that," I said in a small voice.

Whether he sensed my need for reassurance or because he too needed the contact, he placed his palm between my shoulder blades. I leaned into his touch. "You're right. We don't know that. Yet that's not all they managed, is it?"

I curled in on myself and hugged my legs. Laying my cheek on my knee, I focused on enjoying his caress. "No, it's not. The old council was overthrown, and a new one replaced it." They were the ones to benefit the most from my turning. Nobody controlled or even questioned them.

"If your turning was indeed prearranged, they had to be involved. They were supposed to get Willoughby executed and didn't. The same people you went to for help." His tone held no accusation, yet guilt was added to the cluster of negative feelings that made a home in my belly. Alex had warned me not to trust them, but I'd insisted they were the good guys. Now they knew we were on to something.

They probably knew about Alex too, which put him in even greater danger. It was one thing for a single rogue vampire to be after us, and another altogether for the enemy to be the council itself.

"The council wouldn't need to outlaw turnings if they planned on continuing them. They could have found another way to go about overturning their predecessors. This must all be a coincidence." Unless they had another agenda.

He tugged at a strand of my hair. "You said yourself we don't know they're turning the girls. If they are, maybe not all council members are in on it. *Probably* not all of them are in on it, or they'd have killed you when you went to meet them. Still, even one of them is enough of a threat."

They knew where to find us. The lack of a new attack might have been meant to lull us into a false sense of safety.

"There's something else your theory doesn't explain," I said. "Assuming they're taking the girls, why are they doing it?" And what could we do?

"We'll look into that. First we have to find a safe place. Maybe my apartment."

I scrunched my nose. "Which floor is it on?"

"What does that matter?"

"If it's not an underground one, you obviously wanna see me go up in flames."

A vibration made me jump. This time there was no procrastination. I elbowed Alex in the ribs trying to answer it. The call would act as a distraction from the scariness, regardless of who was on the other end of the line.

Only, when the music kicked in, I realized it wasn't my phone. My ringtone wasn't "Paparazzi."

With a fleeting thought at how our provider rocked for allowing for reception in the basement, I looked at the tiny slip of a cell phone inching its way toward the edge of the coffee table we used as a nightstand. The screen flashed an innocent white light.

Alex stared at it too, but he stopped me when I climbed over him to get it. "What if it's him?" He wasn't worried. He was asking if I had a plan.

I knew what course of action would appeal the most to me. "I tell him to give me Dotty, unharmed, or I dust him?" I asked with fake cheer.

Alex reached out and picked it up. After one glance at the display, he shook his head. "Out-of-area." We were both whispering.

"Let it go to voicemail."

We remained silent until the cell stopped ringing. We could have waited for an alerting text, but Alex was no more patient than I was. He narrowed his eyes and pressed 1. The phone looked fragile in his massive palm. When his index pushed down on it, I was sure he'd break it. He didn't, and he managed to turn the speaker on too. I silently prayed Sheena didn't have a PIN for accessing her messages.

Alex pressed 1 once more, drew me so I lay on his chest, and held the phone between our ears.

"I want a blonde tomorrow night. The swimsuit model, if she really is no older than twenty-three. Tell her to meet me in the VIP section of the Dark Sun at eleven. Ask for Mr. Erebus's booth. If she doesn't show, I'll come for you." The voice was flat. Emotionless. Willoughby's.

I shivered, and Alex tightened his grip on me. He waited for a heartbeat, then tossed the phone back on the table, and cradled me. "We'll get him." He kissed my forehead. "We'll get him, and he'll pay."

"How?" The human justice system wasn't capable of containing or handling a vampire, and more innocent blood would be shed when he escaped.

"Same way his friend did."

I was happy I couldn't see his eyes. Judging by his tone, the darkness in his expression would scare me more than the notion of one or more council members being after us.

"So we're going to the Dark Sun tomorrow?" I brushed my lips along his collarbone.

He nodded.

"And until then?"

"We're staying here."

I looked up at him, shocked. "What about finding a safe place?"

"Even if the leak's fixed, my apartment is on the seventh floor and facing east. Windows with gauzelike curtains all around. Yours?"

"We don't need an invitation to enter another vamp's place. Dead people have no threshold to keep the supernatural away." I averted my face when he tried to capture my lips. "We don't have to hide together. You could stay at your place, and I'll stay at mine." Not my idea of fun, but I didn't want to risk Alex's life more than I already had. He was strong and trained to fight, but he was still human.

He cupped my chin and turned me to him, our faces so close I went cross-eyed trying to look at him.

"We hide together, we fight together, and—if we have to—we run together," he said. "Only Willoughby can get in here without an invitation. If he does, we can take him."

He sounded so certain, I allowed myself to relax and get lost inside the cocoon his words and presence built around us.

The semblance of safety and comfort only lasted until he said, "I think we should look through the folder Barbara gave us."

With a groan, I let him get up and bring the blasted thing over so we could flip through the pages. There were ten more entries that only held pictures and numbers. Ten more young women who'd been selected for vampire snacks—or worse. And those were only the ones Sheena's Models had lined up for Willoughby. Nothing assured us my former agent was his only supplier.

"This blonde has the proportions of a swimsuit model." I pointed at a young woman's picture. Her measurements were jotted hastily next to the photo.

"I didn't know models came in different categories."

So he thought I was in the same league as Gisele? Could he be more awesome? I felt bad for having to correct him. "They do. Runway models as a rule are really tall but less curvy. Swimsuit models are curvier and often more athletic." And catalog models, like once-upon-a-time me, can be shorter than runway and more girl-next-doorish.

None of the girls in the pics were among the missing ones, and Sheena had said there weren't supposed to be more, so who were they? *Alternatives*? Had she been presenting Willoughby with a buffet? I couldn't think of what to do about it. We couldn't start calling them and warning them off a potential supernatural kidnapper or killer.

"Maybe you should take this to your guys?" I said. "They can do more to protect them than we can."

"My guys are the ones who told us about Sheena's Models. Roebuck has probably gone by the agency by now and has a copy of this in his hands. I was hoping there'd only be a couple more possible victims so you and I could follow them." That last sentence was uttered under his breath, like he was talking to himself. He closed the folder and dropped it to the floor by the bed.

"So Roebuck knows we've been by asking questions too."

"Yup." The single word sounded like a whip cracking.

"Uh-oh?"

"Uh-oh."

How long would it take Barbie to tell *them* Sheena had called in? How soon would they trace that call to Sheena's house? I hoped Sheena had the good sense to follow my advice and leave town. If not, she'd have some explaining to do. The kind that results in people being locked up in loony bins.

It was the least appropriate time for sex. Someone I cared about was missing, people I trusted had betrayed me, and Alex and I were in grave danger.

But I needed something to keep my body and mind occupied, and I needed that to be Alex. Whatever came next, even if we were both going to die soon, I needed to feel him inside me again. I needed to cling to what we had, before someone took it away or I had to give it up.

Nuzzling his wide sternum, I slyly tugged at the sheet between us with my toes. Even if we did nothing, I wanted to be touching all of him.

He untangled my hair with his fingers, brushing it to one side in the process. "Cherry, that's not a good idea right now," he said, caressing my back.

"Dunno what you're talking about," I muttered against his skin and flicked my tongue over his nipple. Lifting my hips, I pulled at the covers.

When I lowered again and started rubbing against him, he grasped my shoulders. "Stop it. This isn't what you want."

I stopped, but not because he said so. Well, actually, I *did* stop because of what he said, but not because I agreed with him. "Says who?"

"I do." He folded his arms around me and rested his chin on top of my head. "You're not doing this because you want to. You're doing it because you're scared and worried."

"Now you're telling me how I'm feeling?" I rolled off him, taking the sheet with me.

"Don't be like that." He turned on his side and reached for me, but I shook his hand off.

"I'm not *being* like anything. This is how I *am*, which you wouldn't know since you've known me for all of five seconds." I was being unreasonable, but I *was* scared and worried, and I'd been alone for too long to feel comfortable admitting it to another person. Sharing my fears didn't come naturally. I needed action. I wanted sex to keep my mind off all the badness.

"Okay then." He grabbed my forearm and drew me to him, rolling onto his back at the same time. "Hop on." There was no hint of lust in his words.

"Wha—huh?"

He patted his thigh. "Changed my mind. We're doing it after all." Taking advantage of my surprise, he coiled an arm around me and lifted me onto his lap.

"Ah, now you're doing me a favor?" I batted at his arm. "*Lemme go.*" I could have been free in a blink of an eye and across the room in one more, but that would have defeated the purpose of my winning the argument.

He raised his eyebrows, giving me the distinct notion he was mocking me. "Isn't that what you want?"

"Not like this." I'd been upset when he'd declined sex, but my mood now galloped toward *livid*. What was wrong with him?

He didn't let go, stroking my breast with his free hand. "How, then? Do you wanna maybe give me instructions? Write them down, so I don't forget? Since I've known you for all of five seconds."

Narrowing my eyes, I wagged my index finger in front of his face. "Maybe I should. Maybe then you'd get it *right* for a change." It was a stupid, petty, *mean* thing to say, and a lie to boot. When it came to sex, Alex was nothing but toe-curlingly praiseworthy.

I expected him to start yelling right about then. Maybe call me names.

He didn't.

He snatched my finger, which had been left to hover in front of his nose, and bit it.

It didn't hurt, but it shocked me into stillness. I don't know how stupid the astonishment on my face looked, but it had to be very, because Alex laughed.

"God. You'd say anything to pick a fight, wouldn't you?"

Hiding my relief that he didn't take my words seriously, I retrieved my finger and tucked my hand under my armpit. "I wasn't trying to pick anything. You just pissed me off." I halfheartedly tried to slide off him, but gave up when he stroked my hip with his thumb.

"Yes, you were. You're freaking out and wanted to get me to either fuck you or fight with you." He saw right through me. He was all kinds of wonderful, and I was an idiot for being such a bitch.

In lieu of an apology, I muttered, "I'm a little stressed. I didn't mean what I said."

"I know." He gave a smug smile. "I knew from the start."

Men. "Well, then, why didn't you play along and let me have my fight?"

"I promise to do so in the future, once in a while. Sometimes I may even put out."

"*Hey.*" I slapped his chest, but there was no feeling in it. With what he'd said, I no longer needed sex or an argument to forget my fears. He'd mentioned a future and had done so in such a natural way that while I was in his arms, I could imagine us having one together. My bubble was firmly back in place. "Could you put out now because I want you to, because you're very, very hot?" I asked.

He shook his head. "Are you still hoping to take advantage of me? Wouldn't you rather just talk?"

I grabbed my pillow and smacked him in the face. My victory was short lived. He dug his fingers into my ribs and tickled me mercilessly. Attempting to flee his attack without using the unfair advantage my vampiric powers afforded me, I didn't notice him pull his pillow from behind his head until it hit me sideways.

"Oh, now you've done it." I twisted my body so I faced away from him and began tickling him on the soles of his feet and behind his knees, keeping him in place with my thighs. That got me a slap on the butt.

I turned to glare at him, when I made out another sound among his chuckles. "Was that your stomach rumbling?"

He shrugged. "It's long past breakfast time."

"Long past lunchtime too." I pushed at his outstretched form. "Go get something to eat. I don't want you going all scrawny on me." Not that I could fathom the possibility.

He sat up and gave me a quick kiss before getting out of bed. "What about you?"

"It's still sunny outside. I'll be here, waiting for you. In the *nude*." Like I'd give up on early afternoon frolicking so easy.

"Aren't you hungry?"

I was but didn't want to drink from Alex all the time. I'd stick with packaged meals as my regular diet and only feed from him on occasion. "We'll go by my place before the Dark Sun, so I can change. I'll have a microwave dinner then."

"You can drink from me. Always. I mean, unless you don't want to. Don't know if it's a same-meal-different-day thing for you." He said it in a low, unsure voice, and it once again dawned on me that I wasn't the only one with insecurities.

"Blood isn't just sustenance," I said. "It's an experience. Some see it differently, but for most it's sexual to a degree." I tried to find the perfect simile, failed, and settled for a close second. "I remember thinking chocolate soufflé was heaven when I was human. For me taking someone's blood is like eating chocolate soufflé off his naked body, only better. It fills my stomach, but it also turns me on and rejuvenates me. I could never get bored with licking chocolate soufflé off *your* naked body."

I paused to make sure he was with me. "I want to take only from you, but it may hurt you. *I* may hurt you. If this is a regular thing, it may weaken you, or you may become addicted to the endorphins released in your body when I bite you." I was talking as if we could go on the way we were, but I didn't feel like I was deceiving him. Was it possible I was deceiving myself, by thinking I'd walk away after we found Dotty? Not what I ought to be thinking. "Do you get what I'm saying?"

Alex nodded again, yet I saw the *but* forming in his eyes before it reached his lips. "But you don't take more than a pint at a time. That much is replenished within twenty-four hours. And if I was to get hooked on your bite, wouldn't it have happened already? Wouldn't we have seen it?"

The handbook had a section about addiction. It said addicted humans could go through depression or even experience physical pain if they weren't bitten regularly. It also said the craving would show after the first bite. "I guess."

His expression was serious. "There won't be any microwaving tonight."

****

With the door closed behind Alex, I picked up my cell. It wasn't like I was hiding something. I'd just rather escape the awkwardness of talking to my ex in front of my current lover.

Two clicks later, I was dialing Constantine.

It rang for a long time, before he finally answered. "Now, *I* don't want to talk to *you.*" His words were drawn out, like he was half-asleep. His drowsy voice had the same effect on me as Alex's drowsy voice. Maybe I had some condition that caused overhorniness?

"Very mature, Constantine. I couldn't talk earlier. Was it something important? Did the council—"

"You may find this hard to believe, but I really don't want to talk to you right now. I'm in the middle of more pleasurable things." A throaty laugh from the background—correction, a laugh that sounded like the woman laughing had something *in her throat*—accompanied his words.

I didn't have time to be indignant before he hung up.

Ádísa. He was in bed with Ádísa again. Or was it still? Had the two of them jumped into bed straight after our meeting and stayed there until I called? I wouldn't, couldn't, shouldn't care. He was safe and obviously pleasured, if not happy. Good for him. I glared at my phone like it to blame that a certain horny bastard hadn't changed. *So much for him not letting go,* something whispered in my head. I gritted my teeth against acknowledging the thought and the stinging it brought to my eyes.

I was still nude, but my naughty mood was replaced by a murderous one. I wished that she-devil was the council member involved in the whole mess, and that I got to dust her. It'd be a challenge, with her age and warrior past in the way, but I'd figure it out.

"A little help here?" Alex's voice snapped me out of a particularly satisfying daydream that involved Ádísa begging me for mercy.

I ran up the stairs and opened the door for him, careful to stay behind it and away from the sunlight.

He inched in and didn't miss a step on his way down, despite juggling a heavily laden tray. The tray held a bowl of what appeared to be a mountain of cheese and exuded a mouthwatering scent, together with two plates, cutlery, and a pepper mill. A very slim vase with a paper rose in it was wedged snugly between the plates, to be kept from toppling over.

"Pasta and a flower for my lady." He grinned and set the tray in the middle of the bed with a flourish. "I would have gone for a real one, but I wasn't dressed for outside."

Denying the urge to bite his bare ass, I sat on one side of the bed. He took a seat opposite me, cautious not to shake the mattress more than necessary.

"Prepare to be amazed." He filled the plate closer to me and then placed the bowl on top of the empty one. Throwing a wink my way, he stuffed a huge bite in his mouth.

A gorgeous, naked, kindhearted man treated me like a queen, and I was about to give him up because we'd be incompatible at some point down the road. Was that rational?

"Eat. It'll get cold." He spoke with a full mouth, using his fork to jab the air above my plate.

I did as he ordered, but not before I overindulged myself with the pepper mill. I brought a forkful to my mouth under his watchful eye and couldn't hold back a moan of approval.

If his omelet the other day had been good, his pasta was excellent. He'd chopped carrot, zucchini, and onion finely, and as he explained while I chewed, mixed that and an egg with the pasta while the latter had been steaming hot, which effectively cooked the egg and left the veggies crispy enough to make the end result yummy. The whole thing was then buried under an insane amount of cheese and sprinkled with a bit of parsley.

I was halfway through my serving when I realized he hadn't even touched his food after the first bite. "What?" I tried not to display the contents of my mouth.

"I know we said we'd talk about us after things settled, but I called my mother when I was upstairs, to ask where she had the onions—"

He'd talked to his mother? It had to have been while I was talking to Constantine, for me not to have heard him. *Was trying* to talk to Constantine, that is.

"Cherry, baby, you're great, but you need to stop zoning out." He was looking at me with good-humored exasperation.

The rest of my bite went down unchewed. "I'm sorry. I'm sorry. You were saying?" His calling me *baby* hadn't gone unnoticed. There was a peculiar warmth in my stomach.

"Eh, the moment's gone now." He gave me a dismissive wave and focused on his plate.

I was such an ass for not paying attention to the wonderful, beautiful, sexy, intellig—God, I needed to work on my focusing. "No, tell me. *Please.*" Whatever it was he wanted to say would be huge. It would play a major role in something. All my instincts screamed I needed to know.

"It's nothing." He picked a piece of pasta with two fingers and popped it in his mouth. "My mother asked why I was home in the middle of the day, and I told her I took this week off, to spend it with my girlfriend. It was supposed to be a white lie, get her off my case, but I liked the sound of it."

His girlfriend. He thought of me as his girlfriend. I hadn't been something so innocent to anyone in a long while. It was surreal that I could feel happy amid all the danger, and that in turn horrified me. There was so much more than my unlife at stake.

I knew Alex had told me so he'd see my reaction, but I couldn't give him what he wanted just yet. When we'd finally be done with the case, I'd have to decide whether we could be together or I should go ahead with my original plan. He didn't know about that, though, and I wanted to keep it that way.

I began to smile, stopped, and ran my tongue over my teeth to make sure no sneaky piece of parsley was stuck on any of them. *Nope.* I beamed at him. "Did you tell your mother you're not putting out?"

****

I'm a natural blonde. Well, used to be a natural blonde. Now I'm a very *un*natural redhead, a shade so striking, it stays in the mind of the casual observer—also known as any guy I choose not to leave a place with, when I go out for a snack. That's why, on occasion, I do my nightly prowl in a wig.

In that apartment, my wig collection was in the right-hand side of my closet, and it was extensive and fabulous.

I was in a skintight silver minidress and had set aside the killer Jimmy Choos, for which I'd used my vamp gaze on a bank manager just the previous month. The dress made it a bit hard for me to kneel, as did the nice and pointy piece of wood I'd taped to my inner thigh. I managed nonetheless, and was now carefully going over the blonde wigs, trying to choose the perfect one without getting the rest of them tangled up.

"What about this one?" I held out a honey-blonde one with as natural a curl as it comes when wigs are concerned, and looked over my shoulder at Alex.

"What was that?" He lay on my bed propped up on his elbows, wearing the shirt he'd had on the night we met. His hair was tousled to perfection, and his gaze was trained several inches lower than what I was showing him.

I realized the dress was not covering even a little bit of my rear, so I pulled on its hem with my free hand. My efforts at modesty were in vain, but at least Alex looked up. "The hair. Do you think it'll work?" I said. It would, in principle. The club would be crowded and the music too loud for Willoughby to realize the blonde waiting for him wouldn't have a heartbeat.

"It's a bit too conservative for what we're going for." He crossed his legs and returned his gaze to where it had been before I demanded his attention.

I scrunched my nose. "You're right." Looking for something more bleached provided three alternatives. Highlighted, short, and feathery was rejected. Longer hair would hide more of me. The second was shoulder length and light yellow, but one look at Alex shaking his head made me discard it. The last one constituted a *eureka* moment. A near-white hue, it was silky smooth, completely straight, and came down to my waist.

I tried it on and studied my reflection. Yes, I have one. We all do, and thank God for that, or applying makeup would be mission impossible. The whole thing with vampires casting no reflection only held true when mirrors had a real silver coating at the back. I don't know why we can't see ourselves in silver; it's not like we're silver intolerant, like werewolves are. What I do know is that it's a good thing I was turned after that era, because my vanity didn't fade with death, and I don't think checking myself out on other surfaces would have comforted me—not like I could walk around with a window pane or a lake in my purse.

I grunted at what the mirror currently showed me. "I'm like a ghost in this." I looked at Alex, who shrugged.

He was looking at my butt again. I found it endearingly annoying. What was more annoying was that my self-made broomstick-turned-stake dug into my flesh, the way I squatted.

The lighter the shade of blonde, the fewer people it looks good on. Some complexions, mine included, are too pale to pull it off without the end result looking like someone threw them in the washing machine, and others are too dark for the hair to look anything but alien contrasted to them. It was extremely thoughtless of the powers that be to give me the combination of hair and skin they did. Couldn't they have read a copy of *Cosmo,* prior to blending features together?

Still, there was a way for cosmetics to fix what nature had messed up.

I applied foundation, thinking of how that golden-white blonde worked on Ádísa. Not that I'd ever seen her without makeup on. For all I knew, she looked like Scarface in a wig. *Nah.* The woman was naturally gorgeous, and it was a good thing her personality was that of a cockroach. If she were nice, I'd have to despise her more than I already did, and I wasn't up to such a Herculean feat.

Speaking of gorgeous blonds, Constantine would have called back by now if he needed to talk to me. I pulled my phone out of my cleavage and checked for missed calls—not that I wouldn't have felt them buzz. Nothing.

I added blush and proceeded with a generous amount of charcoal eye shadow, ignoring the questioning looks Alex threw my way.

I was done applying a double layer of mascara and about to finish it all up with cherry-flavored lip gloss when Alex said, "Don't. It'll smudge when you feed."

Why didn't I think of that? The upcoming confrontation with Willoughby had killed my appetite, but I still had to eat before we left. "You're a wise man, Detective Marsden." I stood on tiptoes to give him a peck on the lips on my way to the freezer. Out came a pack of frozen blood.

Down on my hand came Alex's huge palm. "You're not eating that."

I withdrew my hand and popped the package in the microwave. "You need all your strength tonight. Make that offer to me again when we get back. I promise I'll say *yes*."

He didn't press the matter more, but I knew he'd hold me to my promise.

Chapter Eleven

We were at the Dark Sun at a little after ten, to scope the place out.

The mountain of a bouncer outside the VIP section raised a meaty palm when we approached. "Reservation only, this way." Sweat glistened on his forehead and marked him as human.

"I'm Mr. Erebus's guest. Is he here yet?" I said.

The guy checked the list in his other hand and shook his head. "Says here party of two." He looked at Alex. "He's not going in."

I looked at him, smiled, and said, "Yes, he is. And you're going to make sure we get no trouble for it." I used my slow, mesmerizing voice. Alex could have flashed his badge, but we were trying to stay under the radar.

"Of course he is," the guy said with a goofy grin. He barked orders into his headset, and a busty brunette with barely more than a bikini on came to lead us to our booth, where a bottle of champagne awaited.

Willoughby's seduction style hadn't changed since we met. I parked my ass on the edge of the semicircular leather couch. Since my maker wasn't there yet and Alex was busy locating the fire exits, I took the opportunity to assess my surroundings.

For a place with such a name, I'd expected the Dark Sun to be a bit less perky. Then again, for an exclusive club, I'd expected its patrons to smell a bit less of perspiration. The stench of it was everywhere, and it was too early in the evening for the sweaty bodies undulating around us. The women wore clingy, sexy outfits, but the majority of men looked bored. I didn't get it. Why weren't they interested? Had to be a case of overabundance of supply, bringing value down.

One pop song followed the other, but my mind wasn't on the ambience. We still had time until the rendezvous, yet Willoughby might have also arrived ahead of schedule. It'd be in my best interest to spot him before he saw me.

"Dance with me." Alex's breath caressed my ear, his whispered words more of an order than a request.

"No." My refusal had nothing to do with the reason we were there. In all honesty, despite the weight loss that preceded my turning, when it comes to dancing I feel like the chubby teenager who didn't get a date for prom. Whenever I think of myself doing anything more than nursing a drink and gently swaying on the dance floor, I get a vivid mental image of the hippo in the tutu from Disney's *Fantasia*. "Cherry doesn't do dancing," I said, trying for a joke.

Alex wrapped his arm around my waist and lifted me so my toes barely touched the ground. "Come on. You're too tense. You're supposed to be a wannabe starlet, out for a good time, not the best-dressed wallflower in the establishment."

He ground his hips against mine, urging me to follow their motion. It should be sensual. It *would* be sensual if I weren't as graceful and pliable as a brick wall. His words gave me an out, though.

"I'm also supposed to be here for him," I said. "Alone. Not dry humping you on the dance floor."

He let me find my footing and withdrew his arm but didn't move away. "Well then, you have to play the room."

I knew what he meant, but that didn't mean I liked it. It had been a long time since I last flirted for the sake of flirting, and I felt rusty and old. I reclaimed my seat. "And *you* have to keep some distance." I wanted him out of the line of fire, so to speak.

His hesitation was evident in his eyes, and it wasn't like I didn't share his worry. Honestly, though, if Willoughby recognized me before he was close enough for me to press the sharp piece of wood against his chest, there was no way Alex would stop him from fleeing. If, on the other hand, Willoughby got close enough and chose to attack me despite the danger to himself, Alex could do nothing to help me.

Speak of the devil, and he appears. As soon as Alex took a couple of steps back, I saw someone swaggering my way.

I lowered my head so my hair hid as much of my face as possible, and looked up through my eyelashes. Yup, it was

Willoughby all right. He was taller than average, but not as tall as Alex, with perfectly parted, chestnut hair and chocolate-brown eyes. He was dressed to the nines, as if he were going to the opera and not a nightclub, and had on that self-satisfied smile that once upon a time seemed classy to me but now paled in comparison to Alex's grin—and even Constantine's smirk. And why did *he* keep popping up in my head?

Willoughby took his time approaching and appraising me at the same time. I sucked in my stomach and made a show of crossing my legs, careful not to reveal my weapon, yet positioning my left thigh so I could grasp the stake easily. I didn't realize my mistake until it was too late. There was no way for him to sit right beside me unless I moved deeper into the booth, and that would give him time to recognize me. It left me with only one option.

The moment he stood in front of me, I looked up and smiled. "Hey, you."

From the corner of my eye, I saw Alex close in behind him. Stupid man. He shouldn't stand between a vampire and his escape route. Without thinking, I grabbed the stake and threw myself at Willoughby. I wrapped an arm around his neck and held the stake between us, pointing it at his heart. I hoped the crowd would see it as an overexcited hug.

"I have a pointy stick between your ribs, and I'm not afraid to use it," I whispered in his ear, certain he'd hear me despite the music. "Now, pretend you're happy to see me and walk me out of here. We have some things to talk about."

"Cherry. Always a displeasure to see you," he said. "Didn't you get my message? I have your friend. If you hurt me, she is as good as dead."

He sounded unperturbed by my threat, so I pressed the stake in a fraction of an inch, hoping it stressed my point. "I think she's dead either way. And who said anything about killing you? We just want you to answer a couple of questions." Uh-oh. *Major* uh-oh. Why did I have to go and say *we*?

He caught my slip of the tongue at the same time I did. He grabbed my waist, spun to his left, and spotted Alex, who with his alert stance stuck out like a sore thumb. "You're actually working with the *human*?" Willoughby asked.

I was grasping for a witty comeback, when Willoughby threw me on Alex, as the latter was pulling out his badge.

I bounced back, and with a fleeting look at Alex, started after my maker, who was getting away.

Willoughby could have fought me and probably won. He was older and stronger, and I gave a damn about the humans around us while he didn't. So why was he running?

Behind me, Alex yelled, "Police. Make way." I didn't turn to see how that worked out for him.

Willoughby disappeared among the humans. I couldn't fly after him, with so many eyewitnesses here. If I failed to brainwash even one of them afterward, our kind might be at risk. So I ducked and I rolled and I sidestepped, and the distance between me and Willoughby grew.

He disappeared through the fire exit, while I still waded my way through the crowd.

I was helping up a girl I'd tripped in my efforts to get to Willoughby, when Alex caught up with me.

His eyes were restless, scanning the crowd. "Are you okay?"

I wasn't sure if he was asking me or her, but I nodded.

"What the fuck is wrong with you?" The girl looked too young to be out and drinking. She tugged her top away from her chest. It was soaked. "My mom will throw a fit if she sees this. Does vodka come off silk?" Yeah, she was okay too.

Alex flashed her his badge. "I think you should go home and start washing it now."

"*Hey.* I'm over twenty-one." She rummaged in her purse, but he stopped her with a hand on her wrist.

"You're not. Don't make it worse by showing me a fake ID." When the girl turned away with a huff, Alex grabbed my arm. "Let's go. We have one more chance of finding him."

I frowned, unsure what he had in mind.

"He thinks Sheena sent us. He's probably going after her now. We can catch him at her place. If she's smart, she took your advice and skipped town, but we have to hurry in case she didn't."

I was slightly upset he thought of it before I did. I let him lead the way out the door but didn't keep my mouth shut. "You know, it was pretty stupid of you to try to block his way out."

"Seriously? You think what *I* did was stupid? You jumped on him."

"Yeah, well, I tried to surprise him."

"And how did that work out for you?"

"He was definitely surprised. And he couldn't dust me in the middle of the dance floor. He could have snapped your neck, though. You didn't have to play the hero."

"I'm pretty sure I've told you this—and numerous times—but I'm a cop. I'm supposed to go after threats to society, and that's what I did."

"Well, you didn't have to. I'd have it under control if he hadn't seen you."

"But he did. And I had to act before he hurt you or anyone else."

I couldn't blame him for that. He'd done his job and followed his protective nature. "I guess we both did what we thought best," I said. "Just please be careful next time."

"You too. No more leaping into trouble. Though you were kinda brilliant." He pulled me to him and kissed me hard, until I found my hips bucking against his.

Seconds later, when I told him we wouldn't be waiting for his car, he retracted his last statement.

Once we were airborne, a thought made it through the adrenaline fuzzing my brain—why was Willoughby shocked to see Alex with me? He'd referred to Alex as my boyfriend when he sent me that threat via Mark.

Altitude doesn't do much for carrying sound, but I thought I'd try to share that thought with Alex. Looking up at his face, however, made me decide to leave it for later. He was paler than me, and his eyes were squeezed shut. He more than *didn't like* to fly.

I was contemplating that, when the wind stole my pretty wig, which had until then been a real trouper and stuck to my head as if with superglue.

Thank goodness Sheena's house was soon within sight. I lowered us as gently as possible and pretended her red doormat held me too entranced to pay attention while Alex emptied the contents of his stomach a few feet behind me.

Chapter Twelve

I had every intention of letting Alex save face after his projectile vomiting by allowing him to kick open Sheena's front door, but he said stealth might be a better option.

I tried the doorknob. Surprisingly it turned and the door swung open. *Nice way of staying safe, Sheena.*

I was prepared for Willoughby to jump out at me, but not for was something solid landing hard at the back of my head as soon as I set foot over the threshold. *"Ow."*

I twirled to see Sheena squinting at me in the darkness, a frying pan in hand. "I thought you were him." Her tone didn't hint at a profuse apology.

"What the hell are you still doing here?" I slammed my hand on the light switch, and the hallway brightened. I heard movement behind me, and out of the corner of my eye saw Alex blocking the entrance with his body, his back to us.

I resumed glaring at Sheena. "I told you I'd kill you if I saw you again."

She didn't seem half as disheveled or as drunk as she'd been the previous night. "Well, one of you's gonna do that, anyway. Better you than that creepy asshole."

I grabbed the pan from her hand and smacked her thigh with it. It was not a playful smack. If I'd gone for her head, she might have gotten her wish to die at my hand. "You shouldn't be here. He's coming for you."

"I thought you didn't care." That sounded mocking.

"She obviously does." Alex sounded pissed off. "Fuck if I know why. So why don't you tell her why you're still here, so we can figure out what to do next?"

Sheena let out an indignant sniff. "Well, I couldn't book a flight out without using my credit card, and my limo can be easily traced." Crossing her arms over her chest, she returned my glare. I noticed for the first time that she was in silk pajamas and high-heeled slippers. The woman had no intention of leaving town.

"You could have taken a bus," I said.

She looked more horrified at that prospect than at having her throat torn out by either me or Willoughby. "A bus? I wouldn't be caught dead in one of those. Nope, I'm staying put."

Uh-huh.

Alex closed his hand around my bicep as I felt the handle of the pan bend inside my fist. I let it drop. It clanged, and I winced.

"Sheena, you're in danger. Don't you get that, you idiot?" I was no longer in control of my voice. A human could hear me from the next house over—a vampire from anywhere within a five-block radius.

She planted her hands on her hips and lifted her chin. "Why do you care? I thought you wanted me dead. I don't want to run, and he won't scare me into doing what he wants any longer. I'm not going anywhere. Let him come."

I had no answer to that. I think I growled. She took a half step back, and Alex turned to face me. The extra space she'd given me wasn't a bad thing; I had some thinking to do. I'd considered killing her myself hours earlier, but the version of her that stood in front of me at that moment was the version I'd known and loved. She was the woman who didn't give up, who fought for what was hers, and I'd considered her a friend. I wanted to keep that woman safe, despite what she'd done.

Once we dealt with Willoughby and I knew the fate of the girls she'd handed to him, I'd see what I'd do with her. In the meantime, we had to forget our plan about cornering my maker at her place. I couldn't go up against him if I had to protect two humans at the same time. My priority became taking Sheena to safety.

Where might that safety be, though?

The answer made me grin so wide, I knew my fangs showed. "Alex, grab her."

Before Sheena could protest or even blink, Alex had her in a hold she couldn't escape. And before *he* realized what was happening, I had my arms around them both and was rushing us out the door.

"Cherry, what the hell are you doing?" Alex asked through gritted teeth.

I gave him a quick smile and kicked at the ground. "I'm taking us up, up, and away."

Chapter Thirteen

According to some vampire lore, turning into a vampire means losing one's soul. That's not the case in reality. We keep our souls and remain the same people we were prior to our turning. What changes is our perception of limits.

You see, humans know their time is finite, and no matter their belief system, the majority go through life keeping in the back of their minds the thought that they'll one day be judged. Vampires consider ourselves immortal. To us, judgment day is so remote it loses its significance.

What's more, remorse goes away with time. If we're not careful, our consciences loosen after the first few centuries, allowing for ever-increasing transgressions. Eventually we act like the soulless monsters we're believed to be, not because we are inherently evil, but because we reach a point where we have no fear of consequences.

Or that's what Constantine told me in one of our first meetings.

I definitely felt pretty evil *and* soulless as I rang his doorbell.

Knowing Constantine's eclectic tastes and need for quiet, I was confident Sheena would get on his nerves in no time, with her flashiness and her incessant chattering when she got excited—and she'd be excited all right. She'd be spending a few days with a drop-dead gorgeous vampire who meant her no harm.

I could cackle.

Alex had taken his second flight a bit better than the first one. No physical reaction this time, but his eyes were glazed over as he stood on Sheena's other side and waited for the door to open.

I reached around her and squeezed his hand. "How are you doing?"

"I'm fine. I may barf on your ex, but that'll make up for the rest of my night." His thin smile took away from his joke.

As soon as we'd landed, I'd explained to him and Sheena that nobody would think to look for her at Constantine's, since he was sleeping with one of the council members. Sadly neither of them was convinced of my ex's loyalty to me. I knew he hadn't been, wasn't, nor would ever be loyal as a boyfriend, but I was also one hundred percent certain he wouldn't betray me when it came to something so important. He'd been there for me from the beginning. Taught me. Supported me. Even after we broke up, he

wouldn't stop checking in, making sure I was doing okay—
when he wasn't trying to get me to give him another chance.

Most of all, though, he'd been the one who'd held me
day after day while I wept over losing everything and
everyone I'd loved. He'd helped me keep my humanity and
not give in to the temptation of the easy way. For that alone, I
trusted him.

The door was finally answered, and Wesley appeared,
his attire crisply ironed, in direct contrast to his wrinkled
face. He gave us a little bow. "Ladies. Sir. May I help you?"

"*Hi.*" I expected him to wince at the informality of
my greeting, since he hadn't at what Sheena and I wore, but
he only quirked his lips upward, so I went on. "Is
Constantine around?"

"I'm afraid not, Ms. Stem." At least this time he
remembered me. "If you wish, I can relay a message,
however."

There went my evil plan down the drain. I couldn't
tell him what I wanted. Constantine would be warned and
have enough time to find an excuse not to take Sheena in by
the time I finally got in touch with him.

Alex jumped in. "This is Ms. Herring, who's wanted
by some *very* bad people." He pushed Sheena a forward. She
batted her eyelashes, and I had to try hard not to giggle.

"Yes. Very bad," I said. "We were hoping
Constantine could take her in for a few days, until we take
care of them?" It was my turn to bat my eyelashes.

Wesley chuckled. "You can tone down the charm,
both of you." I could tell my companions were as shocked as
I was by his temporary slip in decorum. If he winked, I might

faint. His face straightened again. "I will make sure Ms. Herring is made comfortable with us while you go about your business." He took Sheena's hand and ushered her inside. "Come in, dear. Aren't you freezing in those clothes?"

It hadn't occurred to me to feel bad for making her fly in nothing but her pj's. Hey, I owed her for the frying-pan-to-the-head bit.

"We'll find you something warmer to wear," Wesley said to her before turning to me. "I will tell Master Constantine to contact you when he returns. And if those very bad men you mentioned are of your"—he glanced from me to Alex and back again—"*special circumstances*, rest assured they cannot enter this property without my permission. The deeds to the house are in my name."

I muttered my thanks, and the door slid shut.

Alex wouldn't hear of flying again, so we used my cell to call a cab that drove us back to the Dark Sun. By the time we picked up his car, Alex's color was back, as was his usual good mood, so we stopped at a twenty-four hour place and he really did buy the eggs to make me the promised dessert.

When we parked in front of his mother's house, I had on a face-splitting grin, which only got wider when my phone buzzed and I saw the caller was Constantine.

"I know she's annoying, but you have to keep her safe for a while. Just for a few days," I said in lieu of a greeting.

"Hello to you too, Cherry. How was your night?"

If he cared, he could have asked me that when I called him earlier, but he didn't, did he? He'd been too busy with What's-her-Name. "Went from fine to crappy to fine again, thank you. Did you hear back from the council?"

He let out a tortured sigh. "Not exactly. Can we meet?"

"What? Now you have time for me?" Oh shut up. I resent the implication that I'm petty.

"I always have time for you, Cherry. Some things are simply beyond my control."

Right. Like whom he fucked and how he talked to me when he was with her.

"I'm deeply sorry if I offended you." His words were belied by his irate tone. He hated apologizing, but I wouldn't listen to anything else he had to say unless he did so. "Please believe that I had my reasons. I called you as soon as I became available."

"I bet you did. What's up?" My legs were crossed in a very unladylike manner, with my right ankle resting atop my left knee, and I was tapping my foot against the dashboard. Alex clasped a hand over its top and held it immobile.

"Now see who's impatient," Constantine said. "I called you first, if you recall. You didn't pick up. I haven't been home in forty-eight hours because of you, and when I finally get here, I find an insufferable woman waiting for me. She's been my guest for a little over an hour, and she's already emptied half my liquor cabinet, Cherry. You owe me, and you'll repay me by waiting. Tonight I'll come to where your human lives. After sunset all right with you?"

I glanced at Alex, who wasn't looking at me but made no move to get out of the car, either. "You're not showing up here."

Constantine was unperturbed. "Will you tell me where he lives, or will I have to find out by myself?"

Even if I ended up going with the leaving-Alex-for-his-own-good scenario, I didn't want Constantine to know more about him than he absolutely needed to. "Will you shut up and listen to me? I'll meet you if I have to, but somewhere else. I can come by your place." I doubted Alex would appreciate the alternative I offered my ex, but the first option was worse.

"I guess that means I'll have to follow my nose," Constantine said. "This will probably make me testy when I meet him, so you two lovebirds better keep displays of affection to a minimum."

He hung up before I could protest.

I doubted he could really find us; his sense of smell was enhanced, but he couldn't go roaming the city, nose in the air. He could always ask Rowland where he dropped me off after the council meeting, however, and I didn't want to have to test that *testy* thing, no pun intended. If Constantine and Alex had to meet, I wanted things to go down as smoothly as possible.

Beside me, Alex said, "I'm guessing he didn't shut up and listen, huh?"

Texting Constantine with the address and making it explicit I thought he was a giant ass, I said, "He didn't. He'll be by at sunset." Phone stuffed in cleavage once more, I opened the passenger door.

I was out of the car when I noticed Alex hadn't moved from his seat. I walked to the driver's side and threw his door open. "Come on, there's plenty of time until then. Let's make it count." None of the badness could touch us for a little while longer, and I needed to be lost in him once again. Needed to feel his touch, to connect with him one more time before whatever tomorrow might bring.

"He'll be by? Here? How does he know where *here* is?"

There was no use in lying. "I let him know where we're staying." Before the red flush creeping up Alex's face had time to translate into yelling, I added, "Not that it was necessary. He smelled you on me last time we met. If he's half as possessive as he used to be, he's followed your scent here."

"Possessive? Are you his?" His face betrayed nothing. If it weren't for his heartbeat rising, I'd think he was making idle chitchat.

I should have been honest and owned up to how I felt about Alex. I should have told him there was no reason for him to be jealous of my past. I didn't. It was bad enough that I knew. Saying it aloud would make my choice even harder. Instead I threw back my head and laughed.

It wasn't nice of me.

I can totally admit that I loved every minute of his jealousy, just as I loved every minute of Constantine's advances. I was convinced Constantine's interest in me had nothing to do with feelings. He cared about me but wasn't in love with me. He only wanted me because he wasn't used to losing. That didn't make the passion of his pursuit any less flattering, however. It was simple mathematics—one Cherry plus two gorgeous men equaled one giggly Cherry with a heavily petted ego.

Alex didn't see the situation in the same positive light. He grabbed what little fabric was covering my breasts, pulled me down, and crushed his lips to mine for a kiss much more possessive than Constantine's attitude could have ever been.

I didn't stop laughing until his hand found its way between my legs and got rid first of the stake and then of my panties.

By the time our lips parted, I'd made my choice. Not about whom I wanted to be with; there had been no doubt there. I'd decided what I was willing to sacrifice for Alex. Now it was all up to fate.

Chapter Fourteen

The front seat was cramped, but I am nothing if not flexible, so I did my best to pass one of my legs over Alex's thighs until I could make myself comfortable in his lap. Ignoring the steering wheel digging into my back was difficult but not impossible.

My efforts had just panned out and I was more than enjoying myself, when Alex whispered, "Call him back and tell him not to come."

"Come? Who?" There was only one person I cared about coming—*me*.

I sat there and watch my chances of coming fly out the window as Alex withdrew his hand from my pussy and used it to push at my shoulder so he could look into my eyes. "Call Constantine"—he pinched one nipple over my dress— "and tell him not to come here. We don't need more vampires with invitations to this place."

His voice was as close to enthralling as any human's could be, but I didn't appreciate that he used our sexual *connection* like a mind-altering tool.

I got off him as awkwardly as I'd straddled him, which was embarrassing for a vampire, and was out of the car straightening my dress in a heartbeat. "Constantine is *not* a threat," I said. "But I get it if you don't want him inside your mother's place, so I will meet him out here. Is that okay?" Not waiting for his response, I turned toward the house.

"I don't want you meeting him at all. It could be a trap." He came out after me.

"It's not." I let out an exasperated sigh and sat on the hood of his car, elbows on my knees and feet perched on his bumper. "It's Constantine. I've known him for years, and he's not going to double-cross me."

Alex stood in front of me. Every muscle of his body was tense, his wide and generous lips drawn into a thin line. Though nothing could make him unattractive, I didn't like the look of distrust on him. "You said yourself you hadn't seen him in years." The distrust in his voice was no less annoying. "His maker is in the council. For fuck's sake, Cherry, *think*."

He made some valid points. It made sense that Constantine would be in on all the badness. He had the ins with the council and had sort of kept in touch with me via the phone after our breakup, so he knew where I lived. If we went further back, it had been really convenient that I'd gotten such a stud of a mentor, with whom I'd developed a romantic relationship. Assuming he'd been involved with

Ádísa the entire time and that she and Willoughby were on the same team, it could all have been a plan to keep me under his thumb or to keep tabs on me.

Except I knew in my heart that it wasn't.

Constantine had his share of flaws—hell, he had several people's shares of flaws—but he was nobody's pawn. I could see him going above and beyond if the whole scheme had been his idea, but not because someone else put him up to it. And I could definitely *not* see the whole *let' s turn someone people would recognize so we can overthrow the council and install a new one* being his idea, since it didn't make him part of the new council.

Unless he was the brains of the operation, and Ádísa was his pawn … Hmmm. That might be worth looking into.

No. I knew Constantine. He'd helped me fix a bird's broken wing so I'd stop crying. I refused to be pulled into conspiracy theories other than the one we were currently tackling. There were bad guys among the ones ruling our kind, and they were out to get me and Alex—who was still rambling, by the way—but my former lover wasn't one of them. Despite everything, for the time we were together, Constantine had loved me in his own way.

Alex's grip on my arm brought me back to the *here* and *now*. "He could be how they're keeping track of you. How Willoughby knew where you lived and where to find Dotty."

Okay, I hadn't reacted when he implied I wasn't thinking, but bringing Dotty into this was a low blow, especially when he'd insisted her kidnapping wasn't my fault.

I poked his chest with my forefinger, only not hard 'cause that would have either sent him flying toward the house or broken his rib cage. "I trust Constantine." I emphasized each syllable with one more poke. "He's lousy when it comes to fidelity, but I trust him not to hand us to Willoughby or the council. If that was what he had in mind, he could have done so when I told him I suspected there was a rogue among us. He could have killed me before I ever left his place. I'm meeting him whether you like it or not." Kicking Alex's car would be childish, so I refrained. Barely.

Alex grabbed my wrist and loomed over me. "I don't like it, but if you're meeting him anyway, he's coming inside. He may wanna grab you and fly you to the council, for all I know." *Brilliant.* Typical male. He took a predetermined thing, twisted it around in his brain a couple hundred times, returned it to its initial shape, and served it up like it had been his idea to begin with.

I filled my lungs with air I didn't need and let it whoosh out. "Sure. If you insist." No sense pointing out to him *that* had been the plan in the first place.

"I want to keep an eye on him," he said, as though I still needed convincing.

I shrugged. Whatever. If Constantine was up for a fight, Alex would be useless, but *whatever*. I was too tired to get into another argument. Mentioning Constantine's vampiric powers would make Alex think I was putting down his humanity. Male ego, when faced with any perceived threat, can lash out in all directions, and the first collateral damage is usually rational thinking.

I started to stand, but Alex planted one fist on either side of my thighs. "I wanna keep an eye on you with him."

"I told you, there's nothing going on between him and me."

"You did. But there's also nothing going on between me and you, is there?" Really? After being patient for this long, he wanted us to have the talk now? Out in the open?

I feathered my fingers over his cheek. "We said we'd figure this out later."

Instead of replying, he snaked one hand between my thighs and ran his fingers along my flimsy thong. "Do you want me?" he asked. I barely had time to raise an eyebrow in question before he pushed two fingers inside me. "Do you want me, Cherry?"

I swallowed. "You know I do, but—" We were outside his mom's house, on top of his car. Even I knew that wasn't right.

"Because I want you. All the time." He withdrew his fingers and made a show of licking them clean.

Hell, it wasn't *my* neighborhood. "Show me," I whispered, pushing my hips upward. I wanted more of him. I reached for him, but he held me down.

"Sit back."

I did and waited for his next move.

It didn't disappoint.

He grabbed my thighs and pulled me to the edge of the hood. The hem of my dress slid up and bunched around my hips, exposing more of me. I leaned back, propped on my elbows.

"I want you wanting only me," he said. "Thinking only of me." He traced his fingers along my collarbone and slipped down one strap of my dress. "I want you always trembling under my touch." The second strap caressed my shoulder on its way down, raising goose bumps. He cupped one of my breasts, his palm warm against my skin. I pressed against him, and he pinched my nipple until it was hard and aching. "Like you are now."

Alex leaned over me and took my other nipple in his mouth, in turn flicking his tongue over it and grazing it with his teeth. Alternating between warm, wet softness and sharpness kept me on the edge. I pushed against his mouth and whimpered when he stopped caressing my other breast to trail his hand lower, over my stomach, down my belly, and between my thighs, setting each spot he touched on fire.

He raised his head to look into my eyes. "And I want to be the only one touching you here." He stroked my pussy over the tiny triangle of fabric.

My arms quivered, and I tensed in anticipation of more.

"Watching you squirm." He pushed the thong aside and used two fingers to circle my clit again and again.

The pressure was right, but his fingers moved too slowly. An ache in my core screamed for more. I was wet and lightheaded, and I had to have his fingers or his cock inside my pussy before I combusted with need.

He pinched my clit, spicing my pleasure with enough pain to make me moan. I lay back, my arms no longer able to hold my weight.

"I want to be the only one tasting you." He knelt in front of me and pushed my legs up and farther apart before spreading me open with his thumbs. His tongue entered me, and I bucked my hips. He used his warm mouth to map every inch of my pussy, sucking on my clitoris, fucking me with his tongue, grazing his teeth over my inner thigh and labia. My senses were in overdrive. I could smell the night air, see the stars even when I let my eyelids drift shut, feel the tiny speckles of dust beneath my fingertips. Above everything else, though, I feel the heat in my pussy, each touch of Alex's tongue and teeth adding to the pressure inside me.

I brought my legs up and draped them over his shoulders. When he pressed the tip of a finger coated in my juices against my second entrance, I'm pretty sure I dug a stiletto heel into his upper back. I was kind of protective of my ass, but with Alex eating me out the way he was, I didn't resist the intrusion. A second finger found its way past the outer circle of muscle, adding to the burning sensation consuming my lower body. Just when I thought it was too much, he replaced his tongue with his free hand.

I gathered every ounce of strength I could and lifted my head to look down the length of my body. Alex was fucking me with both hands and watching my splayed body with reverence, the likes of which I'd never seen before.

"I want you." My lips and throat felt dry. "Only you. Make love to me." I no longer cared we could be giving the neighbors an after-hour show.

He crawled up my body and undid his belt and jeans. I tried to help, needing him inside me as soon as possible, but my hands felt lax. He entered me slowly, ignoring me when I clutched his buttocks urging him on.

I didn't want it slow, but not because I couldn't deal with the feelings I associated with it. I was just so close, I'd burst if he didn't make me come. "Please."

He wouldn't be rushed in taking his pleasure or giving me mine. His cock slid in and out of my pussy languidly. My body tingled. I mewled and panted and begged, and he still didn't change his rhythm.

The tension inside me reached a plateau. I needed *something* to let it all out. I rocked my hips faster and tried to wedge one hand between our bodies, to rub my clit. Alex stopped me, pinning my wrist to the hood of the car.

I groaned.

"I want you to bite me." He draped one of my legs over his arm so he could spread me even wider.

His cock sank deeper than before, rubbing the bundle of nerves inside me with every down stroke, and I no longer cared about right and wrong. I tangled my fingers in his hair and buried my fangs in his throat, coming the instant his blood touched my tongue. The flavors erupting on my taste buds combined with Alex's thrusts to flood my pleasure centers with pure bliss. I was rolling on a cloud of endless euphoric sensations. My body pulsed with life. I wanted Alex to keep fucking me forever while I drank him in.

I forced myself to let go after a few sips, afraid I'd rip his flesh, the way I bucked and quivered. He thrust faster and harder, until he suddenly pulled out, and I felt warm, thick liquid coat my lower belly and inner thighs.

"I want you to smell like me." He kissed me, effectively silencing any protests.

What he did was petty and childish after what we'd shared, but I didn't mind. Because I loved him, and that meant loving his pettiness and childishness too.

Yes, I loved him. Silly, given how little I knew him, but love can flash like lightning, striking you down in a split second. Tonight managed to wipe out my noble intentions of sacrificing my happiness for Alex's normalcy. If all we had left together was one day, it was still worth an eternity of memories. Up to now, I tried to convince myself leaving him was the safest bet, but my heart would be broken without him one way or another. Perhaps I should take what he gave me and be with him for as long as we could make it work, or as long as he lived.

And perhaps now was time for him to know how I felt.

I took a deep breath, filling my lungs with useless air that felt invigorating nonetheless. "I—"

"It's getting chilly out here. Want to move this inside?"

His question drowned the words I meant to say. They were too huge to be said as an afterthought and too small to be allowed to get in the way of our investigation.

Sometimes there's only one specific moment. One opening. If you lose it, you may lose everything. I knew it, still I chose not to tell Alex I loved him.

"Yeah. I'm sleepy." I yawned. "Dawn is approaching."

He rose and held one hand out to me. I took it and smiled to myself when he wrapped his long fingers around mine. My palm looked small and pale, fragile inside his darker, larger one, and for the first time, I sensed it wasn't just an illusion. Alex's power wasn't physical, but it was there, and he held a ton of it over me.

****

My eyelids had just drifted shut, when an earsplitting ringing assailed my eardrums. It tore me from the blissfully hazy space between wakefulness and slumber. My relaxed state had loosened my control over my senses—Alex's cell ringing an entire floor above us, sounded like it was inside my head and trying to get out.

I tuned it out and half rolled off his prone form, to shake his shoulder gently. "Your phone."

I was sick and tired of getting woken up by phones, by the way. Next time we turned in, I'd personally make sure all telephones in the house had the ringers switched off.

Alex's reply was a mumbled grumble.

"I can't bring it to you. It's upstairs. Sunshine-filled upstairs. Get up." My nudging, not very gentle this second time, had the desired effect of at least getting him to open his eyes. The caller was persistent; the ringing continued while Alex took his time getting to his feet and climbing the stairs.

I could pretend to have learned my lesson and say I chose the high road, but I the reason I didn't listen in on his conversation wasn't about ethics. I was simply too sleepy to pay attention. I made myself as comfortable as possible and dozed off again.

When Alex returned to the basement, I awoke long enough to hold up my arms to him, thinking I'd have to get up too. Instead he joined me in bed once more. "Roebuck warned me to stay away from his investigation," he said. "Either that or cover my tracks better. If he hears about me looking into it again, he'll sic Internal Affairs on me."

Sleep weighed heavily on me, making it hard to remain alert. The possibility of Alex being investigated by Internal Affairs, however, was too important for me to give in to my drowsiness. "Can he do that? What will he say?"

He gave me what looked like the facial-expression equivalent of a shrug. "That I'm acting outside the law. Pursuing my own interests. He doesn't need to make it stick, just have them up my ass."

I felt my brow furrow and consciously relaxed it. Vampires don't get wrinkles, but we do get tension headaches. "Doesn't he owe you?"

"Says it's for my own good. That I'm in over my head, working this alone." He turned me so my back was to him and enfolded me in his arms. The hairs on his forearm tickled my chin.

I found that oddly comforting. "Maybe you should lie low for a while, to get him off your back," I said. "I can take it from here." Not that I knew what there was for me to take. We were more or less running in circles and chasing our tails so far. Sure, we'd made some progress, but until we found out more about which council members were involved, there was nothing we could do.

"We've covered that," he said. "The answer is *no*. Now sleep. I want to catch some shuteye." He kissed the back of my head and tightened the sheets around us.

I pushed one of my feet between his shins. "Yes, sir."

I'd screwed up his sleeping pattern—turned his night into day, and vice versa. It'd be bad when the case was over and we didn't absolutely *have* to spend day and night together.

That last thought was depressing enough to keep me up the rest of the day.

Chapter Fifteen

I doubt Alex would take as long to prepare for a date as he did to receive Constantine.

He didn't shower, and his scowl when I mentioned I'd like to freshen up deterred me from doing so either, but he took his time applying gel to his hair, only to muss it up to what he considered perfection. His hair looked adorable—and exactly the same as before he painstakingly separated and positioned the curls to show he just got out of bed—but I was too busy biting back my comments about what a girl he was being to say anything about it.

The best part was when time came for him to put a shirt on, and he realized he'd have to do his hair all over again, because the neckline of the tight white T-shirt he chosen—with comfort, not muscle definition in mind, I'm sure—dared touch the top of his head.

That was when I decided the sight was too much for me. I put on a pair of skintight jeans and a sleeveless top that wasn't revealing enough for Alex to think I put extra effort into looking enticing for my ex's sake. I did put on some lipstick, though, and I used one of the makeup-removing pads I never left home without, to erase the smudges of eyeliner and eye shadow from the previous night that had formed around my eyes. *Not trying too hard* didn't mean I had to look like a clown.

Alex's deodorant suffused my nostrils. If he didn't shower so Constantine could smell me on him, the deo dulled that effect significantly, since vampires don't have intense body scent to begin with. Still, Constantine would smell Alex on me. I hoped that wasn't a bad thing.

The doorbell rang right on time. My former lover was a gentleman—when he wasn't banging a two-bit ancient whore.

I looked at Alex. I could be at the door before the spray can in his hand touched the shelf above the sink, but the Alpha dog in him would no doubt find that insulting.

He placed his palm at the small of my back. "Let's not keep our guest waiting." His smirk was scary.

I spun to face him. "Promise you won't do anything stupid."

His gray eyes looked almost black. He stared at me for a split second, before the hardness melted from the corners of his mouth and his lips parted in a boyish grin. "I promise not to do anything stupid *first*."

It would have to do.

I stepped aside for him to lead the way, and my gaze fell to the back pocket of his jeans.

There was something there I thought I'd left in the car.

The stake I made for Willoughby.

****

I missed Alex's reaction when he opened the door, because I was too busy doing a double take at the vampire on the doorstep.

It was Constantine all right, but the version of him smiling at us was one I hadn't encountered so far. His hair, loose, cascaded over his shoulders, which were bare except for the straps of his tank top, and his arms hung relaxed at his sides, thumbs in the belt loops of his faded jeans. Tan cowboy boots completed the ensemble. I didn't even know he owned a pair of those, or any kind of shoe that wasn't patent leather and polished until you could see your image in it.

He stood underneath the porch light, the halo forming around him carving his shape out of the night behind him in stark relief. I bet he was fully aware of how the luminescence added to his natural gorgeousness.

"What's with the disguise?" I asked. Focusing on how out of character he appeared was better than focusing on how hot that out-of-character-ness looked. And it looked *sizzling*.

He studied me as if I were naked, and for a moment I felt just that—naked and exposed to his shameless charm, with no defense but the human beside me.

Alex, more polite on his worst day than I was on my best behavior, held out his right hand. I knew he'd rather clench it in a fist, but he kept his tension out of both his posture and his voice. "Alex Marsden." He could afford to be polite; his saliva wasn't threatening to spill down his chin.

Constantine widened his eyes in surprise for an instant, before he shook the proffered hand. "Constantine," he said. He didn't offer his last name, and Alex didn't ask.

When neither of them broke the handshake or said something as dishonest as *nice to meet you* after a couple of very long seconds, I realized the greeting was, in fact, a macho territorial thing. Good thing neither of them was literally Alpha *Dog,* or I'd have a pissing contest to deal with. I hoped Alex wasn't trying to establish dominance by squeezing Constantine's palm, because if Constantine squeezed back, Alex's hand would soon look like raw burger. I listened. Nope. No sound of crunching bone.

I shifted my gaze from their clasped hands to Constantine's face and saw he was sizing Alex up. They were the same height, give or take a quarter of an inch, but Constantine cocked his head back and to the side, so he was looking down at Alex. One glance at Alex revealed he was appraising the competition as well. *Fun, fun, fun.*

I was about to pipe up and ask what the urgency of the meeting was all about, or just tickle their sides—anything to break the stalemate—when Constantine raised one corner of his upper lip enough to show a long white fang. "Aren't you going to invite me inside, Mr. Marsden?" He used his mesmerizing voice.

Fuck. Why didn't I see that coming? Why didn't I warn Alex not to hold his gaze?

Because to me, Constantine wasn't the enemy. What was more, since Alex wasn't my prey, I overlooked the fact that he *was* prey to Constantine.

Before I could snap Alex out of the mind hold my ex imposed on him, Alex said, "Come in, Constantine."

Which the bastard did, sneering when Alex got out of his way and motioned for me to do the same. "You will remember I made you invite me inside but believe this is the last I will mess with your free will," Constantine said. "No matter what Cherry tells you."

Way to cover his bases. Would it be my fault if I grabbed the stake from Alex's pants and went for a certain overconfident vampire's heart? I settled for glaring instead, but with the same lethal intention.

Alex nodded. When he spoke next, his voice was clear. "I believe you, but so you know, I have a stake in my pocket." My man and I were in sync.

Constantine, made himself comfortable in the armchair and stared at the front of Alex's pants.

It was the perfect opening to get back at him for being a jerk. "Stake's in the back pocket. That's all him." I felt both men's stunned stares on my back as I made my way to the kitchen. "Can't do this without a beer. Too weird. Anyone else want something?" I said over my shoulder.

Alex asked for a beer too, and Constantine said he'd like a scotch if I didn't have any blood. Scotch it would be, and I'd be naughty enough to water it, just 'cause I could.

"I'll be right back. Meantime, play nice." Not that I trusted them to do so, which was why I tried to hear everything they said while I was gone.

Unfortunately, keeping the beer from fizzing out of the glass took up enough of my concentration that I missed whatever made Constantine laugh. That he laughed was enough to worry me. Did he decapitate Alex? Was he now showering in his blood, like I bet used to be his customary dance of triumph once upon a time?

Balancing all three glasses on a tray, I pushed the kitchen door open with my foot and returned to the living room as fast as I could without becoming a blur to the human eye or spilling the drinks.

The danger of spillage was more imminent when I stopped than it while I'd been in motion; the sight that greeted me made me think the world was spinning backward. I mean, I asked the men to play nice but didn't honestly expect the level of *nice* I came upon.

Constantine was sprawled in the armchair, looking at the ceiling and shaking his head in disbelief, while Alex half-sat on the armrest of the couch and nodded vigorously. "That's what I thought she was, man. It was an honest mistake. You'd have thought the same."

Hearing me approach, my former lover raised his head in a motion that reminded me of a serpent ready to attack its prey. Did that make me a helpless little mouse? Nah—a bird. Better be a bird.

"Maybe our lessons in sophistication didn't do as much good as I'd thought." He narrowed his eyes, but not before I saw the glint of mirth in their irises.

"Your lessons in landing my mark worked like a charm, though," I said, not skipping a beat. For once I was extremely grateful I had no circulation and was spared the embarrassment of blushing from either the memory of the misunderstanding between Alex and me during our first encounter, or that of Constantine's… lessons. I placed the tray on the coffee table, handed Constantine his liquor, and passed Alex his beer. Then I took my own and sat on the couch next to my current boyfriend, my arm draped over his thigh.

"What were you wearing, that our dear Alex thought you were a working girl?" Constantine was so not dropping the subject. *Argh.*

I'd make him drop it. "How's Sheena doing? Are you two getting along?" If my grin was any wider, my face would split in half and each part would roll off my skull.

Constantine took a sip of his drink and grimaced. "To be perfectly honest, Ms. Herring is a pain. She asks questions about everything, flirts with me shamelessly, demands constant attention, and is *loud.* Other than that, she is fine and sends her regards. She is not why I'm here, however."

"She's not?"

He shook his head. "Ádísa is."

I didn't like the sound of that. Did she send him?

Alex tensed and leaned forward. Out of the corner of my eye, I saw the top of the stake jut out of his pocket. I moved my hand from Alex's leg to his shoulder, then ran it down his back, all the way to his waistband. I didn't think we had much of a chance if Alex was proven right as to Constantine's loyalties, but if it came to that, we'd go down fighting.

"What about her?" Okay, so I couldn't have possibly said *her* any more disdainfully.

"She and another of the current council members are the ones who organized your turning." I couldn't believe his calm.

I curled my fingers around the stake but not so I could free it from its denim sheath. Holding on to it was like holding on to reality itself. Hearing my suspicions confirmed shocked me more than meeting Santa or a village of Smurfs could.

"How long have you known?" I asked. *Please…*

"I found out after you and I broke up, but she'd been the one who insisted I become your mentor." He cradled his glass with both hands, staring at the amber liquid as though it held the answer to some invaluable mystery.

If he didn't look at me soon, I'd get up and slap him. "Did she insist you fuck me too? Say you *love* me?" I all but forgot about the man beside me. His warm presence became nothing more than a part of the surroundings. All I saw, felt, tasted was betrayal. First Sheena, now Constantine. How much of my life before and after my turning was a lie? The question swirled in my head, drowning out another one trying to form there.

Constantine looked to my right, and I followed his gaze to Alex's face. Alex looked grim but showed no intention of leaving my side or changing the route of the conversation. I was grateful for his understanding, and at the same time, wanted to yell at him for having no insecurities when I was teeming with them. I readjusted my grip on the stake, but Alex reached behind him and covered my hand with his.

The stake wasn't my connection to reality.

He was.

"She wanted me to make you fall for me. She hadn't planned on the opposite happening," Constantine finally said.

There was no doubt in my mind he didn't miss any of the interaction between me and Alex. Both Constantine and I knew who the better man in the room was.

"That's why she did her best to seduce me back to her." Constantine downed the rest of his scotch in one big gulp. "Once you and I were over, she promised me power to keep me with her, but when she told me what she'd done… I really did and do love you, Cherry. I'd do anything for you, including sit back and let you be happy with a human."

I waited for a comment from Alex, but none came. Too numb to hold on to my beer, I left it on the table. I didn't know how to react. My eyes burned with the sting of tears, and there was an itch in my throat that would lead to hysterical laughter if I let it out. My ex gave me his blessing and confessed his love for me in front of my current love interest. Who, by the way, took it all in stride and let us talk things out. Civilized, huh?

I couldn't let Constantine's declaration of love get to me. "When she told you what she'd done—what?" His eyes were a stormy blue, earnest and tormented, when he raised his gaze to mine, but I pressed on, keeping my tone cool.

Detached. "You were with her again after the meeting with the council. And last night." My jealousy wasn't the issue; I wanted him to know I wasn't buying what he was selling.

I saw him grasping for words before he said, "I was with her because I had to be."

"Am I supposed to feel sorry for you? Poor thing. It must have been horrible, fucking her again and again." I was disgusted. How could he sit here and expect me to listen to this?

"That's not how it was."

The waver in his voice did nothing to melt the ice in mine. "Who else from the council is in on it?"

"I don't know. I only know someone is, because Ádísa told me so." He held up a hand to shush my protest. "Let me tell you things as they happened, all right? Please hear me out?" At my nod, he went on. "When she bragged to me about how she attained her position in the council by having you turned, I didn't hold back. I made my displeasure with her rather obvious, and went as far as threatening I would tell the council about her actions.

"She laughed and told me to go ahead. That it would be my word against that of two council members." He addressed Alex now, maybe seeking male camaraderie. "That would help neither me nor Cherry, so I tried honey where vinegar failed, to find out more so I could have a case against her. I approached her again, made a public apology, and finally got back into her good graces, managing to pass off our fight as a lovers' spat. I told her what had enraged me the most was her lack of confidence in me." He locked gazes with me once more. "I'm not proud for sleeping with her when you and I were together, but I swear to you, the only reason I ever touched her since was so I could bring her down."

"She bought the love-struck puppy act," I said. His charm was indisputable, and Ádísa's ego wouldn't let her doubt his adoration of her.

He nodded. "She still doesn't tell me about what she does, but she's not meticulous about hiding it, either. She believes I'm oblivious. What I've managed to find out is that Willoughby is her childe too. You're right about him turning young women, although I still don't know why. I followed him once, after he visited her, and saw him take a woman to a house on the other side of town from Ádísa's. I didn't see the woman leave while I was there, and I stayed till just before sunrise. I went back the following day, but the place was deserted. I've only seen him twice since, but he keeps disappearing on me."

Willoughby's threat to Mark came back to me. *Tell Cherry to get her boyfriend off my case.* Could he have meant Constantine? But we broke up years ago. I wanted to slap my forehead. *Years* ago? Willoughby was probably *old* old, both *olds* measured in centuries. Four years to him were like a week to me.

I squeezed Alex's hand. "Willoughby didn't mean you. He knew Constantine was after him all along. That's why he was surprised to see you at Dark Sun." The implications of what I was saying hit me full force, and I turned to Constantine. "He knows you're after him."

"It doesn't matter anymore," Constantine said. "Last night I overheard there are some fledglings and a human in Ádísa's basement."

Alex and I jumped up as one. The human had to be Dotty, and the sooner we got to the fledglings, the less the influence Ádísa and her bastard would have on them. Without the right sponsor, the girls could become remorseless killers. "Why didn't you start with this little bit of info?" I asked with a snarl, as Alex demanded instructions to the bitch's abode.

Constantine's eyes blazed at me, brilliantly blue. "If you answered your telephone, I'd have told you much sooner. And my timing doesn't matter. We cannot go there for at least one more hour. Ádísa wanted to be alone, and she's given her staff the night off. She's going out to feed at nine. I say nine thirty is our best bet for getting in and out of there with as little trouble as possible."

I didn't want *little* trouble. I wanted *big* trouble, and I wanted to be the one causing it. The rational part of me knew he was right. I was dying to know what Ádísa needed her privacy for, but the fewer vampires we had to fight, the better our chances of survival. We couldn't exactly spy on an ancient vampire and expect not to be noticed.

"We leave here at nine," I said. "I need to go by my place first." Once the girls and Dotty were free, we could go back and settle things with Ádísa once and for all. With any luck, the three of us might beat her, but I needed sturdier shoes if I was even going to *try* to kick her ass.

"We're going in tonight because he said so?" Alex indicated Constantine with the hand holding his beer. "If he gives me the address, I can go get Dotty during the day, when it's safe. Assuming she's really there." He looked at Constantine. "No offense, man, but I trust you about as far as I can throw you."

Constantine grinned. "If I said the same, it would be a great compliment."

I scoffed. "Shut up, Constantine. We get it—you're strong. Alex, Ádísa is not defenseless during the day. Even without humans protecting her, she wouldn't have gotten this old if she were stupid." Constantine agreed, and I continued. "She'll be as lethal as always below ground level, which is where the girls are. Plus you can't drag the new vamps out in the middle of the day, and we have to save them from her clutches too."

Alex seemed unconcerned with them, which, to be honest, bummed me out. I didn't want him to consider vampires expendable. These girls were significant to him before their turning. They ought to matter now too.

He did that nibble-worthy clenched-jaw thing. "Fine. Then let's get backup. Aren't there any other vampires you can trust?" His question put him back on my nice-boys list.

Those of the council not working with Ádísa should be the obvious answer, but who was beyond suspicion? "We could try Johnny Boy." I looked to Constantine for confirmation.

He shook his head. "We don't know which of them is on her side."

"One of the council members?" Alex asked, eyes wide. "Haven't we agreed they're not the good guys you thought they were? Think outside the box, Cherry. You've been around for six years. Haven't you made any vampire friends?"

It sounded too much like an accusation for my liking. "Six years aren't an eternity, and we're not the friendly kind. Also, I don't know if you've noticed, but my taste in companions has been sort of poor."

Alex shrugged in what looked like agreement, and Constantine scratched his chin with his middle finger. If I didn't know he'd never stoop as low as that, I'd think he was flipping me the bird.

"You've been around forever," I said to my ex. "What about your friends?"

He stretched and graced me with a bored gaze. "I don't do friendships. I do politics." I ignored the sharp pain through my side. He probably didn't do relationships either. Or feelings, despite his statements earlier. Not that I cared. Whatever we had was in the past.

Alex raised both arms. "Going in with *his* friends wouldn't make me feel safer. We need people we know are on our side."

"There aren't any." There was the police, but— "None we can risk, anyway. We are all we've got. Deal with it." It came out harsher than he deserved, but there was no way for me to take it back. I needed air. It was stupid—I didn't need to breathe—but I needed air. And why were the men being so civilized? Shouldn't they be a lot growlier with each other?

"I still say we're walking into a trap." Alex didn't raise his voice, but there was a finality to his tone. He lifted his beer to his lips and gulped half of it down before setting it aside. It seemed he'd put an end to the subject.

I needed to be out of there, away from the two of them, from the responsibility knowledge brought in its wake, and from the doubt eating at my insides. Alex could be right, and if he was, I was endangering much more than myself by stubbornly choosing to believe Constantine.

But if Constantine was telling the truth…

I worried my lower lip with my teeth, aware Alex wasn't going to like what I'd say next. "I have to go. I *am* going. Can't risk Ádísa moving them." My body gravitated toward Constantine's, which I only realized when I felt him caress my inner wrist.

I pulled my hand away and rubbed the skin, as if he'd burned me. The touch had felt too familiar, too comfortable for my liking. Everything about his demeanor was far too comfortable for my liking. He'd waltzed in here like he owned the place and divulged information that turned my world upside down.

Slowly, with measured steps, I positioned myself so the three of us formed a triangle of equal sides. I needed the distance from both of them if I was to take the best course of action without letting personal feelings influence me.

Alex tried to reason with me once more. "Okay. Try to see things from where I'm standing, please. My vamp girlfriend's"—there was that word again; I smiled despite myself—"undead ex appears at my place to tell her he loves her, has always loved her, but he was planted in her life from the start by the woman who ordered her turning, in order for that woman to gain power."

I was forgetting something. What was it?

Alex was unfazed. "He's still that evil woman's lover—though she's responsible for the turning of more innocents—but he's somehow not involved in the whole mess and wants nothing but to bring the bad woman and her accomplices down. At his own risk. Only it has to happen tonight. How believable is that shit?"

Constantine didn't stop nodding during Alex's recap and jumped in before I could answer. "Not at all, and I more than understand your skepticism. I have no assurances to offer you, Alex. You may believe me, or you may choose not to. The fact is I've told you the truth." Folding his hands on his lap, he perused each of us in turn.

"And if he hasn't and I don't come back, you're going to torch his place first thing in the morning," I told Alex, without a trace of humor.

Constantine let out an indignant protest and was ignored by both of us.

Alex looked at me, one eyebrow arched.

I couldn't meet his gaze. "You're not coming with. If something happens, one of us has to be here, to do something about it all." My arguments made sense, but I knew Alex would think I was keeping him from doing his job.

To my surprise, Constantine did nothing to make the awkward moment worse. Instead he put our discarded glasses back on the tray and headed toward the kitchen without a word. He'd undoubtedly hear us from there too, but his attempt at discretion was unexpectedly gallant.

Alex remained silent until we heard the kitchen door closing. Then he said, "I'm not letting you go alone."

I opened my mouth to point out it wasn't up to him to *let* me do anything.

"It's not a case of *me man, you woman,* and it's not about jealousy. Not after last night. This is about you and me being in this together, and I'm coming whether you like it or not." He frowned and ran one hand through his hair. "Hell, I'm coming even though *I* don't like it!"

"You don't understand. Any self-respecting vampire can sniff out a human. A council member will have you drained in a second if you so much as set foot on their front porch." I might be exaggerating, but they'd at least have his memory wiped, if they felt charitable. Plus Alex wouldn't be of much use if the proverbial crap hit the metaphorical fan; I was much stronger than him. There was no way of saying so without wounding his ego, and I didn't want us to part on such terms, when I couldn't be sure I'd see him again. "We need someone to—"

"Tell the world our story?" He let out a bitter chuckle. "Cherry, if they take you down, I'm next. Not like I can ask for reinforcements. Nobody would believe me if I started blaming vampires for the disappearances. And I'd hate myself if something happened to you and I wasn't there. I know you're stronger, and so is the guy pretending not to listen in on our conversation, but I'm fast and a sharp shooter. Even if bullets don't kill vampires, they can hurt them."

"Alex—"

"You don't even know we'll only be up against vamps, anyway. Maybe she lied about sending her staff off, or Constantine did. I can help. You can take me with you or let me drive around all night, searching for a house spooky enough to belong to an ancient vampire, but I'm not sitting on my ass and letting you do the fighting without me."

He cupped my cheeks with both palms, and I let him raise my face to his. His features looked blurry through the tears fringing my eyelashes. Blinking the tears away didn't help clear my vision as he came closer until our noses touched. "Nod if we're clear on that," he said.

I nodded and smiled against his lips as they closed over mine. What did I do to deserve such a guy in my unlife?

Constantine reappeared a few minutes later, more serious than ever. "All three of us are going, then?"

"Yup," I said.

"Maybe Alex should drive there? We don't know what shape the fledglings and human will be in."

Alex nodded and jotted down the address Constantine gave him. "I'll park a couple blocks away and meet you there."

My ex turned to me. "I suggest you and I fly by your place first, since you want to change, and meet Alex outside Ádísa's."

If Alex had any objections about the detour, he wasn't vocal about them. I suspect his fear of flying had something to do with that. The three of us didn't speak again until the grandfather clock standing on the far wall of the dining room chimed nine.

****

Constantine was uncharacteristically hands-off during our short flight to my apartment.

He held on to me, but not like when we flew to meet the council. Despite our proximity, there was a sense of detachment that wasn't there before. It gave me the chance to clear my head, and I was grateful for it. Instead of breathing him in, I let the scents and sounds of the night fill my senses until there was no room for doom and gloom. By the time we landed, I was ready to take on anything.

He kept a respectful distance while I unlocked my door and entered, unnecessarily waiting for me to ask him inside before joining me in the space that served as both my bedroom and living room. I saw the covert peeks he took at my quarters. He didn't have to be so discreet with his disapproval; I knew my whole studio apartment could easily fit in his bathroom.

He was playing nice, which wasn't easy for his snarky personality, so I let him entertain himself while I looked for my tall buckskin boots. With their thick leather exterior, they were as sturdy as they were cool. I wanted them covered with Ádísa's ashes before the night was over.

I was pulling the left boot up my calf, when Constantine cleared his throat. I expected him to finally stop holding back and say something about how brilliant it was that they now made pocket-sized rooms or something, so I didn't pay much attention.

"Do you love him?" he asked. "Alex?"

I hopped around on one booted foot, to stare at him.

His eyes were the color of the winter sky before heavy snow. He didn't wait for an answer. "If you do, don't miss out on even one moment with him. We think there's always time, but there isn't. And he's human. If he won't turn… Just don't waste time, Cherry."

I crossed the room and hugged him. He certainly wasn't my favorite person at the time—didn't make it into my top ten of favorite people, and I was friendless—but it felt like the only thing to do.

Chapter Sixteen

Waiting for Alex outside the wrought-iron gates gave me all the time in the world to ponder the unfairness of her living in a manor and Constantine having a mansion, when I was stuck with a frigging underground studio. Maybe I'd get to upgrade too, in a couple of centuries. If I survived the night.

And where was that man, anyway?

I sighed with relief when Alex rounded the corner. Nothing could have gone wrong this early in the plan, yet the knot in my stomach had become tighter the longer he'd been out of sight. He reached us and gave me a smacking kiss on the lips, which left me with a silly smile and Constantine with a disapproving frown. I pretended not to notice. Nobody cared about *his* approval.

The gates were to keep humans out, I guessed. I was about to propose Alex hold on to me so I could float us over the fence, when Constantine leaned on the gates, and they opened.

"The latch hadn't caught," was his answer to my questioning look. "You really should be more observant, *Chérie*. Having night vision is a gift. Not using it is remiss of you."

"Good thing you're with us, then," Alex said. "It's so handy that you notice the little things." I'd bet my favorite pair of Louboutins that by *handy* he meant *prearranged*. Judging by Constantine's frown, the implication wasn't lost on him.

No reason to allow things to escalate between them. I weaved my fingers through Alex's and pulled him after me, inside Ádísa's garden.

The beauty that greeted us was like nothing I faced before. Flowers formed islands of color through which meandered cobbled pathways. Grape hyacinths and lavender mixed with blood irises and lilacs, making purple in all its shades the prevalent color. Batches of pink peonies and yellow freesia, hot orange gerberas and velvet red roses broke the uniformity with their vividly contrasting hues. And those were just the ones I could name.

I can't describe how vibrant colors look to us at night. They're not as they appear to humans in broad daylight. It's like the colors are three-dimensional, deeper, exposed through a special filter. The colors of the flora around us, framed in the white pebbles shaping up the pathways, composed what I imagined the Garden of Eden would look like.

And like that garden, this one hid a snake in its heart.

Already distracted by the exquisite panorama, I didn't want to add fragrances into the mix, but my nostrils flared, seeking the scents against my better judgment. The mixture of dizzying aromas affected me the way I expected it to, only about a million times more strongly.

Next thing I knew, Alex and Constantine were shaking me. I forced my eyes to focus and waved off their hands.

"What happened?" Alex was in my face, whispering urgently.

"Sensory overload," Constantine said just as quietly. "Ádísa built this garden as a defense mechanism. I'm sorry. I should have thought to mention it, but I've been here so many times, I'm used to it by now. It masks her scent when she's hunted, and vampires who haven't been here before and don't know to block the stimuli are overwhelmed."

Alex looked around. "By what? Vegetation?"

How could he call the miracle of nature around us *vegetation*? A voice in the back of my mind whispered, *He is human.* I wanted to weep for him. His short lifespan in itself meant he would miss out on so much. Now I realized how much more his mortality deprived him of. There was no reason for me to explain what he could never experience for himself, so I nodded. "Vegetation. She's charmed it."

Constantine kept quiet and helped steady me so we could move on. He squeezed my shoulder after a couple of steps, but I didn't turn his way. Whatever solace he offered was not welcome.

Alex clasped my hand and halted us once more. "But why would vampires cross the garden on foot? I get why *you* have to—human with sensitive stomach here." Wrinkles formed on his forehead, as he frowned in a self-deprecatory manner. "But you could fly if I weren't with you."

"We'd walk anyway." I hoped my smile looked reassuring. "Flying over another vampire's property is considered hostile action."

He gurgled back a chuckle. "And breaking into their home isn't?"

Constantine beamed an unexpected grin. "Vampire law. What matters to us is that, if someone inside sees us fly over, they'll be prepared for a fight and allowed to attack first. The way we're approaching now, our purpose might as well be a social visit."

Alex shook his head. "Vampire law is stupid," he murmured, "and if someone's in there, we'll be getting a fight anyway, the second we pick their lock." Still, he began moving again, squinting against the darkness.

Knowing the power of the garden helped me focus on the task at hand. Extending my hearing and keeping the rest of my senses on a tight leash, I placed one foot steadily in front of the other. No matter how careful we were, I cringed every time our shoes made contact with the ground. The pebbles rubbing against one another sounded to me like a burglar alarm, and any vampire left in the manor would be alerted to our approach.

A few feet before the main entrance, I held Alex to me and flew us over the rest of the distance and the stairs to the front door. Constantine followed our example. We managed a near-perfect landing, but Alex's feet hit the marble deck before mine did, since he was taller.

The thud his shoes made wasn't deafening, but in the stillness of the night it might as well have been a gunshot. Afraid we'd been heard, I pushed him behind me and scanned the periphery, expecting someone to jump at us from the bushes around us. Just as I began to relax, I noticed Constantine stood stock-still, staring at something over my shoulder.

Dread filling me to the point it felt like my heart might start beating again, I turned toward Alex.

The door behind him was ajar, and Johnny Boy's face peeked through the opening, his index finger slicing his smile in half.

I took a step backward and collided with Constantine, who was trying to get to Alex. *Get to Alex.* Alex was in danger. Johnny was too close to him.

I looked at Alex. In the split second it took Constantine and me to find our footing, he'd ducked and pulled his gun on Johnny Boy.

"Alex, get away from him."

But Johnny Boy hadn't moved. The look he was giving us was amused rather than threatening. "When you two are done with the slapstick, get the human and come in. And for God's sake, keep it quiet. I heard you when you were still at the gate."

I gaped at him, while Constantine placed his body between Alex and the door. "What are you doing here?" he asked.

"Same thing you are, I suspect. Looking for condemning evidence." Johnny Boy winked at him and turned to me. "Well, are you coming in or not?"

I took Alex's hand and followed Constantine inside. Johnny closed the door after all of us.

"The rest of the council didn't seem moved by your warning about a rogue," he told me, walking ahead and motioning for us to go with him. "Me—I'm not used to ignoring beautiful women."

Alex groaned. "Oh great. Another one."

Constantine patted his back, which had me doing a double take. Those two were *comrades* now?

Johnny kept talking, as he led us deeper inside the house. "Willoughby was easy to trace, once I got hold of his turning file. I found out Ádísa was his maker and thought maybe she'd helped him evade his punishment. I tried to talk to her several times, but she avoided me, and the council wouldn't condone a formal investigation. So here I am." He turned and grinned over his shoulder. "And here *you* are."

Here we were, indeed. I looked around. The place was the baby of extravagant wealth and abysmal taste. The amazing garden outside couldn't be Ádísa's creation if this room reflected her decorative preferences. The lushness of the setting bordered on vulgarity, with her obvious efforts at a burlesque style drifting toward the grotesque.

Plush fabrics of clashing colors covered the walls, Venetian and Grecian masks pinning them in several places so they formed folds before draping to the floor. Animal heads stared at us with glassy eyes from around the oversize fireplace, and heavy chandeliers, interspersed as much with polygonal crystals as with horns, dangled over our heads, more reminiscent of guillotines than ornaments. And don't get me started on the furniture. Really. *Don't*. A woman who chose to decorate her living room this way wouldn't surprise me if she slept in a bed made of human skulls.

She'd shared that bed with Constantine. On more than one occasion.

Since I couldn't share my distaste with my ex, I aimed my grimace of disgust at Alex.

He mouthed something and tilted his head toward Johnny Boy.

Huh? I mouthed back.

He widened his eyes and mouthed the same four words again. *I don't trust him.*

Well, neither did I—not completely—but there wasn't much we could do. I shrugged, hoping to convey that exact message.

Johnny stopped in front of an open door. "I've checked everywhere else and found nothing," he said. "This leads downstairs. I was on my way there when I heard you. Once we reach the landing, we should split up. Cherry, you and I go left. Constantine and the human can check the other side. We'll meet back here when we're done."

His plan wasn't the best, and not only because it involved my ex and current flames, alone, in a dark basement. I was about to suggest an alternate division of forces, when Constantine said, "I'm not going with the human. He's Cherry's problem."

Not knowing whether to be thankful or upset, I went with indifferent and snatched Alex's waistband. "We'll take right."

Constantine winked as I passed in front of him to climb down the stairway. "Good luck," I told him in a cheery voice.

"You too," replied Johnny Boy. It sounded flat, despite reverberating on the walls of the narrow corridor.

****

That level of the manor was almost barren in contrast to the upper one. The stone walls were naked except for lit torches every ten feet or so, and the floor was gritty underfoot. Despite the years she lived and the fortune she amassed, let alone the furniture she picked for her living room, Ádísa was still a warrior at heart and had chosen a frugal style for her chambers and private space.

I glanced at the lit torches once more. Something felt off, but I went ahead and rounded the bend in the corridor.

I ran into a cold male body, the collision hard enough to make me bounce backward. If I were to judge the living status of the man in front of me by his eyes, I'd pronounce him as dead as his temperature indicated he was.

I knew better.

I tried to scream, but he covered my mouth with one hand and grabbed Alex's neck with the other. The council member who scared me the most had a firm grip on both Alex and me. "Make a sound, and I snap him like a twig," Benjamin said. "Is that clear?"

Alex gasped for breath. He kicked at our captor to no avail. I could possibly get away with nothing but a bruised jaw, but I couldn't do much to help Alex; Benjamin stood with his arms spread, so we couldn't reach one another.

"Is that *clear*?" Benjamin asked again.

It was possible that Constantine and Johnny had heard Benjamin and were rushing to our rescue, but I couldn't afford to wait for knights with sharp canines, who might or might not show up. I nodded. Benjamin's palm was disgusting against my lips. It felt dead-dead. Touching my lips to it was like touching them to wax. Cold wax, not the kind I used to get rid of unwanted hairs when I was alive. It was odd, since he and I had to be the same temperature.

"Will you keep quiet if I let you go?" He dug his thumb into the soft tissue underneath Alex's jaw, making him tilt his head back and wince.

I nodded again, more vigorously, my gaze glued to Benjamin's dirty thumbnail.

"Good." He squeezed my face once and pulled away.

"You're the one working with Ádísa," I said as soon as he loosened his grip on Alex. My tone was as accusatory as I could manage without raising my voice.

He gave me a bewildered look. "I'm here to take her down. The bitch will get what's coming to her. She'll pay for what she did to my daughter."

"Your daughter?" My turn to be taken aback. I never imagined he'd have a family.

Though his eyes weren't as wide now that he could breathe again, Alex looked as shocked. He didn't need to know who the man in front of us was; at first glance, Benjamin seemed incapable of human contact.

"She was killed a few days before you were turned. I knew a vampire had done it, but I could do nothing about it." Benjamin's face now showed more emotion than I thought possible, becoming almost human instead of the carved-stone mask it usually resembled. "The death of a human meant nothing to the council. I wasn't supposed to keep in touch with my family after my turning, anyway. Ádísa approached me the night before Willoughby's hearing and promised me the one responsible would meet the sun if I helped her."

Things were falling into place. "That's why you were the first to attack the old council." I remembered Benjamin jumping up and hurling accusations at them, urging spectators to join him in bringing them down. "The one who killed your daughter," I whispered. "Was it…?"

He nodded. "Willoughby. He was supposed to dust for what he did to my little girl. She was twelve. I only had a year with her before I became a vampire—too little time. I couldn't give her up, so I watched over her and my wife as much as I could. Then he—" His voice cracked, and I was shocked to see a tear run down his cheek. "When you came to tell us he was still around, I confronted Ádísa. She called me an idiot for believing you. I looked into it anyway, and once I discovered Willoughby was her childe, I knew for certain you were right. A maker would never have their offspring killed."

Yeah, tell Willoughby that.

Benjamin shook his head. "She lied to me from the start. For all I know, she was the one who ordered my little girl killed, so she'd get to me. I could be the reason my

Virginia died." His face crumbled, and it was as if he shrank, the wind knocked out of him.

I didn't know what to say. I was frozen in place, watching pain destroy a man I'd considered emotionless.

"We're going to bring him down. Her too. For everything." Alex sounded hoarse. Of course he did. He was suspended by the throat for the second time since we met. Hanging out with me didn't do much for his wellbeing.

Benjamin nodded again and let Alex go. "Come with me and keep your voices down. She'll hear you."

"She's here?" That was bad—so *very* bad.

Benjamin walked by me, toward the direction Alex and I came from. "Yes," he said over his shoulder. "I didn't see her leave. I meant to hide until she was gone, then break in and wait for her to come back, but I didn't have the patience. Thought she'd be underground, but all I found were some newly turned vampires. They may be the girls you're looking for."

What about Dotty? "Did you see the human woman too? Thirties, tall, with short hair?"

He shrugged. "Saw someone. She was restrained. I don't know if she's who you want. She was asleep, I believe." With that he was out of my field of vision, around the corner.

Alex and I hurried after him. I wanted to ask where she was and rush to her, but our chances of helping her and the rest of the girls would be much greater once Ádísa was out of the picture. Then another thought occurred to me, and I wanted to smack myself for not having it sooner. "We need to warn Constantine and Johnny Boy." I stopped Benjamin with my hand on his arm.

He frowned. "Johnny is here too? But he didn't believe you. Or me."

He didn't? Then why was he there?

Oh shit.

I was so stupid, letting myself be fooled by Johnny Boy's friendly act.

He'd conveniently appeared at Ádísa's the same night as us, with a story that would work if he weren't a council member. Why would he be looking for proof of her guilt by himself, when he could order someone else to do it for him?

And why didn't I think of this sooner?

He said he'd looked everywhere upstairs for the girls. If he had, he'd know Ádísa was still inside the manor. But of course, he knew that from the get-go. He'd wanted me to go with him and leave Constantine with Alex, because he wanted to take me to her. He was leading Constantine into a trap.

Unless my ex was in on it.

No. Constantine was the one to insist I stick with Alex. Whether he suspected something or not, he definitely wasn't in cahoots with Johnny. And I had to warn him before it was too late.

"Let's go." I started running toward the stairs, where we said we'd meet the other two, barely holding back for Alex to keep up.

Constantine and Johnny weren't at the bottom of the staircase, and we wouldn't find them in any of the basement rooms. Without thinking, I climbed the stairs and burst into Ádísa's living room of horrors.

****

"I suggest you don't come any closer." Johnny smiled amiably, as always. He sat on the armrest of the chair I noticed on our way in. The thing was uglier than ugly, from its winged back to its clawed feet. Ádísa stood behind it, leaning against its back and tapping her sharp nails on the upholstery. Willoughby flanked her other side, his arm folded around Constantine's chest, the stake in his hand pressing over Constantine's heart.

They made for a very evil—if totally clichéd—tableau. I sort of felt bad for Ádísa. For all she had going, she seemed desperate to prove her superiority.

Still, her guys were armed, so I froze in my tracks, as did Alex. Benjamin, however, unconcerned with my former lover's unlife, shoved me aside and lunged for Ádísa with a roar.

Johnny raised his arm. I heard the *thwack* of the cord releasing but didn't have time to warn Benjamin. An arrow shot out of the mini crossbow in Johnny's hand, sliced the air, and found Benjamin's heart.

Benjamin turned to dust mid-leap. One moment he was lifting off the ground, about to close the distance to the woman who promised him retribution for his daughter's murder but used him as a pawn, and the next he was a thin cloud of dust descending toward the inappropriately colorful carpet.

Alex's gasp reached my ears. It was the first time he saw someone dust, since he'd been knocked out when I offed the vampire at his mother's place. I wanted to make sure he was okay, but I didn't dare avert my gaze from Willoughby's hand.

"Why?" I muttered, unsure of what that *why* was about. Why did they kill Benjamin? That was kind of easy to figure out. Why were they turning the girls? Why was Johnny teaming with Ádísa? *Why...?*

Ádísa replied to the obvious question. "He was dangerous. He had to be put down." She looked between me and Alex. "You are dangerous too."

"We've done nothing to you," I spat out between gritted teeth. She was a council member, and we were nobodies. No reason for her to fear either of us. "You were the one who ordered me turned and had him"—I pointed to Benjamin's remains—"help you overturn the council. And you had Constantine keep an eye on me. Why?"

"I am not going to explain myself to you or to a human." She straightened up and went to Constantine.

"Why take the girls?" I asked, unfazed by her turning her back to me. "Or me? You could have turned anyone. Why set up this scheme?"

Willoughby mustn't have noticed how bad guys in movies die after presenting their elaborate plans to the white hats. "These girls are precisely the type rich, powerful men go for," he said with a grin. "Place them in the right spot at the right moment, and they can bring those men to us."

Huh? "So this was about money?" That was absurd. Ádísa had to be richer than Midas.

"No." Ádísa's tone was scornful. Apparently she wasn't above explaining herself if that meant pointing out my idiocy. "It is about power. Turn a few men at key positions, kill a few more after they sign over their companies to their latest significant others, and we rule the world."

I gaped at her. "You're planning to take over the world with an army of what? Five gorgeous, undead escorts? Ten?"

She scoffed. "You're assuming we limited ourselves to Los Angeles."

"Why didn't you turn those men to begin with? Why involve the girls?"

"The ones we're after are hard to get close to. They have people monitoring their every move. Turning doesn't happen within seconds. It's one thing for Bill Gates to disappear for a whole night after an appointment at his office, and another for him to *ask* not to be disturbed because he's spending the night with a conquest. And the girls are trained to be conquests. Men in power have to hunt their prey."

"Bill Gates is married," was what came out of my mouth. My mind couldn't process what I'd heard.

"Why did you break into my mother's house?" Alex asked from behind me.

Willoughby smirked. "We needed to know what progress you'd made with the case. I followed you there before, and she told us you'd be there alone. We were planning on wiping you, but she"—he pointed at me—"got in the way."

"Well, you shouldn't have messed with me. Why turn me?" They'd turned me and let me loose. I didn't even fit the type they were after.

Willoughby opened his mouth, but shut it again at Ádísa's glare.

"What? No more playing the James Bond villains?" I asked.

Blank looks all around. These people lacked basic pop-culture knowledge.

"You know—answering our questions so we aren't left wondering after we escape and kill you?" I acted braver than I felt, but I wasn't exactly trembling in my boots. Their displays of power made them less scary than the ideas of them I'd had in my head.

"Not as if we're risking anything. You're as good as dead." Ádísa arched two perfectly shaped eyebrows. With an order from her, Willoughby dropped his arm, and I let out a sigh of relief. Imminent danger to Constantine was averted.

Probably.

Ádísa locked her gaze to my ex's and said, "I knew I could count on you to bring her here."

The ground opened under my feet, and my stomach plummeted. Constantine betrayed me? I stared at him, certain Ádísa was playing me. She had to be lying.

Constantine was silent. Why wasn't he denying her words? He smiled at her, and I almost took a step toward him before the memory of Benjamin's perma-death stopped me. I'd have to kill the double-crossing bastard later. Because I *would* kill him, for making me trust him and letting me down.

Again.

Ádísa went on. "I knew you had a soft spot for her. I saw you watching, listening… waiting for the right moment to turn on me. I arranged for that moment to be tonight." She whispered the last part, but all nonhumans in the room must have heard her loud and clear.

A sense of peace washed over me, at odds with the situation. Constantine didn't betray me. She used his feelings for me against me, but it wasn't his fault.

I didn't get to relish my relief.

Ádísa made a show of pulling a sharpened stake out of a hip holster and dragging it along Constantine's cheek. "What is it with the women in your family, Cherry?" she asked.

It took a couple of seconds for me to grasp that she was talking to me. The women in my family? I didn't have the faintest idea what she meant.

"No matter. Your allure worked against you this time. It got you where I wanted you. It's such a pity Constantine will share your fate, but maybe I'll get to keep your new friend." She meant Alex.

I growled. "You'll leave all of us alone."

"Or else?" Her smile was too sweet and innocent to be sincere.

Constantine spoke up. "How could you think I would betray you? After all we've been through? Don't you know I love only you?"

I opened my mouth to say I was sorry, I should have known better, when it dawned on me he was talking to Ádísa.

And then he did more than talk. He cupped her face, pulled her to him, and shoved his tongue down her throat.

Ádísa lowered the stake and plastered her body against his, all but dry humping him.

This was like the set of a supernatural soap opera, with the leading characters changing allegiances and lovers before every commercial break. "Now *that's* been cleared up, will you tell me why it had to be me? I mean, I know you needed someone recognizable for the whole council-overturning scheme to work, but I was a minor celebrity at best. Why not go with a big name?" I said.

Oh, for the love of God, could she just answer me and stop sucking face with my ex?

Nobody paid me any attention except for Johnny Boy, who leveled his crossbow in my general vicinity. From the corner of my eye, I noticed Alex moved so he stood half behind me. He wasn't a coward, to be using me as a shield, so I hoped he had a plan in mind.

"*Hey.* I'm talking to you, you harpy. And what do you know about my family?" I yelled the question, both in hopes the other vampires would turn their attention to me, and on the off chance I got a reply.

It worked. Ádísa pulled back from the lip-lock, clearly about to say something. Only she didn't get to.

Constantine, still cupping her face, twisted.

I heard a *crack.* Her spinal cord snapped as easily as a twig. Constantine kept twisting and pulled upward, until he tore her head from her neck with a squelching, ripping sound.

He *twisted* her head *off.*

Despite knowing better, I expected blood to spurt. There was none. In the blink of an eye, Ádísa's body formed a pile, her stake landing beside it with a dull *thud*. Constantine was left holding thin air, his palms covered in her dust. His face contorted, lines marring his beautiful features. His eyes filled with tears. His pain seemed physical.

I wondered if it really was—if there was some sort of metaphysical bond between maker and childe that hurt when severed. Would I feel what Constantine did now if Willoughby was really executed? I didn't know; they don't cover *maker extermination* in the handbook. I'd find out firsthand, though, if Willoughby did us all a favor and died tonight.

I could ask Constantine later, but I didn't want to. He appeared devastated. Lost.

Then he met my gaze.

Producing a maniacal grin, he spun and caught Willoughby's wrist. He took advantage of the other man's shock, to move the stake away from his own chest.

"You killed her." Willoughby's face was a mask of fury, but his eyes held the same devastation Constantine's held for that split second after he killed Ádísa.

Constantine didn't speak, but used both hands to bend Willoughby's wrist backward. He pushed, and the stake was shoved into Willoughby's chest. Willoughby took a couple of steps back but didn't dust. The stake must have missed his heart. I looked at Johnny as he was about to shoot me. I saw it in the tensing of his eyes, the tightening of his finger on the crossbow's trigger. I ducked to the side at the same moment

Constantine kicked the armchair into Johnny and rattled his aim.

An arrow buzzed by, not close enough for either Alex or me to be at risk. If Constantine didn't jar Johnny off balance, I'd be history. Before relief could settle in, Alex pulled me behind him and brought up his gun. This was why he'd hidden part of his body from view—so the others wouldn't see him reach for his weapon. Well, there was no reason for him to hide anymore. The fight was on.

I tuned down my hearing just in time. Alex's gun went off, and the sound had to be deafening to the other vampires in the room. Johnny looked pained even before Alex planted bullet after bullet in his chest. Johnny Boy's inability to take aim again allowed me to approach Willoughby and Constantine, who were wrestling on the floor.

I grabbed Ádísa's stake from where it lay beside them and crawled toward Johnny. The armchair acted as a shield against stray bullets. Alex was still shooting Johnny when I stood behind the vampire and plunged the stake under his ribs and through his heart.

Something whizzed past my head. My cheek burned. Alex almost shot me. "*Hey.* Watch it."

"Are you all right?" Alex crossed the room toward me, holding his gun up.

"Not thanks to you." I rubbed my cheek and checked my hand. No blood, not that it'd leave a scar even if there were an open wound. Dust clung to my lips and eyelashes.

He stopped a couple of feet away from me and took me in. "You seem fine from where I'm standing."

"I'm lucky you ran out of bullets." I tilted my head toward the other two vampires and motioned for Alex to stay where he was. He nodded, and I rushed to help Constantine. I was looking for an opening, when Willoughby brought up his knee and crashed it squarely into my ex's crotch. Constantine folded over with a groan, and Willoughby rolled him off and took flight.

Constantine was on his feet before I could decide whether to chase Willoughby or look for the missing women. "Go find the fledglings," he said. "I'm going after him."

Dilemma solved, I kicked at Ádísa's ashes, watching as my boot scattered them. I'd wanted her to tell me why she hadn't picked someone better known and what her comment about women of my family meant, damn it. And I'd wanted to be the one to rip her head off—or something less brutal but equally final.

Resigned to knowing I couldn't have everything, I stole a kiss from Alex. "Let's get the girls and get out of here."

****

I stared down the iron door barring our way to the first room in the basement. Anything could be behind it, but I was ready for *anything*, so that worked out fine. "I'm going in first. We can't be sure what shape the newly turned vampires will be in. For all we know, Ádísa, Willoughby, and Johnny have been starving them into obedience. If they're in the room, half-crazed with hunger, you'll be the perfect snack for them."

Wisely, Alex didn't put up an argument.

I put my ear against the door for the third time. I couldn't hear evidence of life on the other side, but that didn't mean Dotty wasn't in there. Even if the door weren't thick enough to conceal a heartbeat, Alex's heart pounding would definitely cover it.

I tried the doorknob, but it wouldn't budge. Not surprising. I didn't expect the thing to be unlocked anyway. "Hello?" I said, and jumped when two distinct voices returned my greeting.

"Hold on, we're here to get you out." My mind reeled at the possibilities of what would greet me when I entered the room. Would the women be chained up? Tortured? The mental picture of naked, bleeding bodies lying on the cold floor made me flinch. *Oh God*. With a curse, I grabbed the knob again and rattled it. Nothing. Alex was out of bullets, so I'd have to break the door down.

"Hold on," I yelled again, swearing to myself I'd make sure they were properly taken care of from that day onward. I'd make it the point of my unlife to help them forget whatever pain was inflicted on them for the first weeks of their existence as vampires.

I took a step back, steeled myself, and shoved at the door with my shoulder, putting all my weight into it. I accomplished jack shit on my first effort, but the second time was the charm. The moment my body made contact with the iron surface, the door gave way, emptying me into the room. I didn't bust in; it was opened. From the inside.

I landed face first on a sheepskin rug, in front of a pair of feet with perfectly painted orange toenails. The legs attached to those feet went up for miles, and from my position I saw more of their owner than I wanted to. I raised my gaze to her face. It looked familiar.

"Oh look. They brought us a chick," the tall girl standing above me in a forest-green silk robe said.

I'd seen those hazel eyes before, in one of the pictures Alex showed Sheena's assistant. Intense eyebrows, short black hair… *Liza. Liza Mills.*

She looked a lot more interested when she took in Alex helping me up. "And who are you?"

"He is off limits." I bounced back to my feet, confusion forgotten at the thought of him being in danger. "Nobody bites him."

"I'd say," Alex murmured.

"I wasn't going to," Liza said. "Like I'd feed on a human."

Huh? Humans are our food source.

I glanced around and saw two more girls watching us. They were dressed the same way Liza was, only in different colors, and looked the exact opposite of the prisoners I expected to find. The room wasn't what I'd pictured, either. It wasn't big, but it was every girlie girl's fantasy, with cosmetics and hair products lining all surfaces except for the two sets of bunk beds. I was prepared for a medieval torture chamber but found myself in a sorority house.

"We're here to save you," I said. Now, how to convince them they needed saving?

"Are you a missionary?" the blonde sitting cross-legged on one of the beds asked. "I've dealt with your kind before. I have to tell you Willoughby says our souls are in no danger from our turning." She was clutching at the lapels of her robe, keeping them closed over her breasts and paying no mind to how much of the rest of her was on display.

The third girl sat at a vanity, braiding her dark chocolate brown hair in a manner similar to how Ádísa often wore hers. "Where is Willoughby? He was supposed to feed us today." Done with her hair, she tossed her braid back and turned toward me.

"Yeah. Did he send you instead?" asked the blonde.

I had no clue why she'd think I was there to feed her, but I was thankful she only asked me, and not Alex. That, and what Liza had said about not feeding from a human, indicated Willoughby kept the girls on vampire blood. It sort of made sense, since vampire blood is more nutritional, but I didn't get why he didn't even tell them humans equaled food.

Willoughby was obviously trying to gain their loyalty. Cultivate an actual maker-childe bond. I wouldn't be resentful just because he obviously took far better care of them. I wouldn't.

Then again, any care was better than dumping someone in an alley after their turning.

All three fledglings looked at me like baby birds looking at their momma. A momma about to tap a vein for them. This so wasn't happening.

I had to tell them the truth, and I doubted they'd like it. "Willoughby took off. And Ádísa is dead."

"Oh my God. What happened to her?" Liza seemed about to cry. "Where did Willoughby go? Is Johnny okay?"

I wanted to bang my head on a wall. Instead I shook it. "Dead too," I whispered.

"We'll tell you all about it," Alex said before I could say more—like how I was the one responsible for Johnny's new status. "First we have to get you somewhere safe."

"Are we in danger?" Liza was the most vocal one. The other two girls approached us, and I didn't like how they seemed to be measuring Alex. Whether they meant to bite him or not, they most definitely seemed hungry for him.

Constantine appeared at the doorway as I took Alex's hand in mine. "He got away," he said, his gaze roaming the fledglings. "Are they all you found?"

"Just told these girls their maker disappeared and the other two people… taking care of them are dead." I spared him a glance that I hoped warned him not to disagree. He nodded, and I said, "Can you fly them to your place? We'll look for the rest and Dotty, and then come find you."

"To my place?" He scrunched his nose in dismay. "Cherry—"

The young vampires hissed in unison. The blonde took a step back. "You're Cherry?" Her fangs were out, but she sounded funny more than menacing. "We've heard about you."

Well, this was odd.

"You want to stake us, don't you?" The brunette stood in front of the blonde. "Don't worry, Sally. I won't let her get to you."

I turned to Liza, whom I deemed the brainiest of the three. "Listen—I don't know what Willoughby and the others told you, but I have nothing against you. They were the ones who took your lives from you. They did the same to me. I'm on your side. I'm here to rescue you."

"From what? Luxury?" The blonde one, Sally, wrapped her fingers around the brunette's bicep, stopping her from nearing me. "Don't, Carrie. She's dangerous."

I was about to throw a fit. "I'm *not* dangerous. I'm not the one who turned you so you could fuck and kill men for their estates."

Blank looks all around. *Awesome.*

Constantine held his hands up. "I will explain everything when we get to my mansion. You ladies seem to need to feed. I will take care of that too. If you'll get dressed and follow me." With a small bow, he stepped outside.

I was waiting for protests, but none came. Not taking their eyes off me, the girls hurried to the closet. Alex turned away, and I was left to watch bouncy boobs getting squeezed into revealing tops and perfectly shaped tummies being sucked in for skintight jeans to be zipped up.

I remembered the plastic surgery I never had, and stood there sulking as the girls exited the room, mindful not to come too close to me.

"Come find us when you're through looking around," Constantine called out over his shoulder, wrapping an arm around Carrie's waist and the other around Liza's shoulders. Sally seemed at a loss for a second, but then she grabbed his waistband and the four of them were soon out of sight.

Alex grinned. "Do you think he'll take care of all three of them?"

I scowled. "We have to find the rest of them and Dotty." Constantine *could* take care of all three young ladies. Also, I could *gag.* Sheena would probably be her annoying self enough to keep any sexing from happening till we met up with them.

And I didn't care.

I led Alex to the next room.

That door wasn't locked from the inside, and it took three kicks and a shoulder wedge for me to open it.

My previous fears came to life when I saw Dotty chained to the far wall, her jeans and frilly blouse torn in several places. She was thinner than when I last saw her. Her nose had bled at some point. Rust-colored stains covered her front, and a crust of blood blocked what I saw of her right nostril.

Her nose wasn't the only part of her she'd lost blood from, though. Even from across the room, I made out the raw and angry bite marks on the insides of her elbows and her wrists. I bet there were more on her neck, but I couldn't see them, the way her head was tilted.

At least her jeans were still on. Whatever happened to her, she at least wasn't violated *that* way. Nobody would have bothered dressing her afterward.

Fury fought with nausea inside me. They didn't need to have her chained up, hanging from the wall like a side of beef; they could have thralled her into submission. They could have licked her wounds closed, for fuck's sake. I wanted to weep for her—for what happened to her because she was unlucky enough to know me.

I wished Constantine hadn't lost Willoughby. I wished he'd caught the sadistic creep and brought him to me, so I could mete out some justice.

"Dotty?" I whispered. "Can you hear me, honey?" Her heart was beating, thank God, and her chest rose and fell, albeit slowly. She was alive, and that was all that mattered.

The shackles looked sturdy. I could probably break them, but I might injure Dotty more. Luck smiled at us when I noticed a small key on the bench to my right. "Help me," I said.

Alex ran to her side and propped her up, while I undid her bindings. She slumped against him, and he maneuvered her so cradled her body in his arms. "I'll wait here while you search the other rooms."

With a grateful, shaky smile, I left him and his precious cargo and went to tear down the rest of the doors in the basement.

I found nobody else. A second preppy room, like the one we found the newbs in, was empty. As, predictably, was Ádísa's bedroom.

I returned to Alex and carefully took Dotty from him.

"You'd better fly her to Constantine's," he said. "She needs to be looked after as soon as possible."

I wasn't sure I could take Alex with. Dotty was still out for the count, and I'd have to hold her with both arms.

He shook his head, as if reading my mind. "I'll bring the car."

I thanked him, and we made our way outside. He kissed me when we got to the front gate. It was awkward with Dotty between us, but he managed a lingering kiss, full of promises.

I reciprocated with equal fervor. With the bad guys out of the way, we had a future, and I was keen on starting on that as soon as I had Dotty restored to her healthy, vibrant self, and back with her son.

I gazed at Alex one last time before I took off. He looked at me with a secret smile that made his eyes twinkle. My chest swelled with love that warmed me up inside. I wouldn't let another opportunity pass me by. When I saw Alex later tonight, I'd tell him I loved him.

I tucked Dotty's head under my chin, smiled back at him, and launched into the night sky.

Chapter Seventeen

I waited at Constantine's for three hours.

I shouldn't have waited that long. I should have known something was wrong when Alex didn't show within the first thirty minutes. I should have felt it.

I didn't.

I was too preoccupied with worrying over Dotty, who didn't wake up even after Constantine and I closed her wounds. Sheena helped me clean and change Dotty into warm pajamas and didn't freak out once during the whole thing. That she wasn't drunk or even tipsy spoke volumes about the truth of her resolution to be strong and finally deal with things she avoided for a while.

I was busy helping Constantine feed the three girls, then explaining to them why we killed two of the vampires treating them as royalty. His patience with them was surprising, as was the firm yet kind way he dealt with all the excitement our revelation caused. They were still wary of me but at least seemed open to the possibility they were lied to by their maker and his friends. It was more than I could have hoped for.

By the time I realized Alex was taking far too long, it was almost two in the morning. I tried his cell phone, but it kept ringing and ringing until my call was forwarded to his voicemail. *"I can't pick up right now,"* his recorded voice informed me, *"but if you leave your name and number, I'll get back to you as soon as possible."*

The pit of my stomach gave way, and the world tilted. I wanted him to get back to me *now*. Where was he? Did he have an accident while speeding to get to me?

"Don't be silly." Sheena stopped my pacing with a hand on my shoulder. "Have some of this." She offered me a cup of the tea Wesley made for us all. The poor man felt useless among the drama until Constantine set him on tea duty.

I didn't take it. The stupid stuff wasn't going to fix anything.

"He probably went by his place to shower and left his phone in his car. Maybe he's set it on silent." Her efforts to reassure me were valiant but ineffective.

"He would have called me." He wasn't taking a shower. No shower took that long. "He wouldn't make me wait like this." I should call his place or his mother's, but I didn't have either number.

I shoved my phone in my pocket and made sure Dotty was tucked in where she lay on the couch. "I'll go find him."

Ignoring Constantine's protests that I couldn't leave him with three pissed-off women and a crazy one, I ran out the door and was in the air in seconds.

****

I could have gone to his mother's first. Hell, I *should* have gone to his mother's first, but I didn't want to waste time doing things in what might be the wrong order. Determined to start at the beginning, I flew back to Ádísa's, landed in front of her manor's gate, and flared my nostrils until I caught his scent.

Nose in the air, I followed Alex's trail around the corner he appeared from earlier tonight and into a well-lit street lined with two-story houses, their gardens trimmed to perfection. There, under a streetlight, I saw a familiar car.

My feet almost kicked up sparks, as I covered the distance to the car at full speed, hoping against hope that Alex was just taking a nap behind the wheel, the exhaustion and excitement of the night having finally caught up with him.

He wasn't behind the wheel or in the backseat. I punched through the lock of the trunk, to pop the lid open. Not there either.

The unmistakable scent of his blood wafted to my nostrils. It didn't come from the car but the gravel. A closer look revealed a couple of dark droplets. Alex had been here, and he'd been bleeding.

Something happened to him as he was about to get in his car. I tried telling myself it could be something as small as a nosebleed, but I knew better than to let the lack of more blood appease me.

I couldn't have been too far when he was hurt. I should have heard him call for help. *No.* I should have been there with him. I should have saved him from whatever harmed him.

Willoughby.

The thought made me panic. Every hint of rational thought I might be capable of got choked out. I tried to think of other possibilities. Alex could have been hit by a car—*no, there would be more blood.* He could have been mugged, although the sight of his gun should be enough of a deterrent for any aspiring mugger, who wouldn't know it was empty. He was a cop; he'd manage to at least pull his gun on his attacker.

If his attacker was human.

I could no longer hide from the truth. Willoughby got to him. My maker came back after he escaped Constantine, and he got Alex alone. In my mind's eye, I saw him pinning Alex to the car and closing his jaws over my Alex's jugular.

Did he kill him? I shook my head. Alex had to be alive. He had to be alive for many, many years. We had to make each other happy.

My vision blurred with tears. Wiping my eyes and cheeks furiously, I let my sense of smell overtake my other senses, not hoping for much. If Willoughby flew Alex out of here, it would take me forever to find him.

The scent hit me again, and I frowned. Willoughby carried him away on foot? What for?

The streetlamps were too bright. A cat howled from atop a nearby trash can.

He did it for me to follow them. It was a trap for *me*.

****

I stood at the entrance of Alex's mother's house, working up the courage to make my way inside. I didn't know what I'd find, and for the millionth time considered calling Constantine. He would be more than useful an ally in a confrontation like the one I was about to have with my maker.

Calling him would be the wise thing to do, but not knowing in what condition I'd find Alex meant I couldn't wait. I squared my shoulders and tried the door. It wasn't latched, which added to my unease as I stepped into the living room.

Empty.

The entire house smelled like Alex, so I no longer trusted my nose to lead me to him. The ground floor was empty. I threw caution to the wind and rushed to the basement, only to find it in the same state I remembered it— bed unmade and Alex-less.

That left the upper floor. Had to be where Willoughby was holding him.

I flew up the stairs, and the stench of blood slammed into me like a sledgehammer. It was no longer a hint or a trail. It smelled like a bucketful or two, and it came from Alex's old bedroom.

But I couldn't make out a heartbeat.

A piece of paper was pinned to the wooden frame of the door. I snatched it.

You took something of mine. Now I took something of yours. I hope he is still alive when you find him, so you can watch him die.

- W.

It was written in ink, not blood, the handwriting sophisticated and elegant.

My fangs dropped.

I didn't bother hiding them again.

"I swear, I'll kill you." My words echoed back to me in the narrow corridor. A low *thump* snapped me out of my shock and led me to the entrance of the room. Another *thump* followed. It *was* a heartbeat, slow and unsteady.

Reluctantly, I opened the door.

I saw him.

My brain at first refused to make sense of the sight. It couldn't accept that the crimson sheets weren't really red, but soaked with my lover's blood. I couldn't believe the naked torso, covered with wounds, belonged to the man I loved. I couldn't grasp that I was seeing his life essence seep away from too many cuts to count. Willoughby didn't feed from him, or there wouldn't be so much blood. No. The sick bastard took his time slicing and biting Alex, for the sole purpose of torturing and killing him.

I hoped Alex had been under a thrall or unconscious during his ordeal. He must have been, or someone would have heard and called 911. On second thought, I wished someone did. Alex's chances of survival would be higher. His pulse was too weak. Even if I called now, they'd be too late.

I climbed on the bed next to him and raised his head in my lap, willing him to wake up. "Come on, baby. Open your eyes. Please, open your eyes and look at me."

I was crying again—still—begging him to stay with me, warning him not to dare slip away from my grasp, when we were so good together. "I want to be with you, Alex. Please, look at me. *Look at me.*" I was rambling. I took off my top and tried to wipe him clean.

I didn't want to lick his wounds closed. I didn't want his blood in my mouth, even if it was to save him. So I spat on my hands and rubbed them on every inch of him, pressing everywhere, to stem the flow. His blood slid between my fingers, too precious and too elusive.

"You can't leave me, not when I just found you," I whispered.

Not a twitch.

"Open your eyes, Alex. Open those beautiful eyes. Wake up. We'll make you good as new. Just look at me. *Please.*" I was lying, to him and to myself. There was no way to make him good as new. Though he wasn't losing any more blood, I could see and hear that there was too little left in him. He had but minutes to live, and I could do nothing but watch him go.

Wrong.

There was something I could do.

Unsure of whether it was the right thing, or if it would work anyway, I used my fangs to pierce my inner wrist. Forcing his lips open with my other hand, I held my wrist to them and squeezed a few drops of my blood into his mouth. If the handbook had it right, that ought to be enough.

It didn't appear to be.

Alex's eyes never opened.

Not when I kissed him and told him I'd rather have another moment with him than an eternity alone. Not when I shook him and watched his curls, usually carefree, cling to his skull, matted with his blood. Not when I finally said I loved him.

I moved him off my lap and lay next to him, turning his face so his mouth was a hairbreadth from mine.

I was still begging him to open those long eyelashes of his, when his last breath caressed my face.

I kept begging long after his heart stopped beating.

Chapter Eighteen

Constantine showed up near dawn. He said he called me several times, but I couldn't remember hearing my phone ring. Not that I'd care, if I did.

"He won't wake up," I told him, trying to clear my throat. It was sore, and I guessed my mourning hadn't been as quiet as I thought. "I tried. I gave him my blood. But he won't—" A sob cut me off, and I shook Alex's still form hard. "Why won't he—"

Constantine wrapped his arms around me, pulling me from Alex. "Hush, baby." He hadn't called me that in years. Once upon a time, I melted when the word escaped his lips. Now I wished it was Alex whispering it in my ear.

Constantine tried to calm me down, but I wouldn't listen. His words couldn't penetrate my sorrow. Couldn't diffuse my guilt. Alex was dead because he'd met me.

"—light outside."

I turned to Constantine in a fury and shoved him halfway across the room. How could he talk about anything other than the loss I suffered? He grabbed my forearms when I went for him again, and held me to him while I flailed.

He didn't let go until I stopped fighting his grip. "We have to go before it's too late." He was right.

I couldn't care less.

He obviously caught on, because he hauled me over his shoulder with an exaggerated sigh and moved to the window. Finding fresh strength, I thrashed and kicked. Not that it did me any good; his grasp was made of steel.

"I'll be back for him." He pinned my legs to him with both hands. "I promise."

I didn't believe him, but it didn't matter. He could take me wherever he wanted. Protect me from the sun. Hide me at his estate so the remaining council wouldn't come after me when they found out I killed Johnny Boy. He could keep my body from dusting, but I'd still be dead inside.

Alex was gone, because of me.

Everything I let myself hope for—love, a future— was wiped out because I was stupid. Alex never heard me say I loved him, because I was too selfish to admit it aloud.

Back at the mansion, I sank into an armchair and curled into myself. Sheena tried to comfort me, but I would have none of it. I didn't deserve to be comforted. I'd brought Alex into a world filled with death and left him there to be swallowed whole.

I was wallowing in misery when Dotty opened her eyes and started shrieking. Constantine was at a loss. Her wails became louder every time he tried to approach her, and she wouldn't stay still long enough for him to catch her gaze. Seeing me calmed her down but didn't help us decide what to do next. I mean, were we supposed to tell her the truth or try the all-powerful mind wipe?

In the end, it was my call to let her choose for herself.

We filled her in on the entire story and let her decide if she wanted us to make her forget.

She did.

She didn't want to remember a single thing she'd been through, but most of all, she didn't want to know there was such a thing as vampires, or that I was one of them. I took her memories of the last few days away and, when she came to, fed her a story about Constantine and me being secret agents who were in charge of solving her kidnapping. Other than being a part of that secret organization, VSS—feel free to laugh—Constantine was also a doctor. He assured her she didn't have to worry about her loss of short-term memory, as it was trauma induced.

She swore not to mention us or our organization to anyone, including the cops. Since Willoughby had an invitation to her home and we couldn't be sure if he'd go after her again, we promised to drive her to her mother's, where her son was still staying, as soon as the sun went down.

She wouldn't wait that long, and I couldn't blame her. I wished I could be there when she was reunited with her son, but my wishes weren't what counted now. I hugged her goodbye, promised to check in on them soon, and called her a taxi, which Constantine gladly paid for.

Dotty and Mark would be fine, and I'd be around to make sure of that. I would accept no more losses.

That last thought landed me back in my reality and snuffed out my glee over seeing Dotty back to her normal self. At least she still had a life and the option to lock the boogeyman out of it.

I *was* the boogeyman. I was the thing hiding under the bed, skulking in the darkness and luring good, brave people to their death. Their horrible, painful, lonely death.

I hid my face in my palms and sat there, praying I could take the last few hours back—or maybe even the last few days. I would have never met Alex, but at least his smile would still be brightening the world.

****

"Cherry, it's time."

I lifted my head and looked at Constantine through blurry eyes. Time for what? I blinked to bring him into focus. Exhaustion must have overtaken me, because I was now lying on the couch. I hadn't realized I drifted off.

Constantine wiped my hair off my face with gentle fingers. "Do you want to come with me?"

I didn't know what he was talking about. I shook my head. I didn't want to move; I wanted to waste away and leave behind the pain tearing me up inside.

"He's going to bring Alex," Sheena said with a tender smile. "Are you sure you don't want to go?" Her palm on my shoulder was more than a show of support. She was gently pushing me up.

"Alex is dead." There were no more tears in my eyes, but they were choking my voice. "I don't want to see him like that. Not again."

Constantine frowned. "Cherry…"

In my sleepy state, it was harder for me to block his voice out.

"Cherry, didn't you hear me earlier?"

Instead of replying, I closed my eyes.

He grabbed my upper arms and shook me gently. "Listen to me. You know newly turned vampires don't rise if their turning was close to dawn, so they don't burst into flames when they greet the morning sun."

I knew that. Three hours from sunrise was the theoretical limit. The meaning of his words finally sank in. "If Alex's turning was successful, he'll only just be waking up now." Alone. Oh God, I should have remembered that.

Constantine smiled gently. "Do you want to come with me?"

I nodded gingerly and sat up, but doubt stopped me from standing. "I can't. What if he's not…?" Not alive. Not turned. Not happy with the choice I made for him. Scratch that—I didn't care if he was so mad at me he never wanted to see me again. All that mattered was for him to still be part of my world.

"I'll bring him to you." The softness of Constantine's tone surprised me, as did his certainty.

"Thank you," I said.

"I would do anything for you. You know that." I did, but I couldn't focus on what it meant.

I could have Alex back.
I could have another chance.
I could even have *forever*.
Soon I'd know if Alex was gone or not.

Epilogue

Less than forty-eight hours ago, under Sheena's worried, watchful eye, Constantine turned my emotional switch from *devastated* to *hopeful*, and then proceeded to make good on his promise.

Alex wasn't gone.

In Constantine's words, "he was looking around stupidly," and nearly ripped Constantine's arm off when the latter tried to feed him. Still, Alex was composed and clean by the time the two came back to Constantine's.

I heard the door open and stopped myself from wearing a moat into the floor with my pacing. Alex stopped in the doorway and met my gaze. It took great effort to hold back from tackling him. I studied him carefully, trying to spot any difference between his new self and the man I knew and loved. I searched his eyes for a hint of resentment. There was none. Only love shown in the smile he gave me.

Unable to put my relief into words, I flew into his arms, which closed around me. "I love you," I said, the words long overdue. I clung to him and kissed him the way he deserved to be kissed, declaring my love every time our lips separated.

Constantine cleared his throat. "I've made arrangements for the young ladies to spend the night in my quarters, so I can ensure they are comfortable," he said. Such an altruist. Snort. "You may settle in the guest wing. Don't make me regret my hospitality." *Or else* was implied.

We didn't.

Not last night, anyway.

From what I've seen so far, Alex has taken to his change well enough. He's tamed the hunger already. I guess his first feeding from one of us and his preexisting ethical code helped with that, but I still dread what will happen if he needs to feed from a human.

The council doesn't know about his turning, and we're planning on keeping it a secret for as long as possible. That way, if he decides to keep in touch with friends and family, he'll just have to come up with an explanation for his newfound intolerance to sunlight. We haven't yet talked about how he wants to deal with work and his mother. We haven't talked much in general. We had other priorities.

Alex refused to give flying a chance, said he's too grounded for that, but I convinced him to let me fly him to his car last night—and I listened to him grumble about his trunk being busted.

We drove to his mom's place. I hated cleaning up the mess in his childhood bedroom. The sheets reeked, and the mattress was soaked all the way through. There was no way the blood would be washed away from them, or from my memory. We stuffed the beddings in garbage bags, which we drove to the nearest dumpster, praying nobody noticed us.

The powers that be were listening, as I suspect they have been since Alex and I first met.

The room stank only slightly less like a slaughterhouse after the second thorough cleaning with bleach, and we decided to leave the windows open for the night, hoping fresh air would help.

I insisted we fly back, but Alex wouldn't hear of it. The lid of his trunk is now kept closed with several layers of duct tape.

Back at the mansion, we ran into Liza, who demanded to know when Constantine would be back.

Who knows?

He's meeting the remaining council tonight in hopes of convincing the dusting of two of their members was necessary. I offered to go with him, but he wouldn't let me.

I hope he succeeds. If he doesn't, we have to go underground for a long time, and by *underground* I don't mean his humongous and luxurious basement.

"The girls are asking for him." Liza pouted prettily.

Right. *The girls.*

All three of them have become far more attached to my ex than is advisable. I wonder what will happen when we find the rest of Ádísa and Willoughby's would-be undead army. Will Constantine start a harem?

He said yesterday that he plans to keep them with him until he figures out a solution with the council.

I think he just loves having three gorgeous women falling over themselves for him.

Let him. I have Alex.

We promised Liza we'd let her know if we heard from Constantine, and pushed our way past her, holding hands.

Sheena was nowhere in sight, as expected; her internal clock is the opposite of ours. Night equals sleep time to her body, and I see no reason for that to change.

She isn't in a hurry to go home. On the contrary, yesterday afternoon she mentioned she'd arranged for some of her clothes to be brought in.

"If you run, I run," she said. "I'm safer with you." I think Wesley gave her the idea. He's taken her under his wing and would probably hate to lose her company.

She doesn't have much to fear. There's been no sign of Willoughby, who probably thinks he's exacted his revenge. It's actually unfortunate, because I want to find him and make him answer the two questions plaguing me. I asked Constantine, but he has no idea why I was chosen as vampire zero, so to speak, or what Ádísa's comment about my family meant.

Sheena isn't concerned with all this, of course. She insists Willoughby may come after her at any second. I think her reason for sticking around is, in fact, also Constantine. The man is going to have his hands full for a while.

I don't feel sorry for him. I'm too busy enjoying my time with Alex.

****

I haven't fed and yet can't be bothered. I'm sprawled on my back in Constantine's bed, trying not to think about where I am and what I'm doing.

I look at the man between my legs and tangle my fingers in his black hair. "We shouldn't." I drift off, pleasure turning my next words into a moan.

Gray eyes meet mine. "Will you relax? He'll never know."

Of course he'll know, and he'll probably kill us both, or hand us over to the council to do that for him.

We were only supposed to go to his room for Alex to borrow clean clothes. But Constantine's bed is just so huge. We were unable to resist.

Constantine was sickeningly nice to me since he hauled me away from Alex's dead body, but I doubt he'll keep being nice once he smells my little carnal reunion with Alex in his bed.

I try extremely hard to care about that, while Alex pumps three fingers inside me, his tongue flicking my clit.

I fail. Spectacularly.

Later, exhausted and sated, I trace Alex's jugular with my tongue. Graze my teeth over it. He grabs my hair and presses my mouth against his flesh, but I just nuzzle it.

"Didn't your mother ever tell you not to play with your food?" he asks.

She did indeed. All the time. I let out a deep, throaty chuckle and sink my fangs into the smooth column, letting his rich blood fill my throat. I have all I need, and I'm where I want to be. I'm happy.

I hope I'll feel the same way when Constantine returns with news from the council.

If he returns.

He still hasn't called, and I can't say I'm not a little worried. For all I know, despite his charm *and the fact that he's right*, the council executed him on the spot and the remaining members are coming for us.

They can't come inside this house, thanks to Wesley.

Even if they do, Alex and I will handle it.

Want more?

Cherry Blossom - Chapter One

I like big beds.

I like wide, comfy mattresses that allow me to stretch to my heart's desire and roll over as many times as I please. What's more, I like bedmates that don't take up the space I lovingly maintain around me.

Alex wasn't that kind of a bedmate.

Alex was a cuddler, which I more than appreciated after naughty-times, but suffocated me in my sleep, when the weight of an arm pressed my chest down or a hard body kept me from turning around.

He also snored from time to time, which made no sense, since he no longer needed to breathe. I guess old habits die hard.

I wouldn't have made a big deal out of any of these things this morning, if I didn't wake up to Alex spooning me from behind, both of his arms wrapped around me like steel bars, and his voice whispering in my ear, "I want you to meet my mother."

And I certainly wouldn't have kicked him off the bed, if he didn't add, "And I want to meet your family."

****

"What did you do that for?" Alex rubbed his head where it had impacted with the wall. He was still on the floor where he landed, staring at me.

I sat up and bunched the covers around me, still not fully believing I did what I did—or that he actually said what I heard.

"Cherry? What's up? And *ow*, by the way." He didn't seem as pissed off as I'd be in his place. "Did you have another nightmare? Think I was Willoughby again?"

His concern made me feel bad. To be honest, I never had nightmares of Willoughby. At times when Alex was too clingy in my sleep, however, I may have elbowed him in the ribs or kicked him in the shin and afterward implied I thought he was my maker, haunting my dreams. He was having nightmares of his turning too, so he believed me.

I shook my head. "Not him," I said. "Different nightmare. About you wanting us to meet each other's folks."

That got him fuming in no time, which worked out quite well, because I wasn't feeling all lovey-dovey.

"Why's that so bad? My mother's been hearing about you for two months now. She wants to meet you." And *this* was a glaring example of why we should let our family think we died after our turning. If the vampire council caught a whiff of Alex's staying in touch with his mother, they might resort to extreme measures.

Then again, they'd have to know he was a vampire for them to even care, so it was a moot point. After the havoc that resulted to his turning, the vampire council reinstated the

Vampire Social Services, to help tighten the bonds within our community. They also decreed a census, to record all vampires currently in the United States. We'd kept Alex's change in status a secret, to avoid dealing with the repercussions of breaking the law against turning new fledglings.

"What if she doesn't like me?" 'Cause loveable as I am, this was always a possibility. I didn't voice my worries that I might not like her. "And you can't meet my family. *I* can't meet my family again. They think I'm dead."

"They think you're missing. Finding out you're still"—he scrunched his face—"*around* would be the greatest thing to ever happen to them." He was using his rational voice on me, something that probably worked when he interrogated suspects, but which I hated when I was feeling unreasonable. He got on his feet and dusted plaster off his hair. "And my mom will love you. Just like I do."

Yeah, okay. Play the *I-love-you* card, why don't you? "We'll talk about it," I said. "I'll ask Constantine what he thinks. He knows the council better than I do, and they like him." If they didn't, they'd have publicly executed him for admitting to killing two of their own. Instead, they had him join them. "If he thinks it's safe for me to go home, we'll visit my family."

There was no way my ex would condone something like this. It was reckless and might endanger us all—plus he might be acting cool and superior, but I could tell he wasn't happy with my relationship with Alex.

Alex must have realized Constantine would say *no*, because he kicked dejectedly at the floor and came back to bed with a scowl on his face. "I'll talk to him too. Maybe I can convince him," he said, standing in front of me in his birthday suit.

He could certainly try. Meanwhile, I'd do my best to make him forget about the whole thing.

I smiled, slid to the edge of the bed, and let the covers drop, to reveal a state of undress that matched his. I traced the lines of his body—hard muscle under soft skin that shivered ever so slightly under my touch.

His gaze was locked on mine, as I replaced my fingers with my mouth down his stomach. I loved the texture, the smoothness of his skin. I feathered my lips along his hipbone and felt his legs tremble. I loved his body's involuntary responses. Smiling to myself, I brought one hand around him and dug my nails into his buttock, pushing him against my face.

He rudely interrupted my efforts at driving him crazy with anticipation, by stepping back, grabbing my knees, and laying me flat on the bed in one smooth move. Before I could voice my protest, he was kissing me.

I arched upward and wrapped my legs around his hips, but he resisted, his body hovering above me. "No." The single word was heavy with promise.

He kissed me again, teasing my mouth open with his tongue and finding mine. The kiss deepened, as did my need for him. When he sucked on my lower lip, I ran one hand down the length of my body and between my legs, where I wanted him the most.

He closed his fingers around my wrist and forced my hand to the mattress. "Be a good girl, and don't move." His cool breath tickled my ear.

It's not like me to submit without a fight, but the lust burning in his gaze stifled my rebellious side. I tangled both hands in the sheets, to keep from touching him.

His mouth moved down the side of my neck, kissing and licking the area over my jugular. I wanted him to bite me. I wanted to push against him. I held back. He barely let a fang graze my skin and chuckled at the whiny sound that escaped my throat.

The bastard.

He made his way down my body with his lips and fingers, pulling sighs and moans out of me with every kiss, every caress, every nip. My nipples hardened at his touch. My stomach tightened. Every nerve in my body screamed for more, but he refused to give it. By the time his face was at the apex of my thighs, I craved him beyond reason. I couldn't be held accountable for my actions if he didn't sink inside me immediately.

Only Alex wasn't done teasing me.

He closed his teeth over the sensitive flesh at the inside of my thigh without breaking the skin, and sucked while pushing a finger inside me.

My hips flew off the mattress, and my eyes watered at the pressure building up in my belly. I needed just a bit more.

More pressure. More friction. I needed him to add another finger and pump them both. I needed him to eat me out. I needed him to—*Oh God...*

He didn't do what I wanted but he didn't withdraw, either. Instead, he splayed the fingers of his free hand on my stomach to hold me down and pierced my skin with his fangs at the same time he pressed his thumb on my clit.

I thought I was going to scream, but only a hoarse whisper reached my ears when I managed to form a word. "Please."

He either didn't hear me or ignored me. He drew lazy circles with his thumb around my clitoris, and slid his finger in and out so slowly, I couldn't get the *more* I needed. He kept pulling at my blood, and the sensation was enough to drive me to the precipice but not to throw me over.

Pleading obviously didn't work, so this time I went with an order. "*Now.*"

Alex was not in a compliant mood. He stopped touching me entirely and raised his gaze to mine, making sure I watched as he licked his lips. Once he had my undivided attention, he lowered his head again and slowly ran his tongue along my cleft.

That was when I stopped being nice.

I grabbed his hair to anchor him to me and began grinding against his face, urging him to go faster. Harder. If he wanted to play *Hold off Cherry's Release,* I'd take matters in my own hands.

I was so close—so *fucking* close—when he forcefully removed my hands from his head and rolled me over.

Now we're talking.

The bed was too tall for my knees to reach the ground, and my legs dangled awkwardly. I tried to find purchase on the floor with my toes, but Alex nudged my thighs apart with one knee, throwing me completely off balance, and pushed inside me.

Can't say I complained about the manhandling. Perhaps I would have, if I weren't enjoying it so much. I've always loved seeing Alex's mild manners put aside and this dominant side of his come out in the bedroom—bathroom, kitchen, public place, wherever.

He dug his fingers into my hips and lifted me to meet his thrusts. I didn't have time to push my body up with my arms. My face was rubbing against the mattress, but all I felt was the fire he stoked inside me with every plunge. Every time he withdrew, I clenched around him, trying to lock him and the pleasure in place. My fangs popped out, and I bit at the sheets, uncaring that I'd leave holes in them. I was nearly there nearly there nearly—

Alex's movements turned jerkier, shorter. He draped his body over mine, letting go of my hips so he could wrap his arms around my torso. I let him draw me to him and tilted my head to the side, to get my hair out of the way.

The moment his fangs pierced my throat, everything I wanted, everything my body craved for suddenly flooded my senses, short-circuiting my brain. I couldn't tell which of us was trembling. All I knew was that, pinned to him, torn sheets hanging from my mouth, I felt my body shudder with waves of pleasure until I could no longer keep my eyes open.

Alex obviously had problems controlling himself, too, because his knees buckled, and we toppled forward, his teeth and cock still inside me.

In my fuzziness, I barely registered his tongue gently licking the wounds he'd inflicted, before he rolled to the side and gathered me close. It's possible I purred with delight. This was one of the times I not only didn't mind the cuddling but welcomed it.

I don't know if I drifted off or just zoned out, but I'd been too engrossed in my efforts to distract him to realize someone else was in the room, until Constantine cleared his throat.

Keep up to date with all the latest news and information from Sotia Lazu at http://SotiaLazu.com

MORE IN THE VAMPIRE CHERRY SERIES

Cherry Vampire, Book 2 – Cherry Blossom

I thought being a single vampire was challenging.
I had no idea.

As if my murderous maker being still at large isn't stressful enough, Alex wants us to meet each other's parents. As per vampire law, I've let mine consider me dead since my turning, but Constantine, my ex and newest member of the vampire council, is suspiciously quick to allow a visit. Perhaps because he knows more about my family than I do.

But as always in Cherry-land, one problem isn't enough. Alex's increasing jealousy of Constantine leads to violent outbursts completely unlike his usual mild manner, there are reports of attacks on women matching my description in the area, family secrets come to light, and feelings I shouldn't be having are messing with my mind.

I need to sort things out, and soon, before I lose Alex for good—worse, before he turns on me.

Cherry Vampire, Book 3 – Cherry Pie

What if you get what you want and it's not what you need?

I never asked to be a vampire, so when Constantine says there's a way for Alex and me to become human again, I jump at the chance. Alex's reservations may have something to do about the process's involving Constantine and me in bed together, but what's one night when I can have my life back?

And I plan to live that life with the man I love. I'll be mortal with Alex, and I couldn't be happier about it. Kinda. This would be much easier if mortality didn't come with pains and aches, and Alex wasn't pressuring me to start a family.

For too long others have made my choices for me. This is my chance to do what makes me happy. But first I have to decide what that is. And then I need to find the strength to claim it, before my options are taken away.

Acknowledgments

Thank you, Marilyn and Lorraine, for working with me for months to shape up this story and for keeping my morale high when I was about to give up.

Thank you, Allyson Lindt, for urging me to stick with Cherry and her world, for holding my hand from halfway around the world through every step of this process, and for keeping me sane(ish).

Thank you, Andrei, for reading each chapter as soon as I stopped typing, and for loving me. I love you!

About the Author

Sotia loves romances with a twist and urban fantasy novels, always with vivid erotic elements. Her favorite characters to write are not conventional hero-material at first glance, and she enjoys making them fight for their happiness.

She shares her life and living quarters with her husband, their son, and two rescue dogs, one of which may be part-pony. Sappy movies make her bawl like a baby, and she wishes she could take in all the stray dogs in the world.

Also, she hates mornings.